THE LIBERA ME DOMINE

Robert Pinget

THE LIBERA ME DOMINE

Robert Pinget

Translated by Barbara Wright

Red Dust New York 1978

Originally published as *Le Libera* by Les Editions de Minuit, Paris 1968.
Copyright © Les Editions de Minuit 1969

This translation published in Great Britain as *The Libera Me Domine* by
Calder and Boyars, London 1975. Copyright © Calder and Boyars 1975

Published in the United States of America by Red Dust, Inc. 1978.

Library of Congress Catalogue Card Number: 78-53831

ISBN: 0-87376-025-5

The publication of this book has been made possible in part by grants from
the New York State Council on the Arts; and from the National Endowment
for the Arts in Washington, D.C., a Federal Agency.

If old Lorpailleur is mad I can't help it.

If old Lorpailleur is mad I can't help it, nobody can help it and anyone who could prove the contrary would be mighty clever.

If old Lorpailleur is mad but is she mad, she is, claims that I was involved either closely or remotely, that I had a hand in the affair of the Ducreuxs' little boy, that I was in league with the police hence my impunity.

Had a hand in the affair of the Ducreuxs' little boy unbeknownst to anyone, my name wasn't mentioned at the inquest then here comes this madwoman years afterwards and tongues start wagging.

If old Lorpailleur is mad I said to Verveine I can't help it, nobody can help it, you must get her locked up, there must be a way, what's the use of being a chemist then, you must know how it's done, you must know someone, some authority, oh come on, you just have to pick the proper channel and then it's all plain sailing, grease the wheels, that's the expression, he answers no, hasn't the authority, anyway not the slightest idea how to, all he can think of if the worst comes to the worst is the family, he'd heard years ago that for this sort of thing, but the family's a long way away how do you expect, a sister in the Argentine, all the rest dead and buried, I said let's think let's think, it's not possible, there must be a way, am I supposed to put up with it, tongues are beginning to wag, in any case says he if they go on you'll have to go through with it, he meant the police, the law courts, so on and so forth, just because of the evil gossip of a madwoman, it's not possible, it's not possible I said.

If old Lorpailleur is mad something must be done at once.

Verveine answers well I can't do anything about it, if you can think of a way carry on, you won't find me meddling in your affairs but is she mad that's the whole point, no no don't get me wrong I'm not saying that you had any sort of hand in the Ducreux affair, all I'm saying is that someone like old Lorpailleur may well have started people talking about you for other reasons mayn't she, don't get me wrong.

Don't get what wrong I said.

Don't get what wrong I repeated, tell me what you're getting at.

That someone like old Lorpailleur at her age, fortyish, may well imagine that you given your character, given your means, I don't know, you used to work together in the old days so they told me, that was it, well then maybe at that moment she might have I don't know, she might have imagined, you see what I mean.

Someone came into the shop, I should have waited, I didn't wait, we left things at that as they say but things never stay left at that for long.

If old Lorpailleur is mad things won't be left at that, we'll find a way, there must be someone, some official channel, then it's all plain sailing, quick, the straitjacket, old Lorpailleur is in good hands.

The Ducreux affair, an old affair, a good many years ago, a good ten years ago, the Ducreuxs' little boy, four years old, was found strangled in Ferret's wood under a pile of leaves, he was wearing his little sailor suit, he'd gone out one Sunday with his parents, they were making their way over towards Sirancy, the parents were having a nap after their picnic.

6

He was wearing his little blue dungarees that his mother had made out of an old pair of trousers of his father's and a little red woolly and shoes of the sandals type, sandals and little socks that his mother ...

A dear little blond boy with brown eyes strangled on the spot near Chatruse, he was found three days later, his parents' grief was terrible, the whole village was talking about it, we hadn't seen a tragedy of the sort since eighteen seventy-three.

We'd never seen anything like it.

Immediately the gendarmerie, immediately the inquest, the witnesses, the neighbors, they'd seen the little boy going out of the yard at about ten in the morning, Mademoiselle Cruze was cleaning her windows, she had a step-ladder on the pavement.

It was in July, a bad month in our parts, every sort of calamity happens to us in July, fires, car accidents, hailstorms, drownings but we hadn't had a murder since eighteen seventy-three, it's still there in the records and newspapers of the time, a fellow called Serinet shot dead by his brother-in-law.

We'd never seen anything like it.

The father was a baker, the mother too, they still are, they're still there, in the rue des Casse-Tonnelles, but the little boy isn't there any more, he'd have been fourteen, such a pretty little boy, they still talk about him even though they've had three children since, little Laure, little Frédéric and little Alfred, all very sweet children.

It's all very well to say they've had three children since, little Laure, little Frédéric and little Alfred, the tragedy they lived through you don't forget just like that, these things mark you for life said Verveine, she was a good excuse for him that customer who came in, he didn't have to answer me, I should have waited, I didn't wait, it's not possible that he doesn't know what to do, madwomen get locked up, wasn't he saying that she wasn't mad, wasn't he implying that I was telling him a lot of nonsense, what a nerve the old bugger has, you won't find me meddling in your affairs, isn't it everybody's affair, a madwoman in our midst.

It's all very well to say they've had three children since, the poor Ducreuxs, it still preys on their minds especially as the killer was never caught, he's still at large.

In spite of the gendarmerie being called out, the inquiries, the official reports, the special tribunals, so on and so forth, it's a very strange thing in this day and age, the killer is still at large, no reason why it shouldn't be little Laure's turn next, for instance, or little Frédéric's, just the very thought gives you cold shivers up and down your spine, it shouldn't be possible, a permanent menace, a poor baker's family, they're still there, living in what might well be called daily panic, no it shouldn't be possible and when the day comes that old Lorpailleur insinuates that Vervein had something to do with it I won't be the one who proves the opposite.

If old Lorpailleur is mad it's nobody's fault and things can be left at that, she goes round talking nonsense, her black dress, her hat with the crêpe round it, her yellow teeth, she lost her mother years ago, still in mourning, a maniac, on her bike going to school at half past eight, an English-type bike with upright handle-bars, she sits up as straight as an i, when the day comes that her crêpe gets caught in a gust of wind and sticks to her face round a bend just when a truck's coming I won't be the one who proves the opposite I mean that the truck was to blame, old Lorpailleur killed outright, lying there in the road, but also that mourning mania don't you feel there's something disgusting about it, dragging your dead around with you at the height of July, two days before the school broke up, she passed the baker's, Mademoiselle Cruze busy cleaning her windows saw her out of the corner

8

of her eye, she doesn't say good morning to her any more, she had her shopping basket on her carrier as she had to do her shopping after school and a few minutes later there was little Alfred coming out of the yard.

Things could have been left at that.

Old Lorpailleur came out of school and got on her bike, she sat down and just at that moment let go of the handlebars, she falls off, she lies there screaming and kicking, the children are frightened, I can still see them standing round her in a circle at a distance with their little briefcases under their arms or their satchels on their backs, when Blimbraz arrives, and then Verveine, they go up a bit closer to her, she's foaming at the mouth, it's obvious that she was mad said Madame Monneau what did I tell you, her bereavement must have unhinged her, what an idea, entrusting children to a madwoman, blind that's what we were, my little boy did tell me she was queer, in the middle of a dictation she suddenly used to call out words that had nothing to do with it, I can still hear him.

The word cataclysm or catastrophe, it seems it preys on their minds, megalomania, calamity mania, they see traps everywhere, they turn every which way to get out of them, to free themselves, to escape, something's going to pounce on them, they feel they're tied up, that's madness for you.

Something like the truck for instance.

She was lying in the road, the kids in a circle at a distance, the poor teacher, how come she did that, the truck driver kept repeating, she just suddenly came straight at me, she came straight at me, he was wiping his forehead with his handkerchief, the doctor who lives at the bend in the road leaning over the dead woman feeling her pulse, listened to her heart and certified that she was dead, there are already twelve people, mothers grabbed hold of their kids, come on don't look, come on d'you hear me we're going home, the kids said then there won't be any more school, in any case you were breaking up the day after tomorrow, what about next year, another teacher, get a move on d'you hear me don't turn round, they'd taken the corpse opposite to the doctor's before the morgue, there were about twenty of them who kept repeating all together oh the poor thing, they were pitying her now, they were pitying the madwoman who'd been bringing us bad luck for years, the gendarme was dealing with the driver, sample of his blood at the chemist's, report, witnesses who hadn't seen a thing but they knew her, everybody, her sister lives in the Argentine with so it seems an actor but personally what I say, so on and so forth, gives you something to talk about, it's always in July that calamities happen to us, drownings, fires and accidents.

Or that she wasn't killed outright.

Or that the truck simply passed her, and that she got to school at twenty to nine.

Madame Ducreux at her window was keeping one eye on little Alfred who was playing in the yard and with the other was sweeping the bedroom, as she was edging the broom behind the armchair she suddenly saw little Louis ten years earlier, the child was hiding, she was pretending to look for him, she suddenly found him and said oh the naughty little rascal you gave me such a fright and pulled him out from behind the chair and kissed him on the mouth, it's all very well to say they've had three since, it was all very well for her to say it to herself, the good mood she'd been in that morning vanished, the old sadness took its place but Ducreux was calling his wife to come into the shop, the girl couldn't cope, it was half-past eleven, all the ladies were fingering the bread in spite of it being forbidden and during this time little Alfred had wandered off, the mother like a madwoman left them all standing, she went and grabbed hold of the child in the yard, he had barely moved, he was making mud pies near the water-tank, come on d'you hear me we're going home, it's time for your soup or whatever.

While the ladies who were fingering the bread saw old Lorpailleur on her bike coming back from school, isn't it ten years since her mother died, dragging her mourning out like that, dragging her dead around with her, you can't tell me she isn't a bit mad.

There'd been a lot of talk about the disappearance of the Ducreuxs' little boy, people had imagined everything there was to imagine, a kidnapping neither more nor less, but it's all very well, you never really get over it, is it normal to have your child strangled, what was behind it, what sort of people did the Ducreuxs mix with, no it's not normal.

Which would have meant that as soon as the customer had gone out again I would have gone back to Verveine's.

And Verveine seeing me back again wanted to change the subject and asked after all my family, questions which I answered patiently, my nieces, my sister in the Argentine, an old retired cousin who used to work with the railways, I could have invented some more since the conversation inevitably had to come round again given its point of departure i.e. crazy old Lorpailleur.

He had known her mother well, a Voiret from Hottencourt, the oldest of eight children all brought up by her as the mother died after the last one, she was a Bianle from Crachon, my mother knew her well, she remembered seeing her fall one day writhing and foaming at the mouth, whereupon I immediately said aren't these things hereditary, nothing surprising if the grand-daughter suffers from the same complaint, when she fell the other day several people assured me that she was foaming at the mouth, to which he immediately replied I tell you she wasn't, I saw her with my own eyes, she was knocked down by a truck, no trace of epilepsy in that, Mademoiselle Lorpailleur has a very strong constitution, I can't understand why you should get so excited about these old maids' tales, do you think we believe them, what are you getting at, I should be interested to know, looking at me over his glasses, extremely interested to know.

The kids in a circle round the victim.

Verveine who had seen her fall rushes over to her and gets Blimbraz to help him carry the injured woman to his chemist's shop.

Mademoiselle Cruze his sister who was cleaning her windows gets off her stool and starts scurrying about trying to make herself useful.

Five minutes after the accident the doctor came up with his bag, he said take her to the chemist's, and there, in the presence of Verveine, Mademoiselle Cruze and Madame Monneau, he examined the victim and said a slightly bruised shoulder, nothing serious, give her a stimulant, while old Lorpailleur was writhing on the divan and moaning as if she were at death's door, all the same I'm telling you, not the slightest trace of foaming at the mouth in all this, ask my sister if you like or Madame Monneau, do you doubt my word, in any case epilepsy just for your information is no less than . . .

The Ducreuxs' little boy, perhaps after all.

The Ducreuxs' little boy may not have been kidnapped.

But Verveine was carrying on about that business that happened ten years ago, he considered it his duty so he said to try and reconstitute the tragedy, is it normal that we never knew anything about it, how do we know whether the parents themselves didn't hush it up, in league with the police, the examining magistrates, so on and so forth, which would explain why they never talk about it, only yesterday Madame Ducreux came in for some aspirins with her little Frédéric, a lovely little boy, it was on the tip of my tongue to say isn't he like Louis, it was Louis wasn't it, I didn't say it but there was something about her look which told me that she understood why I was embarrassed, not that that was the first time I'd seen little Frédéric, it is Frédéric isn't it, but I don't know what it was that particular day that made him look so like the poor little boy who had his throat cut, maybe his red pullover or my own mood how should I know, patience is the only thing that ever gets you anywhere and by dint of cross-checking and imagination oh yes you finally get there, truth will out in the blinding light of day.

As for Mademoiselle Lorpailleur's bruises I don't know if I can tell you, said Madame Monneau, just imagine she got them the day before, she fell off a chair when she was cleaning her windows and dislocated her shoulder, Cruze can't tell you anything about it, it happened at Crachon at her sister-in-law's, in my opinion she just quite simply let herself fall off her bike when she saw the truck coming, either because she was afraid or because she thought it would be to her advantage, that's what I'd be more inclined to look into, she's such a mischiefmaker, getting us to believe the truck had run her over, what could the driver say, even so it's a bit much that there wasn't a living soul in the street at that hour to be a witness, Mademoiselle Cruze didn't see a thing whatever she may say, she was going into the baker's, you can't see the bend from there unless you've got eyes in your behind, excuse my language.

And to come back to old Lorpailleur's machinations because machinations they were, may I drop dead if I'm telling a lie, instead of considering her mad couldn't we just treat her as a scold and whip her, that's what's wrong these days, we don't flog people in public any more, they weren't so stupid in the middle ages, all that to get the truck driver put behind bars, you must admit there'd be good reason.

That day Madame Ducreux, the baker's wife, had taken a

bit longer doing her bedroom, she was cleaning the windows standing on a stool) when she saw little Alfred, such a good sensible little boy he was usually, going out through the yard door, she rushed down, she ran out into the street, she grabbed hold of her little boy, her husband called her into the shop, it was half-past eleven, she went into the shop with the child and all the ladies went into ecstasies about how well the brat looked, all of them stopping themselves saying what was on the tip of their tongues i.e. that he looked like the little boy who was dead, the assistant couldn't cope, a girl from Hottencourt who has neither hearth nor home, orphanage, she's been working there for three months but she still can't tell the difference between a well-baked loaf and a not very well-baked loaf, Madame Ducreux said to her you take him, sit him down in the kitchen and amuse him, I'll be back in a moment.

Or that there wasn't a single customer in the shop at the time but that as the girl had to go out for some reason or other Ducreux called his wife, he'd just seen her coming down, otherwise would have served them himself and left the mason a minute in the kitchen where they were discussing the estimate for the shed they were going to have built in the yard and Madame Monneau apparently called out, knowing they were both busy, don't let me disturb you, I'll come back in half an hour and as she went out apparently saw old Lorpailleur sitting up stiffly on her bike, she was on her way to school, half-past eight.)

But the children saw her get up, pat the dust off her skirt and get back on to her machine, she wasn't the person they'd been standing round it was the driver of a truck parked outside the Swan café, dead drunk on the pavement, so you see.

While little Louis went wandering off, the parents fast asleep, these country picnics they tire you out, both lying on the rug, she with her fat legs exposed, her skirt above her knees, he with his back to her curled up like a gun dog, a branch of a walnut or some other tree was tickling him and he brushed away this imaginary fly in his sleep, the child went wandering off, she had put him down to rest first, he hadn't gone to sleep, he'd got up, he went wandering off, the forest is dense once you get thirty yards in, they never saw him again.

A peasant out picking mushrooms had seen him something like thirty yards away, he'd recognized him, thinking his mother was with him, he was the only witness but witness to what, all he'd seen was the little boy going further into the forest with his imaginary mother but at the inquiry there were heaps of witnesses who'd seen the boy that morning, who'd seen him the day before, who'd seen him the week before at the baker's, who'd seen him the day he was born, who knew his parents, his grandparents, his cousins, so on and so forth, none of which stops the killer still being at large.

A little grave with two geraniums and a little cross, it breaks your heart. She was watering the geraniums, she pulled up a weed, she was crying quietly in the morning sunshine, Louis Ducreux, 1948–1952, these things make you think, don't they, an innocent little creature, one of God's angels, but it was nearly half-past eleven, she must hurry, she crossed herself and went back to the baker's where the ladies were fingering the bread, the assistant wasn't very bright and couldn't cope with all the customers, there are always a lot at that hour on a Saturday, Madame Ducreux said as she went in I'm so sorry I was at the cemetery and the ladies adopted the appropriate expression, they didn't dare go any further though, little Frédéric is the spitting image of the other one, he was playing in the room at the back of the shop, every so often he would peep into the shop making an adorable little grimace, he suddenly said wee-wee and the mother said to the girl carry on will you I'll be back in a moment.

And yet said Madame Monneau they never talk about it I can quite see that it would just be rubbing salt in the wound but even so is it normal this strangler they never caught, still at large like any common rabbit-stealer, wasn't there anything else they could have done, gone a bit further, the police, the law courts, so on and so forth, they seem to have forgotten pretty quickly, between you and me what sort of people used they to mix with, the Ducreuxs, you haven't the slightest idea, I remember a fellow called Vernes who lived in Chatruse, he used to come every Sunday to stock up with bread, you remember, as if there wasn't a baker's in Chatruse, is it normal, he used to spend half an hour chatting to Madame Ducreux, you aren't going to tell me you didn't notice, you can't blame people for wondering, it's sad for the parents but there's still something.

But that the picnic was just rumor spread by God knows whom, the Ducreuxs have never picnicked anywhere, the father can't bear them, the only way he likes to eat is with his feet under the table and with his slippers on them at that, winter and summer alike, as for the mother she hasn't had a Sunday out for well nigh twenty years now, that's how long her sister and mother have been coming to see her on that day, all she wants is a rest, the very most they do is sit out in the yard when it's fine, in any case just the very idea of going to sleep in a field beside her child has always made her shudder, such a thing has never happened to her, picnic or no picnic.

But Verveine wasn't convinced, he kept Madame Ducreux talking after the aspirins, he was trying to worm her secrets out of her, this was a few days after the funeral, she was in such a state, wanting to know yes or no did her sister come on the Sunday of the crime with a stranger, a young man who wasn't from these parts who'd been walking with the ladies in the avenue or had he got it wrong, Madame Monneau said she'd seen him with them, perhaps a passer-by who'd stopped to ask them the way or something, no, she didn't answer, she was crying her eyes out, kept blowing her nose, I can still see her, a little handkerchief that had belonged to her grandmother the sort they used to make years ago for mourning, with a black border, however he didn't like to press her too hard, beating about the bush, asking vague questions while he was pretending to make up a prescription, all of which gave the defendant plenty of time to answer with groans and nose-wipings a little handkerchief that had belonged to her grandmother quite so.

Pity added Madame Monneau that we can't question the sister, she's in the Argentine and the mother died quite some time ago, what am I talking about the mother, the step-mother, it was the step-mother who came on Sundays with the sister, she didn't get on with her mother, she was always telling me so, her step-mother quite so Madame Degrange she's dead too, pity we can't hear what she would have had to say about it, a young man of twenty or so who wasn't from these parts, I don't remember the witnesses saying anything about him, there you are you see, one more oversight on the part of the lawyers, I reckon there were a good many of them.

I'll come back in half an hour.

It was such lovely weather, it was the middle of May, the first fine days, you're not afraid of going out without a woolly in the morning, you open your door to let in the sun, it's already so hot that you say it really is summer, it's taken us by surprise, you see your neighbor perched on a step-ladder cleaning her kitchen windows, she's starting on them early today, and the schoolmistress sitting up straight on her English-type bike, her mourning veil floating behind her, going to school, half-past eight, her shopping basket on her carrier, she'll be going to do her shopping at eleven and the little Ducreux boy is it Frédéric or Alfred trotting about in the yard under his mother's eye, she's at the window, what can she be doing, she looks as if she's dreaming, it isn't every day she can, she works her fingers to the bone, poor woman, what with all her housework, her three children, the bakery, the trouble she has with the shopgirl, odd that they're always changing, do you think it's normal, they hardly ever stay more than a year or even six months, they go elsewhere, don't they like it at the Ducreuxs', do they make life difficult for them, he's not a bad sort though, and well-bred at that, excuse the pun nor is she so far as I know, maybe a bit highly-strung, a bit tired, not surprising with her three kids one after the other, she works her fingers to the bone, what with the housework, the bakery, the shop-girls, odd that they don't stay isn't it, we were just talking about it Hélène and I, she maintains that she's jealous of her husband, Madame Ducreux I mean, and that she's the one who sacks the girls when she thinks there's something in the wind but really you know, even though I'm no better or stupider than the next one I don't believe it, Ducreux is a good husband and a good father, the home-loving type, hasn't got that sort of temperament, don't you agree, unless unless ... maybe he could have changed in that respect, they do say that that sort of misfortune the loss of a child I mean can alter your character, it upsets something, it releases something, and yet he was such a good husband, such a good father, but that doesn't prevent his feeling, how awful, do you really think.

Such lovely fresh weather, contrary to all expectations, June had been so hot and then suddenly such a lovely July, the beginning I mean, ushered in by all those storms at the end of June, it wasn't normal, we certainly took advantage of it, opening our doors in the mornings as if it were May, the first fine days, a friendly sort of sun, it was already quite hot, in the kitchen-gardens, vineyards and orchards, when you're not afraid to go out without a woolly, you know what I mean, that was how July began, it wasn't normal but with the propensity people have for letting themselves be lulled into a sense of false security we didn't even remember that it's always in July that calamities happen to us, a car accident, someone drowned, a fire, it must have been a Saturday, I can still see Madame Ducreux cleaning the bakery windows, she was starting on them early, Madame Monneau who arrived just at that moment earlier than usual on a Saturday, much earlier, she works her fingers to the bone, what with her housework, her children, her clock shop, she stopped at the foot of the step-ladder, Madame Ducreux was going to get down to serve her, she was holding her sponge which she'd just dipped in the bowl on top of the step-ladder, she was looking round at Madame Monneau when she, Madame Monneau I mean, said don't let me disturb you, I'll come back later, I know what housework is, whenever you have a minute you know, can you believe it what wonderful weather, personally I can't stand the heat, you'd think it was May, it must be last week's storms, by the way how's your little Alfred, is he better, because the previous Sunday he was playing in the yard when all of a sudden the storm broke it was preceded by a thunder clap which had so frightened the poor little boy that he had started running as you might say and he slipped and fell and slightly dislocated his shoulder, there's nothing serious, the doctor said it wasn't serious, his mother is treating it with cold compresses, in short she isn't worried about him and just as she was asking the baker's wife about him little Alfred went out of the shop, his mother immediately leapt off the

19

step-ladder, she grabbed hold of her little boy, she pushed him back into the shop and said to the girl look after him will you, he's such a fidget, whatever happens don't let him out into the street, she can still see her other little boy, the one who was run over by a car ten years ago, what a blow for the parents, serve Madame Monneau she went on, I'll be back in a moment, but the customer said don't let me disturb you, I'll come back in half an hour, what am I talking about run over, that was the little Bianle boy, his poor mother can still see the truck coming round the bend, just as old Lorpailleur was passing on her bike, the child was waiting on the pavement and only looked on his side, he didn't see the truck and that was it, killed outright.

Just as old Lorpailleur was passing, Madame Ducreux sponge in hand, Madame Monneau going into the baker's, then changing her mind I'll come back in half an hour, with the glorious morning sun, all the ladies ready to go out, it was market day, young Bianle with a friend already down by the river, he has an absolute passion for fishing, his mother used to say that seeing how little gifted he was at his lessons she'd make a fishmonger of him or something of the sort, and what a job it had been to persuade Mademoiselle Ariane ten years later to take him into her service and put him in charge of the Grance ponds, she likes them to be full of fish and regularly cleaned out, there are at least six to the east of the forest in the bit between Fantoine, Malatraîne and Crachon.

The baker's wife on her step-ladder was telling the new one to serve Madame Monneau, a girl who'd only been there two days, odd that they don't stay but Ducreux has other interests, his wife doesn't know anything about it or if she does have an inkling that something is going on her suspicions are misplaced, just imagine the picture, the husband lumbered with a mistress and the wife regularly sacking the wrong one while the other one has never had it so good.

Because to say that she was passing on her bike at this moment and that Madame Monneau had looked the other way as usual and was carrying it off by chatting to the baker's wife was one of Lorpailleur's tricks, she had seen the customer coming out well before she got to the bend, she was still outside the café because she had had to stop to fasten here basket on to her carrier, young Bianle was there with a friend, he was trying on his float before he went to school, he couldn't wait to go fishing after lessons, then passing the baker's hadn't seen anyone, Madame Ducreux still doing her housework on the first floor day-dreaming by the armchair where the child was hiding, identical circumstances at different periods of time, unforeseeable, so that one drags out one's existence with a stab-wound in one's heart, then coming round the bend and noticing little Frédéric in the yard making mud pies by the water-tank and saying to herself he's the spitting image of the one who was strangled.

A white marble grave with three pots of artificial cyclamen, they make such pretty flowers nowadays, no need to water them, they look clean and tidy all the year round.

In spite of his lack of success Verveine didn't let up, he even went so far as to hazard a few roundabout questions to his customer about her sister in the Argentine, hadn't there been some talk about her coming back about ten years ago, he seemed to remember, was it Monneau who mentioned it, was it your step-mother, a girl we used to know so well living abroad such a long way away it was quite natural but young Pinson went abroad at that time too, he might have met her in those far-off countries and told her the terrible news, how did she react, to which the defendant continued to reply with sobs and hiccups, a subterfuge, her little handkerchief was soaked, she was trying to find another in her handbag when little Alfred coming up on tiptoes knocked a whole lot of tubes of toothpaste off a shelf, the mother jumps, Verveine says, I can still hear him, don't bother it doesn't matter, comes out from behind his counter and starts picking them up still only thinking of his last question and trying to find a new angle to make the unhappy woman talk.

And one thing leading to another, spending most of her evenings reconstituting the tragedy, Mademoiselle Lorpailleur became convinced that there must have been some connection between young Pinson and the sister in the Argentine, still not seeing the connection with the murder nor the possible motives behind their actions but not despairing of discovering them.

In her haste to reassure her Madame Monneau couldn't think of anything other to say than what can you be thinking of, oh but come this is madness, be reasonable, the poor woman was in such a state you couldn't bear to look at her, thinking, the poor mother, because of the sudden silences that greeted her when she met her neighbors, that tongues were beginning to wag about the circumstances of the tragedy, the relations between the Ducreuxs at the time, the congenital disease the child was suffering from, and God knows what more besides.

In her haste to contradict her old Lorpailleur started stammering well whatever next but this is a plot do you think I'm mad, I tell you it was a Thursday, there was no school, without convincing Verveine who got out his diary and read for the year 1952 Saturday July 12th disappearance of the Ducreuxs' little boy, saw Mademoiselle Lorpailleur just miss a truck at the Casse-Tonnelles bend, a sudden gust of wind had blown her crêpe over her eyes, and I even he added remember thinking it was dangerous and that you ought to tuck it under your coat or pin it down on to something quite so.

Her mother old Lorpailleur's that is, Madame Aristide, died in May fifty-two, two months before the tragedy, which explains why the daughter was in mourning when she came to offer her condolences to the Ducreuxs, a woman who wasn't in the least like her daughter, Madame Aristide, very kind, very sympathetic, even a bit gaga towards the end of her life which dragged on for a good ten years, she had a filthy sort of illness that no doctor could ever cure, they put her in her bath-chair in the sun and the children came and pinched her sweets from the basket beside her where she also kept her knitting and a thermos flask, she was very fond of little Louis who was their neighbor of course, their yards adjoined each other, when she died old Lorpailleur moved to the rue de Broy at the other end opposite the Chestnut Tree café, these differences of character between mother and daughter are something very strange, the mother was as kind as the daughter was vicious and embittered, which to a certain extent can be explained by her disappointment but there's more to it than that, it could have been quite the opposite, when her engagement to Georges Magnin was broken off it must be twenty years ago now, if every girl who got jilted ended up like her life wouldn't be worth living, the house belonged to the mother, the father had nothing, he'd been a mason but from forty on after his accident he didn't do anything, he had a pension which brought him in next to nothing he died when he was sixty i.e. ten years before the mother who died at seventy-five, she was five years older than he, the daughter immediately sold the house and went to live in the rue de Broy right at the end opposite the Chestnut Tree café, she's far from being hard up, makes you wonder whether there isn't something vicious in the fact that she carries on with the school, just to torment the children, the parents thought of getting up a petition, that must be a good ten years ago, nothing came of it, some parents like the Bianles for instance and the Magnins didn't want to sign, you never know, if it makes a stink in high-up circles you can say good-bye to your subsidies, all this because the mayor, who was he at the time, was on old Lorpailleur's side, anyway she stayed, they'd got into the habit.

It would be more likely to be on the side of her uncle Voiret that we should look for similarities, you remember Armand Voiret, a right bastard, always bickering with everyone, that business of the easement with old Surot what a bore that was, they could never agree, yes you might look in that direction but there's more to it than that, she's more than a mischief-maker she's plain vicious, only the other day young Bianle came home in tears, she'd kept him in on the Thursday because he'd made a mistake in his recitation, do you really punish a child for getting a word wrong, the parents wanted to get up a petition, she can't even stand animals, every time she gets a chance to lash out with her broom at Mademoiselle Ronzière's cat she takes it, and her mother's canaries you remember what happened to them, no, whatever you may say, there's more to it than that.

Sitting up straight on her English-type bike Mademoiselle Lorpailleur was going down to do her shopping, it was a Thursday, the children were playing in their back yards, she passed the Swan café where young Bianle was tying a hook on to the line of his fishing rod with a friend, they looked away, at the corner of the rue Neuve she stopped to fasten her basket on the carrier and as she was just about to get on to her machine again Madame Monneau was going into the baker's which caused old Lorpailleur to make a detour, she went down the rue du Couteau and it was there that from twenty yards away she saw the truck just miss little Frédéric, the mother grab hold of her child and then go into the chemist's where she apparently waited two or three minutes, Cruze was in the café, and then left without her aspirins, went back to the bakery and said to the girl serve these ladies I'll be back in a moment, the customers were arriving, it must have been half-past eleven.

Because you can be mildly mad or stark staring mad, she belongs to the latter category.

But Cruze alias Verveine had the nerve to answer me you won't find me meddling in your affairs.

Now *I* say that old Lorpailleur is mad.

Reconstituting the tragedy in question bit by bit in her spare time, insinuating that I must have had something to do with it and not only I but the parents themselves, the poor Ducreuxs, the mother will make herself ill over it, isn't it a disgrace to let that fanatic spread rumors and set people against each other, we know how these things end.

No one went to see her in the mental hospital, in any case it was advised against, she was given cold showers and put in a strait-jacket on some days and had electric shock treatment and drugs, all of which took a weight off people's minds, we breathed again, the children's writing improved, their arithmetic too, just imagine that in old Lorpailleur's day at eight years old they didn't know how to add twenty-five and twenty-five, I found that out with young Magnin, yes good riddance, her sister from the Argentine or goodness knows where came back to the district, she got rid of the flat and bought back the family house for a song, a sensible girl and still not bad-looking, a brunette with blue eyes, I'll draw a veil over what they said about her morals over there, people are such scandalmongers, in any case nothing to complain of here, perfectly well-behaved, apropos of the flat she found it in such a state just imagine, with medicine bottles and barbiturates as they call them in every corner, and filthy, it made you want to vomit she didn't bother to go to the lavatory, I'm talking about the madwoman, she just did it on the floor, at the foot of the bed, and manuscripts everywhere, loose sheets covered with her illegible writing, really just the very thought of our having put up with a creature like that in charge of our children for fifteen years, it makes you want to tear your hair.

And it seems that it was only after, quite some time after young Bianle's accident, he was run over by a truck, that we heard that old Lorpailleur had seen it from a distance and could have been a witness for the truck driver because it wasn't his fault and saved him from getting his year's suspended sentence or whatever it was, the child got over it, fractures aren't so serious at that age, but the poor man was terribly upset, he visited the boy in hospital every day, in his free time, or sent his wife with chocolate and oranges, which was why they pulled down number twelve on the corner, a building that belonged to the parish, they weren't using it for anything, not enough room for the village hall that they built in the rue Gambetta on the site that used to belong to Amorinz, he did very nicely out of his compensation that fellow, what it is to suck up to the council, the visibility is all right there now even though the mayor talks of pulling down number two rue Ancienne as well, in short she probably saw the whole thing, can you imagine such wickedness.

So that since her sister couldn't come back from the Argentine she had all the time in the world to fix things with the lawyer so that he didn't drag the case out but settled the inheritance to her advantage, there are some things that you only discover when it's too late and which are not at all to the credit of you know whom, quite so the lawyer.

Such lovely weather, the first fine days.

That morning the roadman who acts as rural policeman in his spare time or vice versa apparently heard someone shouting in the wood, it must have been half-past eleven, there was nothing extraordinary about that on a Sunday

when so many people go out to enjoy the fresh air and picnic in the country, what sort of a shout, a child calling out,
first he said yes then he said no, getting the different times
muddled up, which is excusable given the hour and the season, can you really expect Blimbraz to make a list of all the
noises he hears in the forest what an idea, in the middle of
July, what with all the people out walking there, how did he
know the time, because he left the village at eleven just work
it out, he may well have stopped for a moment at the bistro
but when he was asked later the owner of the Swan didn't
remember having seen him at all that day.

It was such lovely weather, contrary to all expectations,
from one day to the next, the beginning of May right up to
the second half had been remarkable for all those frosts and
that perpetual wind the like of which had not been recorded
since eighteen seventy-three, Bianle and Ducreux, the fathers
that is, had gone over to Malatraîne with their sons to look
out the boundaries of the field that Armand and old mother
Surot are always bickering over, she claims she has a right
of way, an easement as they call it, through Voiret's land,
at the edge of the forest they saw Auguste Serinet the
brother of the chap who was killed, Ducreux had been talking to him the day before about the shed in his yard, Auguste is related to Madame Monneau through his sister-in-
law the widow but they aren't on speaking terms any more.

When she got to the baker's Madame Monneau apparently
told Madame Ducreux that Auguste had been flying a few
kites in the direction of his sister-in-law the wife of the one
who was killed about their quarrel which was really without foundation, it dated back to Antonin's death, something
to do with the division of the property, Serinet hadn't at that
time been willing to let old man Monneau have his field in
exchange for the plot they didn't know what to do with,
but everything must have worked out all right at the time of

27

the re-allocation because the exchange did in fact take place, they still weren't on speaking terms though, which worried Auguste less from the sentimental angle than from the business one because the Monneaus had decided on the extension I told you about to their house, they were thinking of getting a builder from Agapa to do it and Madame Monneau was discussing this with the baker's wife and wondering what might follow from a reconciliation, wouldn't it encourage young Serinet's designs on her sister's daughter, her niece that is, who didn't want him at any price.

They saw Auguste and Ducreux asked him whether he wasn't somehow going to come to terms with Madame Monneau, it seemed to him that it would be a pity if he were to lose the order on account of such an ancient quarrel, but Auguste didn't want to make the first move, he wasn't short of work, they'd soon see what trouble they'd run into with that builder, not a reliable firm.

When she got to the baker's Madame Monneau apparently told the baker's wife that she'd seen Serinet at the corner of the rue Neuve and one thing leading to another that she would never make the first move, she wasn't the slightest bit interested in what might follow from a reconciliation, do I care, have I ever bothered about what people say, it just doesn't make sense does it now, as if the scandal-mongering of a madwoman were going to change the face of the world, neither of the adjacent parts of the two properties was of the slightest interest to her, when you think of all the misery there is in the world how can people possibly waste their time on such nonsense, village tittle-tattle, she was being philosophical and Verveine suddenly asked himself the question, should he or shouldn't he.

Such lovely weather, it was the end of June, there was a truck parked outside the Swan café, the Bianle and Voiret boys were on their way to school, it must have been half-past one when all of a sudden the truck driver comes out of the café, he feels giddy, he collapses on to the pavement, the children come up, soon there are about ten of them in a circle round him, the chemist comes hurrying over, we'll take him says he to the doctor's he lives opposite, that was where they took the sample of his blood, the man wasn't drunk, he was just liable to fits of giddiness, the subject came up again later apropos of little Frédéric's accident, it was Frédéric wasn't it, the road wasn't wide enough at that spot, it was dangerous if anything was parked there and there wasn't sufficient visibility, pull down number twelve that was what they should have done but they only did it afterwards, too late, the parents were left with only their eyes to cry with, such a sweet child, six months later, it was the end of July, the month of catastrophes.

Fires, people drowned, car accidents, so on and so forth.

They saw Auguste and Ducreux didn't mention the matter to him for fear of upsetting old mother Monneau who had put him in touch through her brother-in-law, a relation of Voiret's, with Magnin's firm, they were prepared to do the work for half the price but he hadn't committed himself to Auguste.

As for the hearing it did indeed take place, I'm referring to the Bianle affair, and it resulted in the driver being given a suspended sentence, because the Ducreux affair never got beyond the inquiry stage, the killer is still at large.

And ten years later Etienne Bianle, he was eighteen entered Mademoiselle Ariane's service, she's never had any fault to find with him, he's still there as gamekeeper, and apropos of that I'd like to point out that the murder of Serinet by his brother-in-law could well have simply been an accident, it was July, but no one had any doubt about the guilt of the accused, not a single witness in his favor, it's enough to make you despair of there ever being any justice.

It was one day during this same fine weather, great big midday July sun, they brought Serinet's body home from the woods in a coffin, he had been killed the previous evening about seven the doctor said, when he wasn't back by the time the soup was on the table his wife thought he must have stopped at his brother-in-law's and had dinner with them but when he still didn't come home she began to get worried by about eleven, she went to her brother's and found his wife there alone and in the same state as she was, Simon hadn't come home either, the two of them went to notify the gendarmes who didn't start looking for them till the next day round about ten o'clock, they said they must have gone on the spree to Agapa or elsewhere, their wives had a bad night torn between fear and fury, at first they had been more or less inclined to agree with the gendarmes then their fear got the upper hand, they'd already stopped believing in the spree explanation long before the cops finally went into action with Blimbraz, they followed with some of the men, they went straight to the wood where the missing men used to go poaching, there was no alternative but to admit it, they searched for about two hours and found Serinet with a bullet through his heart, no trace of the other, but given the time it took to get hold of the doctor who certified that he had been dead since the day before, and then the carpenter who always had a spare coffin reserved for the next comer, it was quite three o'clock when they brought Antonin back home, not midday, but the sun, it was enough to make you ill, the procession crossed the square, the funeral would take place the following day, the poor widow was in such a state and her sister-in-law the same worse even she didn't know what had become of her man, they'd searched the wood for him too after they'd discovered Serinet, which meant that it was quite six o'clock when they decided to call off the search and take Antonin home but being July if you went by the sun you might have thought it was midday, I can still see Topard the gendarme wiping his forehead and Madame Simon all red, her sweat mingling with her tears, her hair so dishevelled, a pitiable sight, the widow too, still in her apron, she hadn't taken it off since the day before, she was going home with a husband to weep for instead of a libertine to beat, if only the gendarmes had been right when they decided they couldn't be bothered to put themselves out immediately but there you are, life had decided otherwise, they stopped outside the church where the curé gave the blessing for those who depart this life without the sacraments and then they took him home seeing that he only lived a few steps away, if he'd lived miles away they'd have put the deceased in the crypt till the next day but the poor widow who wanted to cry her fill at home in their love-nest as they say, they hadn't been married three months, funny sort of anniversary.

As for Simon, three days after the funeral they ran him to earth in Douves where he was hiding in an hotel, it's my opinion that if he had been guilty he'd have gone further away, he'd have crossed the frontier, he'd lost his head, never having had it screwed on very tightly anyway and already foreseeing that he wouldn't be able to defend himself against all the accusations, some weak people react in unexpected ways which convict rather than acquit them, let's suppose as I believe to be the case that his emotional reaction was responsible for his running away after the accident, then the inquiry and the assizes and life imprisonment, that makes two widows as you might say, the amazing thing is that they didn't become mortal enemies, on the contrary their grief united them, never a Sunday but what they go out together, which sets the tongues wagging too, whatever happens to us it's always for the worst.

Or if the curé had in fact casually suggested a modest

little blessing just to be going on with, and if Madame Antonin had refused saying that there'd be plenty of time the next day or not saying anything at all, just a simple gesture on her part and the curé would have realized that he mustn't insist, she was too distressed, unless the abbé had followed the procession and said a makeshift prayer at the murdered man's home and then immediately gone back to the church and given the verger his instructions, having extracted an order for a first-class funeral from the widow, Serinet had the wherewithal.

As for Mademoiselle Ronzière, she wrote the event up in both *Le Fantoniard* and *Le Petit Photographe*, thus cutting the grass from under the feet of old Lorpailleur who had to fall back on an epistle on the subject of Providence and Misfortune, it's a very strange thing these old maids on our local rags, you might almost think we collected them on purpose, as if the nonsense they try to get us to swallow was their revenge for their cumbersome maidenhood or whatever, the whole thing would be laughable if it didn't have such a noticeable effect on the way our papers are run.

Germaine Ronzière is retired, she used to work in the post office, that wasn't where she got her talent from, she's always flirted with the Muse, she knew our Poetess Louise d'Isimance well, they collaborated it must be ten years ago now on a little volume of the poets of our region since the XVIth century, there are nine counting Louise and Germaine, all much of a muchness, singing of roses and vines, except that in the old days poets like Mathurin Saveur and Valère de Bonne-Mesure for instance were inclined to put in bits about the light at dawn whereas these days it's the light at sunset, that's the main difference, this Valère as everyone knows was an ancestor of Mademoiselle Ariane, she still owns the first poems he wrote, in his own hand, the rest disappeared during the Revolution, the manuscripts I mean, because the actual books, you can find them in the Agapa library but isn't that a real old maid's idea, publishing a volume like that that no one's interested in and Verveine and I were wondering if it wasn't a very bad idea at that, it gives a rotten impression of our province, people might get the idea that the thinkers in our midst never got any further than their own back gardens or vineyards, hang it though we certainly have produced men of quite another stamp, as for instance at the turn of the century Ernest Magnin the mayor who all his life fought to bring water to the parish and electricity as well, if it hadn't been for him we'd still be in the middle ages or squabbling over our different religious or political views in the parish council without ever progressing an inch, but there you are you see, really intelligent people don't put pen to paper.

Really intelligent people don't put pen to paper, that's what Monnard says, he's our clerk to the parish council, an educated and very sociable man, we all try more or less consciously to model ourselves on him but he takes no particular pride in this or at least if he does he doesn't show it, according to Verveine subtlety of mind is something that works all ways and is also active therefore in the field of our awareness of ourselves, I consider this a debatable point, in short Monnard who is only semi-retired from the teaching profession, he had to give it up after a serious operation and he's still only about fifty so you see he's no richer or better-born than you or I, is an attractive character, he stood for Mayor ten years ago several people advised him to but he wasn't elected because of an intrigue that would take too long to explain but which certainly came from high-up circles given his tendencies, this didn't worry him in the least however quite the opposite as he isn't ambitious and he still fascinates his little circle just as he always used to, which is why Verveine says that this too argues calculation on his

33

part or rather affectation, intelligence doesn't insulate anyone against humiliation, that too is debatable.

It was apropos of old Lorpailleur that he came out with this
gem, a few of us were at the *mairie* discussing the parish
loan when the question of the advisability of putting an ad-
vertisement in the local rag came up and one thing leading
to another we went on to discuss the scope of the printed
word in general and our literary hacks in particular not
forgetting Lorpailleur, Monnard contrived to make his
remark just when the schoolmistress's name had been mentioned, not immediately however so as to put them off a bit
but near enough for the less uncouth to make no mistake
according to Madame Monneau he is one of the ones old
Lorpailleur is supposed to have turned down in the days of
her youth but I don't believe it for other reasons, not that
Monnard's natural elegance is one of them because there
have been examples of people with distinguished minds being particularly apt to go off the sentimental rails, I'm not
making it up, in short Monnard is a bachelor which, still
according to old ma Monneau, is one of the reasons for the
failure of his candidature apart from that of his advanced
ideas, there's plenty of room for discussion there, personally
I should rather have thought that being a bachelor should
have weighed the scales in favor of his holding office but
everyone has his own opinion on this point.

The parish loan went very well and the village hall is being built, we decided to put it alongside the football pitch,
the contract for the masonry went to Mortin though he
very nearly saw the work going to Charpy, it was all
settled at the last minute, one more proof of the inefficiency
of our institutions or let's say of our administrative procedure which however codified it may be is nevertheless only
too often of an extremely improvised nature.

Or this remark about really intelligent people could have

dated from some time previously, it's not impossible, Monnard may very well have been drawing neither on his own experience nor on his reading but have been quoting his father old Monnard who didn't have his son's distinction but who was quite as intelligent, he had been mayor, I remember my father telling me Monnard has had another go at so and so on the council, one of his particular *bêtes noires* was Latirail who had literary pretensions and who was always coming out with quotations, as for Latirail junior the schoolmaster he's the living image of his father and his contributions to *Le Fantoniard* don't exactly err on the side of modesty, he has influential friends, the son, politics have dessicated his mind, he's as cantankerous as a squint-eyed mongrel so that whatever the sex or degree of culture of their authors all the various items in our newspapers reek of old maid, there's food for thought there, given that maidenhead or whatever is not really the *sine qua non* for anyone who has some sort of style or particular way of life.

As for Mademoiselle Ronzière she wrote a report of the event, I'm referring to the laying of the foundation stone on the site of the village hall, thus cutting the grass from under the feet of Latirail who had to fall back on a political or whatever account, referring to a remark of his father's about the ballot at the mayoral elections but giving it a left-wing slant, thus allowing it to be understood that Mortin's getting the contract could well have been the result of an intrigue in high-up circles, in short a bastardly sort of article that revolted old Lorpailleur because of the odd insinuation here and there about the teaching in primary schools and the conclusion that existed between ...

In short a bastardly article that aroused old Lorpailleur's indignation to the point where she ...

In short, an article.

Or if after the curé had suggested to the mayor that the

schoolmistress might use her influence to get the children to go to the catechism class and she hadn't taken kindly to this unwarrantable interference in her affairs, not that she was against religion but she thought she knew where her duty lay, she didn't need anyone to remind her of it, she had alluded to this in her Saturday article by means of a reference to the remark made by Monnard's father whose opinions she distorted, something that the most ignorant amongst us presumably noticed the next day and which must have deprived her of what little sympathy we may still have had for her.

Sitting up straight on her bike the schoolmistress came down the rue de Broy and then took the Sirancy road to the newspaper office where she had to deliver her copy, at this time of year there was a delay in the postal deliveries, it was a Thursday and it was as she was passing the Tripeaus' general stores that she apparently saw Magnin standing on the pavement talking to the driver of a parked truck which driver seeing the little Ducreux boy just about to cross the road apparently held him back at the last second, old Lorpailleur couldn't see the child as he was hidden by the truck, which apparently caused her to stop suddenly in a great state of excitement, to thank the truck driver and scold the child, one of her pupils, I'm talking about little Frédéric, seven years old, then climbing back up on to her machine again apparently rode off while Magnin was reminding the truck driver of the dramatic disappearance of the brother, the killer is still at large, adding to the story his own doubts about the morality of the Ducreuxs, the sort of people they used to mix with at the time and how it could have been in their interests according to him for their oldest son to disappear, Mademoiselle Moine was at her window and apparently heard every word of the conversation.

And as she disappeared round the corner at the quai des Moulins Madame Monneau who was watching her out of the corner of her eye came out of her house she had been doing everything she could to avoid her ever since the allusion in the local paper of the twelfth of June to fields, easements, rights of way and other grounds for the bickering and law-suits which are everlastingly poisoning our neighborly rela-tions, she regarded it as a dig at her, excuse the pun, as she had advised her brother-in-law not to give in to Magnin, she had even worked herself up into a terrible state over it, the thing was common knowledge and old Lorpailleur had certainly taken advantage of this to display her superficial erudition and moralistic hypocrisy in the newspaper, Ma-dame Monneau would never forgive her, she came out of her house, then, she shut her door and as she was bending down to pick up her shopping basket from the pavement she heard shouts coming from the quai des Tanneurs, from behind her that is, which made her turn around but it was only some children playing, then as she passed the butcher's she no-ticed the butcher's wife at the back of the shop cleaning the windows of the communicating door, standing on a stool, which was what made her say to Madame Ducreux a few minutes later that it would be better if the butcher's wife took more trouble over her steak and less over her house-work, her meat was becoming uneatable, to which Madame Ducreux apparently replied that she patronized the other one but that the quality couldn't be much better, it's all to do with politics, what does the government think we are making us put up with such stuff, it wouldn't matter so much if all the taxes didn't keep going up, it all boded no good, she broke off at this point as she heard screams coming from outside and they both went out, Madame Monneau saying that she'd heard something as she was shutting her door from over in the Tanneurs direction, that was where it was coming from all right, and then the cries stopped.

Children playing, it was a Thursday.

During which time Ducreux was in the yard discussing the estimate with the mason, he was all for something prefabricated to avoid expense, which the mason was more or less disputing, there's no shortage of stone and as for the labor we can come to some arrangement, young Verrière's out of work, he'd like nothing better, he could spend as much time on it as was necessary, you aren't going to worry about a day or two.

Talking about all this ten years later Mademoiselle Moine said that it was precisely twelve noon when the accident happened, she'd heard the child scream, getting both the day and the time wrong but nobody remembered that, she happened to be at her window, Ducreux had even come out with his baker's cap on and he'd been the first to approach the little victim, Cruze had only come up afterwards, she remembered having seen the apprentice running to the chemist's and then to the doctor's, the doctor was still at the hospital at that hour, they carried the child over to Cruze's while they were waiting for him but it was too late, the truck driver was tearing his hair, no punishment can ever be too severe for these road hogs, he must have been half-seas over, she'd seen him so she said coming out of the Swan a few minutes earlier, which was impossible as number twelve hadn't been pulled down at the time but nobody remembered that either.

Mademoiselle Moine had come down too, she had some shopping to do near the bridge, she went down the rue Neuve which leads to the crossroads and just before she got to the chemist's she saw a drunken man trying to open the door of his truck, she immediately crossed the road as she'd been afraid of drunkards ever since the time when Maillard had nearly killed her, he was on his way back from the bar and in the dark he mistook her for his wife, they lived on

the same landing, she was on her way back from the sewing-
bee, normally the ladies never stay there after ten o'clock but
what with the jumble sale they were having to work their
fingers to the bone, even so Maillard had never been cured
of this propensity of his in spite of having been convicted
of grievous bodily harm, that was another July misdeed, and
so it was when she got to the other side of the road that she
saw the truck driver collapse on to the pavement, Chinze the
shoemaker called his apprentice to help the toper to his feet,
he didn't know what to do with him, it was Lorduz the
gendarme who settled matters by taking him to the station,
he happened to be passing, Lorduz remembered this ten
years later even though arrests of the sort are far from rare
but the driver was Polish or whatever, didn't speak a word of
French, this was confirmed by the lessee of the Chestnut Tree
who ought to have been fined for serving a customer in that
state or going on serving him, he got off scot-free.

Or that Mademoiselle Moine had only come down a long
time later and that she saw the pool of blood on the pavement, young Bianle having been made mincemeat of, his
brains were splashed all over the bakery wall, sights of this
sort remain engraved on your mind for ever, people remembered that too but some said that it was the end of June
whereas it was nearly a fortnight into July, the school broke
up two days later, fine holiday he'd had poor angel, Blimbraz
swept up the brains with the grocer's dustpan and brush, the
horrible things you do in such circumstances but what else
could he have done, he lost his head, I can still see him, not
knowing what to do with the debris.

The doctor bending over the little victim, all he could do
was certify that he was dead, the poor mother was in such
a state, just imagine the picture, Bianle sweeping up the
brains, the brothers and sisters poor angels sobbing in the

arms of their grandmother, his mother that is who is off her head anyway, whether from sorrow or senility we don't know, she's getting on for ninety-three, and poor Blimbraz who never stopped repeating that if only the parish council had allowed the credits we'd been demanding for the last two years for the alterations to the crossroads it would never have happened, it was enough to make you die of despair, the curé is inclined to pile on the horror on these occasions, he mumbled a modest little prayer, the funeral would take place in two day's time, he had extorted a first class one from poor Bianle who had lost his head, Mademoiselle Moine still remembered how many vases of flowers and wreaths there were, we hadn't seen the like since . . .

A cat burying her mess, that's what Mademoiselle Ariane was looking at, it always made her feel sentimental, how well Nature has provided for these things really hasn't she, when you think of the way we, eh, you see what I mean, yes really Nature, to which the curé replied it wasn't nature, nature is an atheist's word, it was the good Lord Mademoiselle, to which Mademoiselle losing her temper, she's naturally irascible, replied the good Lord, Monsieur le curé, has other cats than this one in his bag, he has to watch the way plenty of other cats than this one jump, in short let the good Lord mind his own business in so far as cats' business is concerned, this was very shortly after the little Ducreux boy's funeral, the curé is so tactless, in any case so naive, the strangest thing in all this is that Mademoiselle de Bonne-Mesure always falls for it, someone of her eminence, and yet she isn't against religion, she goes to eleven o'clock Mass every Sunday with Mademoiselle Francine, she adores cats, she keeps half a dozen, she was watching all this one fine July day from her terrace, Minouche was doing her business in the hydrangeas, it was the first Saturday in the month and therefore shortly after the funeral, the day she traditionally invites the curé, they're a very old family.

Sitting having coffee on the terrace with Monsieur le curé and Francine on a July day, a torrid sun which was so different from the weather the previous week which . . .

Sitting on the terrace with the curé and Mademoiselle Francine, they were all three waiting for the luncheon bell, just a finger of port in each glass, on a beautiful July day, during the first week, they were discussing the previous Sunday's sermon given by the Reverend Father, the Mission preacher, its tone had somehow displeased Mademoiselle Ariane, was it a little unctuous, Mademoiselle her niece was yawning with her mouth shut, it was nearly one o'clock and the curé was weighing his words before replying but couldn't find anything to say other than he's an excellent man the children love him, then all of a sudden there's a movement in the box-tree where Minette had been concealed, she starts scratching in the flower-bed intending to deposit her mess therein, Mademoiselle Ariane interrupts herself and goes into ecstasies, the fact is that Minette was a stray, Mademoselle Fancine went pssht pssht and clapped her hands, thus cutting the operation short, which made her aunt protest, oh you naughty girl, when you think of the way we and so on, the curé as if nothing had happened carried on about the marvelous weather which was so different from, in any case great big clouds were gathering in the west, the storm wasn't far off and Minouche was digging her hole elsewhere.

That the good Lord was present even in the most insignificant manifestations of nature, whether tactlessness or naivety, Mademoiselle started guffawing with her mouth shut, she had been keeping one eye on Minette who under that of Providence was depositing her mess in the kitchen-garden, Mademoiselle was most displeased, most, ding ding, they got up and went over towards the door into the lounge which is on a level with the terrace, Marie in her white apron greeted the curé and stood aside to let her mistress pass which mistress entered followed by the ecclesiastic and the niece, crossed the drawing-room to the dining-room where she sat down and there surprise surprise was Minette depositing her mess in the window-box that Mademoiselle tended so lovingly, it's under one of the dining-room windows, she cultivates ferns in it and sort of little artichokes, very rare ones, indignation from the aunt, chuckles from the niece with her mouth shut, pssht pssht, she fled to the kitchen-garden.

Present in even the most insignificant manifestations of nature.

Then Mademoiselle Ariane said I should very much like to know your opinion of that preacher, there's something about his manner that I don't much care for, adding ten years later, she had just repeated her phrase, I told you so I told you so, but the curé that day had no reason to complain of the Father, he said, taking a second helping, an eel matelote, very good with the children, and he let the spoon slide down into the sauce, nothing to apologize for Monsieur le curé, Marie picked it out with her finger-tips, the big double doors had been left open so the reflection of Mademoiselle Ariane and her two guests could be seen from a distance in the drawing-room mirror with the servant in her white apron, a picture that set you dreaming about the good old days, they took things easily in those days, they weren't in such a hurry, but the doctor says that where hygiene was concerned they weren't quite the thing, that was what was responsible for the greater part of their illnesses, he's always going on about it, he's taught our women to wash, you see what I mean, the sort of thing we think of willy-nilly when we see such a scene on a July day, going to so much trouble to keep the house cool, blinds drawn, smell of melons and old wardrobes, not a sound.

Out in the garden under the plane tree the flies were wallowing in the dregs in the port glasses, a cock was crowing, the heat was setting fire to the air over the harvested crops, it was summer.

Or when they came out of Mass Mademoiselle Ariane took off her silk coat and Francine her head-scarf, what a heat, we hadn't seen the like since eighteen seventy-three, Madame Monneau and Madame Bianle and the choir girls were standing round the curé who had hurriedly taken off his vestments in order to enjoy the company of the ladies out in the square, it must be mentioned that there was a collection for Peter's or someone else's pence to be organized, his housekeeper was most indignant about the the stinginess of the faithful, I can still see her a slight little figure in light gray, the curé requested her to be so good as to keep quiet oh come now Marie, assuming the air of a humble, meritorious man who was glad to submit himself to the Ways of Providence, bowing very low to Mademoiselle Ariane at whose house he had been doing himself proud the day before, I'm talking of the Saturday before the cat-shit, the ladies hurried off to the baker's to buy the tarts they treated themselves to on Sundays, so that the shepherd found himself discussing the murder in question with his flock and repeating the Ways of Providence, Madame Monneau was furious, the housekeeper added render unto Saint Peter or something of the sort.

Or that Mademoiselle Francine bicycling from Malatraîne to see her aunt, an old English-type bone-shaker that she uses for short distances she says it's good exercise and in any case you see the countryside better but she uses her car for longer ones when she goes into town for instance, caught sight as she was coming out of the cross-path of a man just going into the wood on her right, that she said to herself from this distance he looks like old Chottard, then branching off to the left i.e. in our direction thought she heard a child calling out, she couldn't catch the words, there's an echo at that spot but if you don't happen to be in the direct line of the sound waves far from clarifying people's voices it confuses them, she imagined it was a family having a day in the country, the mother looking for somewhere to have lunch, a bit weary what with the picnic basket to carry, her son quite some way behind her, he would have been following the father at first but then when he too got tired would have decided to wait for her, in short the sort of scene a passer-by might conjure up from merely hearing some sort of sound on a sunny day on the outskirts of the forest, it was a Saturday, she hadn't a care in the world, I'm referring to Mademoiselle Francine, other than to arrive on time at her aunt's, that is, she was quietly pedalling along, she was admiring the ferns which abound all the way to Bonne-Mesure, she was drinking in the pure air and the birdsong, she was already imagining Marie on the terrace arranging three chairs round the iron table, was the curé going to hold forth about the jumble sale again, she refuses to allow herself to be roped in like poor Odette Magnin who is the same age as she is or even Laurette Vinet who neither of them have the slightest hope of getting married, it's the beginning of the end when you start devoting yourself to good works, there would be plenty of time for her to lend a hand as they say on such occasions but in a casual sort of way with the elegance of the lady who has nothing against being charitable when she has nothing better to do, thoughts of that sort, she arrived at the gate which Amédée had opened that morning in her honor, she got off her bike as she couldn't ride over the gravel, the old manor appeared before her with all its windows open to the eleven o'clock sun, it was already hot,

44

was her little blouse stained under the armpits, she stopped, the perspiration was in fact apparent, never go out again without something to change into, and it was at this moment that Amédée who was clipping the hedge round the kitchen garden saw her from a distance and called out good morning to her, these old servants take touching liberties with you, she gladly forgave him, after all when she was a very little girl she used to follow him everywhere as he went about his work, she used to pinch sweets out of his pocket, essence of pine they were, he had always been subject to bronchitis, thinking as she answered him from a distance good thing I wasn't smelling my armpits it's a bad habit I've got into but at that distance he wouldn't have been able to tell, even so one ought always to be on one's best behavior you never know.

While in the village Madame Ducreux was recounting the Bianles' adventure of the previous Sunday, they'd set off on their tandem with their youngest on the carrier, they were going to picnic in the forest, they stopped at the clearing and went into the wood, her husband was pushing the machine and she was holding the little boy's hand, here and there the path was overgrown with brambles which meant that she wasn't making much progress, brilliant idea that was of yours making us get off there she was saying to her husband instead of going on to the crossroads and then taking the little path that goes straight to it, but pig-headed as he is he was apparently pretty fed up with her moaning, you can see his point of view too, all day in his workshop he needs a bit of movement the poor man, he needs a bit of adventure, you remember what a gay dog he was when he was young, wasn't he the one who ran away from home for three days with Edouard Vinet, no that was his brother, in short she was explaining to Madame Monneau that at one moment she let go of her little boy's hand, he wanted to be with his father who was some way ahead, she was quite

45

willing and they both disappeared into the wood, she wasn't worried she kept stopping to put the picnic basket down or to look at some leaf or other, she doesn't have such a marvelous life either what with her dressmaking and her housework, she felt free, a bit tired already but relaxed, you get moments like that, they're rare though, when a pleasant sort of floating feeling comes over you, all the more so as just going into the country is a pleasure in itself, she added that when a calamity befalls you at such a moment it upsets you all the more and that we would do better if we were always a little bit worried somewhere so as not to lay ourselves wide open to the workings of Chance, this showed that she'd previously given these matters a good deal of thought, and at one moment she found herself alone in the middle of the forest, the clearing was even farther away than she'd thought, brilliant idea he had making us get off there, he'll always be the same and that's a fact.

And it was as she was making this observation to herself that she heard the little boy calling on her right, was he saying Mummy or Daddy, there's an echo at that spot that confuses all the sounds, she got into a panic and called back here here where are you and started running in the direction leaving her picnic basket on the ground, luckily the boy wasn't far off but he was all by himself, she asked him where his father had gone, the kid was crying, he didn't know, so she started walking blindly relying on the position of the sun, a thing she remembered from the days when she'd been a scout-mistress and it was only a hour later that she found Edmond fast asleep in the clearing, how can he be so irresponsible she wondered, let's look furious when we wake him up because the picnic basket God knew where she'd left it, he'd be furious.

Telling this to Mademoiselle Moine who was passing her door she added it makes me go hot and cold all over just thinking about it, God knows what might have happened to the child, can you understand how men can be so irresponsible, no one can take a mother's place, do you suppose he said he was sorry when he saw the state I was in, and who had to go and fetch the basket with the boy, I did, he was asleep again when we got back, we had our lunch it must have been two o'clock at the very least, don't talk to me about picnics, I'll never set foot there again, meaning in the forest, you get much more of a rest at home, what she was forgetting to mention was that her husband hadn't felt very well that morning, she was the one who had insisted on his getting up, it was his duty to take the child out and let him get some fresh air, seeing that the older one had been at his grandmother's since the day before, it was she who was responsible then and she knew it but like all the women around here she was trying to put the blame on her husband, it's more convenient, men don't go in for so much thinking, they don't split hairs and if you rub their noses in their own mess it works nine times out of ten, they don't remember they'd been feeling poorly that morning and when I say their own mess it isn't precisely their own, well this time it hadn't worked and when the grandmother heard about it the next day when she brought the older one back she was so furious with her son-in-law that she told Madame Monneau, the mother, Augustine's mother-in-law that is, that Edmond had tried to lose his child in the woods, he'd never wanted a second one, who knows if he won't murder him one of these fine days, it was her duty to have the child to live with her but her daughter wasn't convinced she said she was exaggerating, Edmond is a very good father when he's not feeling poorly, which is something that happens to him more often than it does to the rest of us, the after-effects of all those fevers he caught over there, a family permanently on the *qui-vive*, when I think of my other daughter, that must

47

be even worse poor thing, the one in the Argentine, the letters she writes me if you only knew, her husband drinks, it's my opinion they'll be divorced before two years are out, just imagine the sort of offspring they're liable to have, it seems that their eldest he wanders in his mind, psycho psychi what do they call it troubles, marvelous old age I've got ahead of me, because like all the women round here she was incapable of seeing any problem except in terms of herself, she pretended to be worried about her family's health but she was far more concerned with her own well-being.

Or that it could have been Bianle who happened to be at the crossroads at that moment, he was on his way to his brother's to discuss the Voiret easement which doesn't in the least suit his book ever since he's decided to build, he apparently saw Francine taking the right fork, he took her for Mademoiselle Ronzière because he's short-sighted and especially as he didn't know that Francine used a bike for short distances, he's always seen her in a car, his house isn't far from the town, it couldn't have been anyone other than him that Francine saw since he was coming from the Crachon road which is in the opposite direction but he hadn't heard a thing from the woods, it's true that his moped makes an earsplitting din, all the more reason then, but Mademoiselle Ronzière had been questioned at the inquiry, she hadn't gone out until half-past eleven that day she'd had all her washing up from the night before to do, she'd had her cousin Romain and his wife plus the Alphonse Monneaus, she had felt obliged it was only polite to return their hospitality what with them inviting her to little Alfred's first communion, it did make quite a crowd but she preferred to work them all off at the same time, not that she said that of course, which proved that she couldn't have met Bianle, she hadn't head anything either but she did say that she had wondered why people didn't take advantage of such a morning to go out for a bit, in her day the forest had always been full of people, true that with a car they often prefer to go over Chatruse way.

As for Doctor Mottard he's a cousin by marriage of the watchmaker, he married Victorine Laruaz who died oh it must be ten years ago leaving him with a lame daughter, it's not for nothing that they say that the cobbler's wife is the worst shod, they spent a fortune on the poor girl but she still limps, how old can she be, about forty, she practically never leaves the house she does everything for her father, the housework, opens the door to the patients, acts as his assistant, he absolutely adores her it's quite touching, he calls her Poulette and then this great big girl appears, obviously though as she doesn't take any exercise and is well fed she's a bit like the Christmas goose but really very nice, she's very fond of plants and small birds, there are flower-pots at every window and there are three canary cages, one in the waiting-room so that the children don't get impatient, one in the dining-room to amuse Dad at meal-times and one in the kitchen for her that's where she spends most of her time but it sometimes happens that a pot of petunias or whatever takes a header on to the pavement or that when she's watering them it goes over someone and the neighbors that puts their backs up, there's nothing they can do about it seeing that the doctor's so dedicated, in any case if anyone remarked on it to him he'd start laughing and call Poulette to laugh with him, he sees no evil anywhere apart from the nasty things his patients have wrong with them, they don't make men like that any more, that's why it's just slander the gossip Madame Monneau and old mother Piédevant come out with, that old Lorpailleur's mother apparently quite so with the doctor when she was young, filthy things like that.

Or else that he was supposed to be against locking them

49

up because his own sister, Mademoiselle Mottard who died oh it must be ten years ago now, was a schoolfriend of old Lorpailleur's and her best friend for more than twenty years, he could have refused to take action against her in memory of his sister or been afraid to do anything to give credence to the old gossip about the two friends, ma Monneau or Mademoiselle Ronzière being the first to shout from the housetops that she wasn't normal that way, you see what I mean, as if the doctor bothered his head about that sort of thing, really some people certainly do have time to waste.

When you think of how lovely the country is round our way, the shy sun when you open your window in the morning, the honeysuckle in the backyards, the glorious scents and birdsongs that carry us through from hour to hour until nightfall when the frogs croak themselves hoarse at the edge of the forest, so much loveliness, and of how we're always ready to do any little thing for each other, how we laugh together at the Swan café, how we all feel the same grief when someone is in mourning, how can anyone be so vulgar as to see nothing but filth in everything, I'm quite willing to admit that there may be some but all the same what a sin against Nature, as the doctor says everything you can ever think of saying about her is always true which means that everything you can possibly think of is to be found in her, you can quibble till you're blue in the face but that's the proof of her existence.

Or that it would be too good to be true to spend your time opening your window in the morning and waiting for the frogs in the evening, misfortune exists, such as work with the sweat of your brow, death lying in wait everywhere and leaving us uncertain of our fate, in short just the opposite, it's difficult enough to get by but as the roadman says it's much better to stick to the things that make life pleasant and we haven't got time to waste over people who are in mourning for their illusions.

Our acrobatics in this hornets' nest.

Or that another day, Mademoiselle Moine was having her siesta in her deck-chair, and that little Frédéric was run over by the truck while she was daydreaming about the beauties of nature, children singing hymns in the morning sunshine, such lovely weather.

As for the Father's sermons we never knew where we were, we almost couldn't even be bothered to go and listen to them, what an idea too to send such a queer type to preach to us, and to think what's more that some of his customers went on racking their brains, as if you couldn't interpret his addresses in any way you liked, that was the doctor's opinion, much the same as you can with Nature, which was no excuse.

Such lovely weather, you stood at your front door, you stretched your limbs in delight, a lull, it was the first Saturday of the month, the day the curé visits Mademoiselle Ariane, he came out of his presbytery into the garden, he took his moped out of the shed, he opened the gate, he sat on the saddle, he pedals three times and that's it, the engine goes pop pop and the curé takes wing, old Lorpailleur was writing her article in her little house, I can still see it, a round table covered with a crocheted table-cloth, a Voltaire armchair its seat raised by two plush cushions, in the corner of her dining-room, under the clock that's going tick tock, all she can see of the road when she raises her head is the Oublies crossroads and then not the whole of it, its west corner consists of number twelve so it's quite impossible to keep an eye on anything going on in the rue Neuve or in the rue de Broy or even in the rue des Casse-Tonnelles, and even less so as it was getting dark, it was winter, five in the even-

51

ing, on her table she had some newspaper cuttings of the period, a history of France and a treatise on ethics, there was some holly in a little vase and an all-pervading smell of eucalyptus coming from the sick-room i.e. the mother who wasn't much longer for this world, when suddenly a ring at the bell . . .

What it was that prompted old Lorpailleur to reconstitute the tragedy ten years later without a particle of new evidence nor even sufficient knowledge of the old evidence, Verveine has his own opinion about that.

Or little Louis's mother, busy doing the bedroom on the first floor and the little dining-room and its round table covered with a crocheted table-cloth, what they needed was a sideboard, coveting Mademoiselle Laruaz's, she'd been talking of getting rid of it for years, Antoinette never knows where to put the china away after she's washed up, she has to keep to-ing and fro-ing from the kitchen to the dining-room but for a young couple they really weren't so badly off, they'd got a proper bedroom suite and a very beautiful pink silk eiderdown on their bed with four rows of stitching plus a flounce, it had been very difficult to get the material to match but she had set her heart on it and when she's really determined there's no stopping her, in the end she'd found a rayon the same shade at Tripeaus', her furnishings are in such good taste, and yet it was her two little bedside tables that she liked best of all, their tops were in imitation marble and they each had an adorable little drawer over the space where the chamber pot went, they'd come down to them from his grandmother so they were antiques, she'd had to clean and disinfect the insides, it's the most difficult of all smells to eradicate, going about her household chores, then, after she'd woken, washed and dressed the child and put him out in the yard by the pile of sand that had been left after the preliminary work, the child could spend hours making sand castles or mud pies, it had got to the point when it was almost becoming alarming, was he backward or what, in general at that age they can hardly ever keep still for a moment, the strange thing is that no one saw him go out, not even Madame Bianle and yet she lives opposite and hardly ever leaves her window when it's a sunny day, I'm speaking of the grandmother who's dead but she had invited her sister to lunch that day and had work to do and her shopping as Madame Monneau testified, she'd seen her at the baker's at a quarter-past ten, as for explaining how the child could have got the other side of the crossroads to number twelve that was impossible or at least no light had been thrown on it at the inquiry, would you believe it, a baby all by himself in the road that's something you can't help noticing, no one had seen him in his little red woolly and his blue trousers, barely three years old, a blond cherub, I can still see him with his little chain round his neck and his little shoes . . .

His little boots rather, they grip the foot so well, and his socks which were always sliding down under his heels so that you might have thought he wasn't wearing any but he was, his mother testified to that at the inquest.

Poor little boy with his blue woolly and his red socks, look now he's lifting up his little behind, he gets on all fours and then oops he tries to stand up but he doesn't make it, he falls down, he starts all over again and oops the same movement, he's on his feet now, he tries to look up at the window where his mummy ought to be, she'd only just changed him but he'd done it again, he was covered in wee-wee, he probably felt uncomfortable, how do we know what goes on in their little heads so as to know what goes on in their little pants, he wanders up and down, he's trying to pick a stick up off the ground and he falls over again, he starts sticking his little behind up in the air again and oops

53

there he is on his feet, he's forgotten the stick, he wanders up and down, he tries to look up at his mummy who ought to be at the window, he raises his head and there he is on the ground, in short these little maneuvers two or three times and he starts crying, he wasn't a cry-baby though, a good little boy, a docile little blond cherub, his mummy had just changed him but he'd done it again, he's trying to look up at her it's as if he's asking her to come and do something about it but how can we know what was going on, maybe he wanted someone to help him pick the stick up but she wasn't at the window any more she was doing her housework she was in the dining-room where the child had just done wee-wee, that was why she had changed him, was he going to start all over again, he began to wander up and down a bit and then with the little stick in his hand he started trying to scythe like his daddy, he lifted his little arm and oops there he was on the ground but quick as you like he's stuck his little behind in the air then he's on all fours then he's on his feet again, was he really trying to scythe, he must have forgotten, he wandered over to the sand pile and at that moment a butterfly settled on it and the child tried to catch it but the insect had already flown away, flitter-flutter right and left, rather as if it had been drinking, it whirligigged, it was a white and black cabbage butterfly, twirl-twirl, on the honeysuckle, on the sand, gathering its spoil, in the shy sweet morning sun, it flutters over to the gate quite drunk with flower-sap and sometimes it must be admitted with delicious dung-sap too and maybe even with the little pee-pee penetrating the little poppet's pants, that was why when the child was trying to catch the butterfly on his little behind he found himself plonk on the ground again but oops up he gets again, the butterfly flutters out through the gate, the child follows it along the pavement and that's where it all starts, the tragedy starts there, a child all by himself in the road on a beautiful July day with his little stick in his hand and scraping it against the walls as he went along, it goes crss crss, or was it a toy windmill, whirlabout twirlabout in the light morning air, from flower to flower, what goes on in these delightful little butterflies' heads.

While his mother quite unawares was going about her household chores in the dining-room, she was rubbing at the wee-wee stain on the armchair with warm water, it had been a mistake to stop putting him in his little plastic or whatever pants, was he normal her little boy still wetting himself at his age but Madame Monneau had told her that hers was still wetting when he was five, the thing is to train them to use the potty right from the word go but her little boy is such a darling and he cries so even though he's not a cry-baby that she hadn't the heart, she mustn't make excuses though, she'd start again tomorrow, she'd be firm, the stain just wouldn't come out, the color of the armchair was coming away with it, bad quality this material, she went back to the kitchen and fetched a basinful of warm water and then went back into the dining-room thinking about a flowered cretonne she'd seen at Tripeaus', would Louis be capable of covering the chair, I'm referring to the father, that would be a saving, and one thing leading to another back to the armchair she used to play in when she was a little girl and the sweets her grandfather used to give her, he'd pull them out of his pocket, all the time telling herself that she was late, her husband would be calling her into the shop about half-past eleven, the ladies busy fingering the bread in spite of it being forbidden, good thing the girl was looking after the child, she doesn't seem very bright but for all we ask of her no need to be especially brilliant.

Going out of the gateway following a butterfly but the insect was already some way off, it settled on the honey-suckle, a geranium, a delphinium, the little gardens in our village, they're so simple, so gentle and friendly, hardly ever a little fence even, all their flower-beds spilling over on to the pavement, and then flew off towards the Bianles' where a finch snapped it up, the little boy had forgotten it, he was trailing a toy duck behind him on the end of a string, it kept jumping up and down as it went along, it was fixed on to a curved hub, what adorable little things they invent for children, on the left there was a field full of daisies with a little sainfoin here and there and on the right one full of poppies with some oats here and there, not counting the lucerne and the bugloss and the bladder campion that makes such a nice little noise when you pop it, real country, and such lovely weather, with its far-off bluish hazes and its cows down by the river, and everywhere within your field of vision pardon the pun, a perfect picnic place, on he went, the little boy, hippety-hop, with his imitation crocodile school-bag under his arm that his mummy had given him for his seventh birthday with his little comics in and sweets stuck to the bottom and pink stones and an owl's feather, the treasures of a child of that age, his daddy wondered whether he was normal, he looked more like a little girl what with his fair hair and his little cries of surprise and his adorable smiles, but he remembered that his friend Bianle had told him that his had been just like that till he was nine, even so it was probably about time to start breaking him in, to get him to understand something about life, work, responsibility, military service, so on and so forth, in which respect anyone might have thought that his daddy was really going a bit far, Nature has her fantasies however much the world may dislike them, in short all the clichés you can think of on this and so many other subjects, while the kid was standing there with his legs apart holding the end of his kite-string, there a very strong north wind, you could see it high up in the sky with its pink and blue paper frills, then all of a sudden it came crashing down in a turnip field, the boy ran up to it and discovered that it had broken in two but that the canvas was still intact, he picked up the kite, got on his bike and rode off towards the forest.

While his mother who hadn't managed to get the stain out was daydreaming as she went about her housework, cut-price cretonnes, broken kites, adorable mornings, picnics in the blue, the whole weight of things which means that one day you wake up with an aching heart, a dessicated butterfly on the wall, a little sock hidden away in the drawer, holding her broom by the same armchair, you can still see the stain, and that shopgirl who isn't up to it, another one we'll have to sack, it must be half-past eleven.

And once he was in the main road, not a care in the world, he apparently started humming and then one thing leading to another reciting improvised poetry about how blue the clouds were and how pink the summer mornings, secretly giving free rein to everything his daddy would have considered suspect, imitating one after the other the voice of the lover under the window of the beloved and the voice of the beloved answering the lover and the voices of the poppies and the oats and the bladder campion pop pop, even so Nature really is something.

But what was inexplicable was that no one had seen him going out, a child all by himself in the road that's something you can't help noticing, no though, he went running after the butterfly or if he'd forgotten it he must have been up to something, as Mademoiselle Moine said how do we ever know what's in their minds, and that's where the tragedy starts, it must have been a quarter-past eleven, Madame Monneau came into the baker's, Mademoiselle Cruze was cleaning her windows, Ducreux was discussing the estimate for his shed with Magnin, the ladies saw the truck stop at the crossroads and the driver get out outside the Swan café and other people saw him climb back into his machine and then take the bend so quickly that Madame Piédevant said just look at that, if there'd been a child round the corner it would have been mown down, couldn't they demolish number twelve once and for all, there's no visibility there, or that they ought to make fundamental alterations to the crossroads, something along those lines.

Step by step, with soaking pants.

But Verveine didn't split hairs and when Madame Monneau after she'd been to the baker's went in for her aspirins the first thing he said was to be wary of Madame Piédevant, at all events the time wasn't ripe yet for their deductions, for a new inquiry to be started there must be some certainty, some evidence, he himself was on several different tracks at the moment, he was wondering for instance whether there wasn't something to be cleared up in Monnard's direction, whereupon mother Monneau exclaimed what, the clerk to the council, what an idea, such a distinguished man, really Monsieur Cruze what's got into you, Verveine not a whit disconcerted said that that was just it, his distinction, his correctness in every little thing, his over-refined sense of humor, he was beginning to find them suspect, no one's perfect, only too often the worst vices go hand in hand with the best appearances, as for the others there were according to his way of thinking Topard the gendarme, he'd play anybody's game, young Pinson, Mademoiselle Ronzière and a certain Vernes who used to take such an interest don't you remember in Madame Ducreux, in short the killer or his accomplice is lurking less far away than we thought, Madame Monneau left without her aspirins and immediately went and called on Sophie, Cruze was in a bad way, old Lorpailleur was ripe for the asylum, there was madness in the air, that's where we've got to, now Sophie was not particularly surprised, she'd had her suspicions said she and especially of Mademoiselle Ronzière who always used to suck up to everyone, hadn't she changed since, I'm not saying that she had a direct hand in the affair but that she must have had wind of it, her nephew the one who came to visit her every week was a friend of young Pinson's and of the Lorpailleur sister and when I say friend, actually what did become of her, speaking of Clotilde Lorpailleur, after their mother's death the sisters quarrelled over the inheritance then she got a job as a nurse in a mission in the Argentine or somewhere, something to do with the government, that was when she must have met young Pinson who was the secretary or something of the sort, they left together, then, a few days after the tragedy, strange that Henriette didn't make the slightest allusion to this at the inquiry seeing that she was at daggers drawn with her sister, but it must be said that we didn't know anything about it till much later, shortly before Clotilde came back, through old mother Pinson in fact who up till then had held her tongue hoping that her son would marry his colleague, but their liaison didn't last given the way the Lorpailleur girl behaved over there . . .

Or that Henriette Lorpailleur herself could have gone and seen Cruze and told him of her suspicions, she had discovered that not only did Mademoiselle Ronzière's nephew visit her regularly but that she herself also went to see her sister at Crachon every week, she hasn't been back there since, strange that we never realized the connection, all the more so as from that moment, give or take a month or two, the Vernes fellow never set foot at the Ducreuxs' again, what did he think of that, Verveine noted it down in his little book and wrote under the twenty-fifth of June look into Vernes-Lorpailleur and Vernes-Monnard relations, all the while appearing to agree with the madwoman's line of argument, he wasn't born yesterday.

Unless she went to call on Simon Vernes and went round by the rue Neuve and the rue du Nid-de-Poule to put people off but then she would have had to branch off not far from number twelve in the direction of Malatraîne, and the child's school-bag on her carrier didn't contain her copy for the paper but a resumé of the famous day hour by hour which she may well have left with Vernes so as to give him time to annotate it, and then came back round about half-past eleven with the empty bag which was apparently found near the scene of the accident, which would have accounted for the difficulty the examining magistrate had in identifying the bag, the child in his hospital bed didn't recognize it, either as his own or as belonging to a school friend with whom he might have swopped it, but when the mother was called upon to produce it she apparently couldn't find it anywhere, so the point had to remain in abeyance.

For what was actually in the bag they found at the scene of the accident was not a schoolboy's homework nor the little things they treasure at that age such as comics, sweets, stones and so on, but a detailed plan of the village and a list of names which included those of Mademoiselle Ronzière, young Pinson, Topard the gendarme and Cruze the chemist alias Verveine, but nothing to enable them to identify its origin, which was why the examining magistrate had such difficulty in getting the mother, Madame Ducreux that is, to admit that her child ...

Now on this Thursday the twelfth of July the lawyer and Judge Maillard who had got up earlier than usual to discuss Eugénie Doudin's inheritance, a complicated business which they wanted to deal with outside working hours, were at the judge's, it must have been half-past eight, when they heard the mistress of the house exclaiming in the next room but it's Etiennette Piédevant and immediately launching into a conversation with the person so named who had come back

60

after being away in a far-off country, her mother had been afraid for her health, for her virtue, so on and so forth, but she had come back safe and sound judging by how well she looked and by her self-possession which she hadn't had before, she had taken a job as a nurse with a government mission over there, Madame Maillard wanted to hear all about it, what the country was like, whether the food was good, whether there were any crocodiles there, because her favorite reading is hunting or whatever stories about the customs of the natives, savages whose stomachs are blown out like balloons through stuffing themselves with maize or millet and who have diptheria or dysentery not to mention all the rest, apropos of that is it true what they say, the little girls become prostitutes almost from infancy, even so you aren't going to tell me, a whole population subjected to shameful diseases and diarrhea, what had she seen, what had she observed, was she at least properly remunerated, and Etiennette was replying that it had been a most interesting experience but as for the crocodiles or whatever there weren't any, any more than there was any maize or millet, the aborigines made do with rice, now Madame Maillard did know that the aborigines still existed, isn't it terrible in this day and age, the two of them stayed there talking until the moment when Madame Maillard said but do come upstairs, you'll have a cup of coffee won't you, and Etiennette went upstairs, she was wearing a very pretty dress made from some stuff she'd got out there with a bold floral pattern, Madame Maillard asked her if it had been properly disinfected, you never know, but Etiennette smiled the smile of the much-travelled, they went on talking for a good quarter of an hour about the experiences of the mission from the ethnological point of view as the traveller put it, that makes an immediate impression and Madame Maillard didn't dare say any more about the natives.

So that the lawyer and the judge were disturbed by this

conversation, they began to feel uncomfortable, Monsieur Maillard opened the door and requested his wife to move into the kitchen at the same time shaking Etiennette's hand, didn't she look well but business in business, he would be delighted to have a chat with her some other time and he shut the door again but when the business discussion was over and the lawyer had gone Madame Maillard gave her husband hell, who did he think he was, being told off like a naughty child in front of that chit of a girl, and from his own point of view what sort of a way was that to treat people, what would Etiennette Piédevant who had travelled think, a vulgar provincial like him who hasn't even got a study to talk in without coming and telling his wife to keep quiet, all very well to say that's the way it is, unfortunately that *is* the way it is, that's precisely where he makes a mistake, letting everybody know it, and anyway these appointments at half-past eight what sort of an impression does that give you of a lawyer, all set to feather his own nest again that fellow, as if there weren't any others in the district, their blue blood's running thin in that family what with his daughters that haven't a thing to wear, I'd like to know what happens to all his fees and when I say fees, not that there's any secret about it, they get spent in Sirancy quite so, at the hôtel des Chasseurs where he and the rest of his ilk go on the spree, it's a disgrace in this day and age, a whole family ruined by the sordid goings-on of the father, not that she had any sympathy for the lawyer's wife, that bigot, but it was the principle of thing, so don't try and tell me, eh, I'm not going to put up with it any longer, neither this nor that, to the point where the judge took his hat and went off to the court, it was ten o'clock.

Or that Etiennette Piédevant could have been passing the Maillards' house and met Mademoiselle Doudin who was going to see the judge at that unseemly hour to parley with him about the inquiry that had been started into some fraud to do with the inheritance, a complicated business that the judge was going to explain to her, quite against the rules, before the court sat, and that the said lady was embarrassed at meeting Etiennette and chatted to her about this and that, nothing to do with the case, and then just to put her off went with her as far as the baker's and Madame Maillard who was spying on her from the window apparently saw her coming back by way of the rue Neuve rather than the rue de Broy which was already quite busy at that hour.

Or that Judge Maillard coming out of his house, he was on his way to the court, may have met Etiennette Piédevant who apparently stopped him quite shamelessly, she's been like that since she came back from the Argentine, and asked him what the present position of the Doudin affair was, she seemed very much interested, to which Maillard apparently answered that matters were taking their course or something of the sort, according to Madame Monneau who was observing them from one of her windows, she was cleaning them.

But it is only right to add, still according to Madame Monneau, that this fraud to do with the inheritance was not unrelated to the Ducreux affair, a thing no one had any suspicion of at the time, and that Etiennette before she went away had had dealings with the Doudin family, had quarrelled with the mother, Eugénie that is, and that it was to some extent because of that that she embarked on . . .

But it is only right to add that this fraud to do with the inheritance was not unrelated to Etiennette's abrupt departure because she had quarrelled with Odile Doudin after some very odd family business and when I say family I mean the father and when I say very odd business . . .

Now Madame Maillard was not aware of all this filth and if she stopped and spoke to Etiennette it was in all innocence, she was simply curious to hear the girl's impressions of her travels, about her relations with the natives and about the crocodile hunts she dreamed of, most disappointed she was when the traveller informed her that there weren't any in the country she had been to, in any case the only thing that interested her was her work as nurse or laboratory assistant with the government mission, an ethno or ethni question, something of the sort.

According to Mademoiselle Ronzière Etiennette only passed the baker's at eleven o'clock, she was on her way back from town carrying a big cardboard box that came from Brivance's, a new dress, she's always so smart, the ladies couldn't contain their impatience to see her open the box, it was a previous season's model that she'd got at a discount as she knew one of the girls who worked there, a yoked bodice with a fully pleated skirt in a purple and aubergine flowered material on a gray background, of such elegance that you had to be Etiennette to dream of such an extravagance, when and where would she be able to wear it but a young woman never asks herself that question, I can still see the ladies going into ecstasies over it, caressing the material and trying to make out how the sleeves were set in and the yoke and the very tricky bias of the skirt, and it was only after the dress had been put back in its box that the conversation one thing leading to another came round to the Doudin inheritance, Etiennette played it very cool, she didn't know anything very much except that the Maillards weren't necessarily above certain irregularities, she didn't mention the word fraud, which would explain mother Maillard's high and mighty air these days, when people start getting haughty you'll always find there's something more to it than meets the eye.

However that may be Mademoiselle Cruze who was cleaning her windows apparently saw Etiennette coming out of the baker's and going down the rue Cachepot and just before she came to the crossroads meet Odette whom she hadn't seen since Eugénie's death, she stopped, she put her cardboard box down on the Bianles' window-sill and they chatted for a good ten minutes, she could still see them Odette with her mourning crêpe, self-effacing and dignified, Etiennette nervy but looking younger than ever, and yet they're the same age, very much the wrong side of thirty, and it could well have been only after that that she went down the rue Neuve and into the other chemist's where according to young Pinson she bought some toothpaste, the question of why she had quarrelled with Verveine not having been raised, what I mean is young Pinson didn't have a chance to answer it, Mademoiselle Cruze has her own opinion, you know her.

That on the other hand it would be quite unwarranted to suspect Monnard, I'm referring to our parish clerk, of having been either closely or remotely connected with the affair, such a distinguished man, totally disinterested and aiming at something quite other than profit or honors, he had put all his idealism into teaching and literature, hadn't he been working away for years on his monograph on the Bonne-Mesure family and completely in the background at that, he'd even refused to be introduced to Mademoiselle Ariane and her circle, it was a good opportunity though, all the nobility of our district are connected to her through blood or courtesy, no, the only thing that Monnard gleaned from one side or the other was the indispensable information, he reserved all his efforts for his research in the record office by special permission of the minister, to which it should be added that Mademoiselle Ariane was amazed at this modesty, that she had made several unsuccessful approaches either through her niece or the lawyer's wife who was a relation of hers, or through the Baroness who is perhaps the person with whom Monnard feels most at ease ever since the jumble sale where he . . . .

No really it didn't exactly become that bigot to start making insinuations about Monnard, when you think about her attitude to the heirs to the Doudin estate, she may well have expected to inherit something from Eugénie it's quite possible but whichever way you look at it she hadn't the slightest right to anything, why wasn't she mentioned in the will, well there was food for thought there, the way she'd been making up to the deceased, the way she'd been bringing her pots of jam and sponge-fingers for years and years, the old girl wouldn't give up the ghost, and do you remember how she use to take her niece there in the Dondards' new car, she used to keep the old lady company, under the pretext that she was only doing her duty to an old friend, there's no doubt that that business with young Sureau had something to do with it, just think back to the time when Clotilde had made that remark apropos of his so-called fianceé, the old lady couldn't make head nor tail of it, she was very much in favor of the association on account of what Jean-Claude would get out of it and you really couldn't blame her given the family resources, well this remark upset her, they just didn't seem to think she was all there any more, she unbosomed herself to Mademoiselle Moine on the subject and her reasoning was anything but gaga, it's my opinion that that's where it all started.

Because Mademoiselle Moine was very good friends with Eugénie, they'd been at school together during the second Empire or whenever, that's going back a bit, which meant a lot of memories in common, a lot of afternoons recalling the past, old mother Chottard, the Moineau family, picnics in the forest of Grance, they'd come into fashion well before nineteen-fourteen, that story about Sergeant Paqueron I've heard it at least a hundred times and the one about Madame Piédevant, the grandmother that is, who was for ever starting on the same sock for Jean-Jacques, she was so lazy that the child had had time to grow an inch every time he tried it on, and the story of the curé's housekeeper who got hold of all the Peter's pence and called them her savings, ah yes poor thing she certainly did have some memories, well notwithstanding all this Mademoiselle Moine was still not mentioned in the will.

Poor Mademoiselle Dondard she was the butt of the entire Moignon family, they lived on the same landing, you remember the Moignon children, a dozen of them, it's my opinion that they had worms, thin, fidgety nervy, even so they haven't turned out any worse than anyone else, isn't the oldest one the manager of the spaghetti factory or his cousin, the second one is head nurse at the hospital, Gaston quite so, the third is Alfred the one who upset his mother so terribly when he married Eliette Mottard, the cousin of the doctor, she gave him three lovely children, so you see the worst . . .

The fourth what was his name now, Hubert, Albert, something ending in Bert or am I wrong, Adalbert that's it, what became of him, wasn't there some question of his going off with young Pinson on that government thing to the Argentine or wherever, no that was Rodolphe the fifth or sixth a red-head, what can have become of him, the sixth or seventh was Jean-Claude who gave his grandmother so much trouble . . .

Young Jean-Claude then the seventh or eighth that is, who gave everyone so much trouble, he was the one who had worms, he had them throughout his childhood, I can still see him, thin, fidgety, nervy, even so he hasn't turned out any worse than the others, what became of them all, the oldest one let's think isn't he head chef at the hospital and the second one Albert or Rodolphe that is isn't he a male nurse

67

at the spaghetti factory and the third the red-head Gaston quite so who gave that poor Eliette Mottard so much trouble, he's given her three lovely children so you see ...

Poor Mademoiselle Mottard, she was inexhaustible with the little Moignons, they lived on the same landing, how she loved them, how she spoilt them, they were her whole life, well you see they haven't turned out any better than the others, wasn't the oldest one ... Mademoiselle Mottard Eliette Mottard that is who gave her poor mother so much trouble, what became of her, the doctor's sister-in-law who had the twelve children who all had worms, I can still see them, they lived on the same landing and there were rows every day, they were always ready for a fight, whether they turned out better or worse than the others I couldn't say, we all make our own way in life and then we meet them again ten years later with beards and moustaches or else looking like perfect cretins yes really Nature.

Poor Madame Moignon, she was a Mottard quite so, Sigisbert's sister he's the one who's the child's godfather, they didn't know what to do with him, I'm referring to the godson, what a lot of trouble he gave his parents, should he stay on at school, should they apprentice him somewhere, they were thinking of an artistic profession at that time, they'd always cultivated a certain way of life, well ten years later he hasn't turned out any worse than the rest of them and his marriage to the Pinson girl is the height of respectability, Monnard the step-father, Odette isn't his daughter, owns that spaghetti factory in the Argentine or wherever.

Or then again Monsieur and Madame Chottard apparently saw her passing the baker's, I'm referring to Etiennette, they were sunning themselves on the little terrace Magnin had built for them overhanging number twelve, they hardly ever leave the house any more but at that distance you may well wonder, they may have thought she was Eliette, they look much the same.

And apropos of Jean-Claude, the eighth or ninth that is, he had apparently quite so with the youngest Moignon girl, which would explain her hasty departure to the Argentine, her parents explained it away by saying that she'd got a job as a nurse with her uncle Piédevant who owns the spaghetti factory, you see what I mean.

Poor Mademoiselle Mottard.

And apropos of young Jean-Claude, the ninth or tenth that is, she'd known him well as a child, he had a bent for poetry, a rather slow, contemplative child, perhaps a shade narcissistic but it was so charming, the father was making himself ill about it you know, his son would go mad from ... doing I don't know what to himself, poor darling, as if the things adults do to each other destined them *ipso facto* to poetry, he's married now and his bent has vanished, she was working herself up, she was getting red in the face ...

That the truck driver after he had stopped his engine may have kept his seat for a short time while he was consulting his map of the district, and only afterwards got out of his cabin, yet there was still according to Mademoiselle Mottard someone else beside him, a younger man so it seemed to her, who took his mate's place when he left it though no explanation of this act was offered at the inquiry by the accused, I'm referring to the young man, and yet it wasn't difficult to recognize the fact that from the driver's seat he could see the crossroads better and that it was at this moment and not at half-past eleven that Mesdemoiselles Piédevant and Mottard, the niece that is, crossed or may have crossed the road on their way to the chemist's, a thing that couldn't leave a young man cold, seeing that these young ladies, and when I say young ladies, their vital statistics were no less interesting than those of any others, all the more so as at that hour there were hardly any women about, it must have been half-past eight.

And it was from her window overlooking the Swan café that she apparently saw the driver getting out of his stationary truck, and his seat immediately being occupied by his younger mate who was apparently not interrogated at the inquiry; odd, this, but there were many irregularities in the proceedings to say the least.

Unless not wanting to lean out of the window ...

Or the other Mademoiselle Mottard her cousin whom we used to see pulling her little cart along the road, she used to collect all the animal droppings for her garden armed with a shovel and a rush broom, what a lot of dirt to say the least she's collected in the course of her long existence, so humble in her black overall, her little bun coming undone and falling over her shoulders and when I say shoulders, her hump rather, she was so hunchbacked that it broke your heart, they could have done something about it when she was young but she was born too soon, they can perform miracles in the osteo ostei what do they call it line these days, like club-feet, or those deformed people who look like little storks, calves no bigger than that, she went out at dawn like other people go out to pick raspberries for their dessert but not she, that wasn't what she was after and with good reason, and yet the pleasure in the discovery was the same and not rare I can tell you in our part of the world where livestock abounds, some unkind people used to say she didn't even turn her nose up at christian stuff which isn't rare either, people squat all over the place and especially in the cherry season, nothing like cherries for giving people a good bellyful so that they often do a great pile with the pips in as well, we have such gluttons you'd never believe it, they hardly ever use a scrap of paper either, more likely a few leaves that happen to be within reach, Mademoiselle Mottard was getting on in years maybe she didn't realize the difference, she threw herself on her spoil you ought to have seen her, and back in her little garden at about half-past eleven she used to smear the lot over her strawberries and peas, she had her say at the inquiry too, she said she'd seen Odette pedalling in the direction of Crachon, she was mixing her up with Mademoiselle Ménard, it's true they are alike . . .

Which would have meant that Magnin on his way to the Ducreuxs wouldn't have been wrong when he stated that he'd seen Mademoiselle Mottard with Etiennette, the party concerned, I'm referring to Mademoiselle Mottard, having remembered that in fact the cyclist had stopped within yards of her to re-tie her scarf, Magnin was going by just at that moment on the Sirancy road, so it was to be concluded that two cyclists had gone by, the schoolmistress and Mademoiselle Poussegrain, which was perfectly plausible at that hour, it was a Thursday, old Lorpailleur would have been on her way not to the school but to the newspaper office and Eliette . . .

Now Verveine had got to the point where he was doubting Madame Monneau's word on the one hand, how could she have met Etiennette that day seeing that the party concerned went out at eight and not at eleven, and on the other hand that of old Lorpailleur who swore she had gone out at eleven whereas Verveine had seen her at half past eight.

As for Latirail the boys' teacher they could congratulate themselves on the fact that he was away at that time, he was suffering from dysentry and had had to have someone to replace him for a month because that swollen-headed busybody wouldn't have missed the chance to contribute his little drop of poison the way he did during that other business the . . .

The way he did during that old business, making us all suspect one another and then ten years later we wondered how we could possibly have felt like that it all seemed so trivial but people get worked up and lose control of themselves and that's when you get revolutions.

Poor Mademoiselle Crottard.

In point of fact Etiennette Passavant didn't know Latirail as she'd only recently come back but she remembered him as a child when he was in the orphanage and used to go round collecting Christmas boxes with a school friend, nevertheless she hadn't seen him since those days something like thirty years it was and knew nothing about his education or profession if you can call it that, which didn't prevent the accused, I'm referring to Latirail, from treating her at the inquiry as an old acquaintance, insinuating that she knew a great deal about him and he about her, the reasons she went abroad et cetera, what a nerve eh, but how could she defend herself, it was established that she knew him as a child and the magistrate didn't raise the question again.

As for Mademoiselle Crottard she had missed her Mass owing to having stopped shortly after she'd passed Eliette and Madame Monneau in front of number twelve, Madame Monneau had plied her with questions about Verveine, she was throwing doubt on his qualifications, now Mademoiselle Crottard had always dealt with him, he treated her very well for her dysentry as he had treated her mother who used to suffer from the same complaint, it was a point of honor with her to defend Monsieur Cruze but she made up for it after the service by making an act of thanksgiving that lasted a good half-hour, Magnin was able to confirm this because he passed her as she was coming out of the church, it must have been half-past eight.

What she hadn't said was that she had cut short her thanksgiving because of an irrepressible colic, her congenital complaint was playing her up, no doctor had been able to cure her of it, the chemist least of all, and had gone and taken refuge in the presbytery where the housekeeper who was an old hand had opened the privy door for her before you could say knife, one more second and it would have been too late.

Poor thing when you think of how she spends her days, she's very deserving, after Mass when she hasn't cut it short because of you know what she goes back home where her mother is still in bed, as often as not the first thing she has to do is clean her up because the old woman suffers as I said from this congenital malady, the grandmother had it too, no doubt about it it's a real cross, next she sits her in her armchair and gives her her rusks to nibble while she's waiting for the coffee, that's when she herself doesn't have to leave her there and rush off you know where, she heats up the coffee and takes it to her mother who as often as not has done it again while nibbling her rusk, she still has all her wits about her, she explains I was nibbling my rusk and plop I let off and out it came, I'm so sorry darling, darling starts cleaning her up all over again, she gets a bit irritable and puts the packet of rusks down in the pile of you know what, during this time the coffee has got cold and she has to start heating it up again and it sometimes happens that for the third time the old woman when her daughter comes back with the coffee says oh darling, darling starts all over again from scratch, rereheats the coffee, then if all goes well she does some light housework interrupted as often as not by her own colics and if all goes well she finds herself at noon having her lunch in her mother's room with mother neverendingly nibbling her rusks, this makes an unbearable noise which poor old Crottard bears with for the love of God while thinking about her communion that morning and plop the old woman's done it again, even so there's no denying it, this malady is a cross, the poor woman starts cleaning up all over again if all goes well for her and so on if all goes well until the evening and then Mass the next day.

Or that that day the curé's housekeeper didn't see poor old Crottard arriving all dishevelled and thought to herself that she must be better, there was some improvement, she would congratulate the chemist, being in the secret if you can call it that of the treatment he was prescribing for the unfortunate woman, and went out round about nine to do a little shopping and then met the doctor who was on his way to the hospital and pointed out to him the truck parked in front of the baker's, it hardly left room for a hand-cart to pass, saying when you think of the tragedy of ten years ago talk about a disgrace they still haven't demolished number twelve, you'll see there'll be another calamity at these crossroads, by the way how's Mademoiselle Mottard, the poor lame woman was quite well thank you, it looked to him as if with the passing of time her nerves were settling down, she has plenty to do at the moment with her plants, her canaries, her needlework, so on and so forth, to which the housekeeper apparently added that there's something fey about Mademoiselle Mottard, I've seen her embroidery, she was talking about the jumble sale, such fine work, a real miracle, being perfectly well aware that none of her frippery had been sold and that it would turn up on the same stall the following year but the doctor wasn't listening, he was waving to Magnin who was supposed to be coming to see him that evening about a building job, repairing an old wall and an adorable little window where the lame woman would have all the time in the world to arrange her potted plants which would then fall head-first on those of the passers-by, he's such a good man, our doctor, and as he left Mademoiselle Moine he enjoined her to take care of her liver, nothing fried, no sugar, no nothing.

Unless Mademoiselle Moine with her customary lack of discretion had stopped him in order to talk about Mademoiselle Crottard's mishap earlier on, what can be done to relieve her of that cross, it came upon her right in the middle of communion, such a deserving person and all the rest of it, to which the doctor may well have said she'd better come and see me, we'll look into it, it may be chronic appendicitis, she'd better come and see me, which he oughtn't to have said but with such an old acquaintance he wasn't on his guard, for Mademoiselle Moine had time in between nine and ten to talk to everybody about this incurable malady which by half-past eleven had practically become a shameful disease, so that when towards the evening poor old Crottard went out again to buy some jam for her mother's rusks people were hardly even returning her greeting and when she got home she was so upset that she barely had time to dash into the privy, one more second and it would have been too late.

But Madame Monneau had only been half-listening to the servant and a few minutes after she had left her . . .

In the middle of stirring his powders, bicarbonate plus magnesium, coming to the conclusion that Madame Monneau knew all about young Pinson's relations with the Ducreuxs, husband and wife, there was food for thought there.

So that when the said lady going into the baker's and not seeing anyone there apparently called out I'll come back in half an hour and went out again just as Eliette was passing number twelve, i.e. on the other side of the road with the truck parked in front of the Swan, Ducreux who had heard her and was watching her from the yard could well only have called his wife as a matter of form seeing that he knew from Verveine that Mademoiselle Poussegrain had sworn by all she held sacred that she would never again set foot in the baker's shop and that this had horrified Madame Monneau, that creature trying to tell us how to behave, something of the sort, in other words he wanted to know, I'm talking of the baker, if the party concerned, I'm talking of Madame Monneau, would draw herself up to her full height and give Eliette a withering look or on the other hand chase after her and tell her a few home truths, something which had its importance given the family ties that existed between Madame Monneau and Magnin who was due at any moment for a discussion about the estimate, the hunchback had tried in every possible way to disparage his work so that this big contract should go through young Pinson to a builder in the town the one whose relationship with her people had been wondering about for years and who, this without prejudice of course, might not have been totally ignorant of the intrigues that preceded the tragedy, what's more the truck driver was his employee.

Or that the driver could have parked his truck at that precise spot on the orders of his employer so as to be able to observe at his leisure Madame Monneau and Magnin who were supposed to be arriving at Ducreux's together, and then having inadvertently missed Madame Monneau by a few minutes and only in fact having seen Magnin arrive half an hour later had pretended to be drunk so as to provoke the incident in question and delay the moment when Verveine would be informed by Mademoiselle . . .

Had pretended to be drunk so as to provoke the incident in question i.e. the crowd outside the chemist's and delay a bit longer the moment when Mademoiselle Mottard who had left home at eight and couldn't walk very fast in that heat would tell Verveine in confidence what she knew of the relations between Monsieur and Madame Ducreux and young Pinson since in any case the builder must have had all the trumps in his hand to be able to offer him the job, the doctor having told her of the rumors that were going around about Mademoiselle Crottard's illness, a thing that should never have occurred even with an old acquaintance, you can never be too strict in these matters but he's such a good man our doctor.

Among the meadow-sweet by the Grance ponds there he went the little angel, hop skip and jump with his butterfly net, our roadman can still see it as if it were yesterday, how could he doubt that his mummy was right there beside him. he was on his way back after going his rounds over Bonne-Mesure way, he acted as rural policeman as well, on his old English-type bone-shaker which he tucks away in a thicket in the mornings and picks up at eleven, he hardly bothered to look round, it seemed quite natural to him seeing that it was a Thursday, his very words at the inquiry, yes but it was a Saturday and that's where the tragedy begins.

Hopping, skipping and jumping among the meadow-sweet like a butterfly little Alfred, it was Alfred wasn't it, was getting farther and farther away from his parents, they'd fallen asleep after their picnic, he was getting dangerously near the ponds, he made an adorable little fishing rod out of a reed and a piece of string, he was mad on fishing, his mother said so again at the inquest between her sobs, I can still see her dabbing her eyes with the little black-bordered kerchief that had come down to her from her grandmother, a lamentable sight, it's all very well to say that they've had three more since then, what an ordeal for the parents.

Coming up all woebegone poor woman and shouting out my child's been drowned.

A crowd outside the chemist's caused by the ghastly business of the little Bianle boy being run over, I can still see the people's horrified reactions, two tragedies one after the other, what an ordeal for everyone, it was July, the season when misfortunes happen to us, accidents, drownings, fires, we didn't know which way to turn, the firemen went over Grance way with the mother, the chemist made an emergency telephone call to the hospital.

A day like today, the sun was enough to make you sick, everybody on the *qui vive* waiting for the inevitable tragedy, our despair suddenly made tangible, death was in our midst.

But we had to pull ourselves together, ten years later we had to pull ourselves together, make the effort, extricate ourselves from the nightmare . . .

As if the years then had never been, and that that frightful July . . .

Death was in our midst.

The fire-engine driving off into the sun, I can still see it, talk about lugubrious, it must have been half-past eleven, the distracted mother had followed the firemen in Dondard's van, he had immediately offered to take her, but round about three they came back empty-handed, they were going to extend the search as far as the lock, Madame Monneau, who with five or six others stayed with poor Madame Bianle, they'd sat her down in the chemist's while they were waiting for the morgue or whatever, the father wasn't there, he only came back at seven in the evening, they'd sent him a telegram, said, I'm referring to Madame Monneau, that she'd had a presentiment of the accident, she's supposed to have second sight or at least she claims she has, a sudden spasm that she'd had the day before while she was cleaning her windows, something quite out of the ordinary, she'd had to sit down, which was confirmed by the two tragedies one after the other, what was intolerable was the way she extracted a sort of kudos from it, they'd ridiculed her enough, hadn't they, with her predictions which turned out to be unfounded more often than not, this time she was exultant.

Or that years before, some ten years, with that horrible

business of the child being run over, people may have been reminded of the time when the Magnin boy, it was Magnin wasn't it, was drowned, they just fished him out in time, difficult to remember, the fact is that it was July and that people were overwrought and saw some menace lurking everywhere how right they were, apparently no one could recollect it ten years later, some said it was at the end of May, others at the end of June, but Cruze had no doubt about that either when he looked up his diary.

In point of fact Etiennette Passavant had heard cries but either she had thought it was just children playing or she'd been in a hurry to show off her dress . . .

In point of fact Doctor Mottard on his way back from the hospital at about half-past eleven and seeing the crowd in question . . .

But Judge Maillard told the lawyer once again that if wilful misrepresentation concerning the inheritance was proved no one would hesitate to hold Mademoiselle Doudin responsible, everyone knew why, her more than ambiguous relations with her step-father and the latter's plans to extend his premises beyond number twelve, almost two blocks further on, this was before the demolition, half of the end building belonged to Monsieur and Madame Véron and the other half to the heirs of the Chottard estate, a matter which Doudin had raised, I'm talking of the possibility of their selling the whole building, now the heirs were against this, the builder would have to be content with the Véron part which he intended to use still according to Mademoiselle Moine as a warehouse, this project had set all the tongues wagging and with good reason, and that there would therefore be grounds if there had indeed been wilful misrepresentation for bringing a joint action at the opening of the inevitable lawsuit, which would dangerously postpone the said liquidation or something of the sort, which the lawyer wanted to avoid not so much on his client's behalf as on his own given the family connection that existed between his wife and Eliette, that on the other hand he prided himself on having found a precedent in a similar case where a penal action had ended in a nonsuit, this conversation was reported by Madame Maillard who was listening in the next room and who you know how stupid she is had quite simply mixed it up with that old business of the Polish truck driver.

Because Eliette as she was passing the chemist's had seen the poor mother in the shop talking to Verveine and hadn't had anything better to do than to pass it on straight from the horse's mouth to Antoinette Doudin, you must admit that when it comes to perfidy . . .

As ma Moignon was saying speaking of her daughter, the fifth or sixth the one married to Mortin the builder, a childless couple, they'd tried everything even the waters at Lourdes and a somewhat nearer pilgrimage to Rottard the spa where there's a miraculous virgin on the hill who is much frequented by people taking the cure they like to kill two birds with one stone and maybe it works for them, it didn't look as if associating with Eliette had brought her luck, speaking of her daughter, then, and convinced as she was that Eliette had the evil eye or something of the sort, which could be interpreted in various ways which in any case were mistaken because the Moignon girl was as serious-minded a young thing as you could hope to find, just not so narrow-minded as her mother and sisters, she refused not to see Eliette merely on the pretext that she was rather ostentatiously free in her behavior, goodness and intelligence don't pay in our parts, what's more Eliette didn't frequent the Moignon girl after her marriage, something which could also set tongues wagging, so much stupidity is certainly not calculated to give anyone a particularly fascinating idea of our local women.

Because Verveine, who knew from Madame Maillard that Doudin, I'm speaking of the widower, had already mentioned his building plans to Magnin, was wondering whether he couldn't worm some secrets out of Eliette using as a pretext something that her step-father had told him in confidence, not daring to confess that he had heard this and that from Madame Maillard, that would have been asking for trouble, that's precisely what he must have tried on a few days later when he saw Eliette going by, he was alone in the shop and she was carrying her Brivance cardboard box, good excuse for him.

And in fact he called out to her, the door was open what with the heat, Eliette had nothing against a bit of a gossip, she went in, old Lorpailleur heard about it from Mademoiselle Moine who was at her window, and putting two and two together . . .

And in fact he called out to her, he was at his door chatting to Mademoiselle Moine, Eliette had nothing against showing off a bit with her cardboard box under her arm, she even suggested that they might like to have a look at her dress, they went into the shop, which didn't escape the eagle eye of Madame Monneau, she was about twenty yards behind Eliette, on her way to the baker's, which she then passed on straight from the horse's mouth to the ladies, there were three or four of them fingering the bread, that's how news spreads and that's where the tragedy begins.

What she didn't say, I'm referring to Mademoiselle Moine, was that old Lorpailleur had confided to her just a few minutes previously that she had been invited with the curé to Mademoiselle Ariane's, a most unusual occurrence, an event for the schoolmistress, it must certainly have been a Saturday, then, the first of the month.

Now the best witness of the scene at the manor was Marie. When Mademoiselle Francine had arrived pushing her bike over the gravel in the drive she had heard her greeting the gardener then she'd seen her going along the rhododendron walk on the right instead of carrying straight on up to the manor house, which meant that she would then take the path on the east side which comes out not far from the outhouses at the corner of the terrace, so it was obvious that from a distance she had caught sight of old Lorpailleur sitting in the sun with her aunt and the curé and wanted before approaching the guests to make some enquiries of the cook, to find out why the schoolmistress was of the party, possibly having a presentiment of a reason which she didn't admit or didn't dare admit and pretending to Marie that she didn't know anything about it, now Marie had overheard just a few days earlier between the niece and the aunt, Mademoiselle Francine having come to the manor during the week which was not her usual practice thus arousing the curiosity of the maid who had probably listened at the door but she didn't say so, a conversation in which the question of the Doudin estate was raised and also the relations between the Ducreux at the time of the death of their eldest with a certain Vernes or Vernet so she said whom she didn't know. Francine was speaking softly as was her aunt but she nevertheless let two or three exclamations escape her which didn't explain still according to Madame Monneau what old Lorpailleur had to do with the business nor why the moment Francine caught sight of her she went round by the outhouses, Marie's assumptions considering that she had never once heard the schoolmistress's name mentioned could therefore have been interpreted as pure fantasy if Mademoiselle de Bonne-Mesure had not invited the schoolmistress to lunch a few days later.

What Marie assumed.

She had replied evasively to Mademoiselle Francine, assuming her most innocent look, saying that no doubt

Mademoiselle was just being polite, she set so much store on good neighborly relations, imbued as she was, this she didn't say either, I'm referring to Marie, with the ancestral duties of her race, a persistence of the protective or christian spirit of the nobility towards those who are under an obligation to them to say the least.

And Francine had told her that she felt rather uncomfortable, she was perspiring in her little blouse, and as she hadn't brought anything to change into she would go and look in her aunt's wardrobe and see whether she couldn't find something adding no one should ever go bicycling without a change of clothes, she apparently went up to the first floor, found what she needed in the hanging cupboard, then did her hair and went down to the terrace, kissed her aunt, handshakes with the guests, then immediately cutting short old Lorpailleur's compliments turned to Mademoiselle to excuse herself for her presumption, she'd got a mulberry stain on her blouse as she was coming along, she would never go bicycling again without something to change into, Mademoiselle Ariane replied that she must always feel at home at the manor, no need to apologize, by the way does Marie know you're here, we were waiting for you to go in to luncheon, knowing that Francine had gone round by the rhododendrons to see the cook first, she suspected that her niece was worried by the presence of old Lorpailleur as she hadn't mentioned her when they had met during the week, this was not premeditated according to Francine who had afterwards unbosomed herself to Eliette on the subject, she had only decided on it the day before i.e. on the Friday, finding herself as she did as if by chance face to face with the schoolmistress in the rue de Broy, a Bonne-Mesure being entitled to the luxury of this sort of distortion of convention, I'm referring to an invitation for the next day, because she couldn't wait to confront the party concerned with the curé, counting on Francine's diplomacy to worm her secrets out of her, I'm referring to old Lorpailleur, it was a heaven-sent opportunity, and as an extra excuse saying that in August she would be going to see her sister-in-law the Baroness in Douves, now she'd been wanting for a long time to have a little chat with her and Monsieur the curé about the good work she was doing with the children, it was in the bag, the schoolmistress accepted on the spot as you can well imagine.

What Marie assumed.

Or that Francine had lingered rather longer with Marie and then upstairs, Mademoiselle Ariane could have called the cook and asked her whatever her niece could be doing, she was always so punctual, now she had seen her turning into the rhododendron walk but didn't want her guests to suspect that anything might be going on, actually they had their backs to the drive, and asked Marie even before she had had time to answer or else she'd winked at her to ring the luncheon bell, Monsieur the curé had to be at Crachon at three for his catechism class, Mademoiselle would come when she came, and it could have been only after the guests had sat down to luncheon that Francine, apologizing to her aunt both for being late and for having borrowed one of her blouses put in an appearance in the dining-room, the reason she was late was actually the fact that she had discovered a letter on Mademoiselle Ariane's dressing table which she had read from beginning to end.

Which would imply that Minette would only have deposited her mess in the box-tree when they were having their coffee, the guests were back on the terrace . . .

Which would imply that if Minette was only depositing her mess in the dining-room window-box as Mademoiselle Ariane was taking her seat, Francine would not have been there yet and so would have had no opportunity to guffaw with her mouth shut and that Mademoiselle her aunt . . .

And that Mademoiselle her aunt, turning to the guests who were looking at the rare artichokes and hence at the cat, would quite simply have said Minette is a stray, she hasn't learnt how to behave yet, with a dry, icy little laugh which rubbed the two guests' noses in their own mess as you might say, people who know how to behave look the other way, so that the stray cat became not the one we're thinking of, I mean the party concerned, but the two plebs.

Or it could have been that Francine came straight up to the end of the drive, paid her respects to her aunt and the guests, and asked them to excuse her while she went and tidied up a little, adding as an aside to her aunt may I go and change in your bedroom, to which Mademoiselle Ariane would have answered but of course you must always feel at home here but don't be too long, darling, Monsieur the curé has to leave at three o'clock, we'll wait for you, in which case Francine would have come in through the drawing-room but instead of going straight up to the first floor would have made her way to the kitchen . . .

Would have come in through the drawing-room and gone straight up to her aunt's bedroom where she would have found a letter on the dressing-table . . .

Would have gone upstairs to change her blouse and do her hair and then quickly come down again and joined the guests on the terrace and had a mouthful of port with them a few minutes before the bell was rung by Marie who had been watching for her from the corner of the terrace because the luncheon was ready, sitting on her little chair in the contemplative attitude of someone who has done her duty, a familiar attitude but one which was often misjudged by Mademoiselle de Bonne-Mesure who imagined that there was something shifty about it, now Marie according to Francine's sworn evidence at the inquiry was one of the most straightforward and honest people imaginable, and it could have been during these few minutes that she Marie the cook had wangled to allow the new arrival to swallow a finger of port before going in to luncheon that Minouche could have deposited her mess in the hydrangeas, which would have caused Mademoiselle Ariane to say her piece about Nature and all the rest of it, the curé his about Providence and Francine pssht pssht, while old Lorpailleur didn't open her mouth but on the contrary kept it pursed up like a chicken's hole, she was trying so hard to look refined.

But Mademoiselle Ariane was highly displeased to see Francine being so hard-hearted with Minette and turning to old Lorpailleur, I'm sure you at any rate Mademoiselle love animals don't you, the schoolmistress said yes and started blushing, she who had let her dear mother's canaries perish and who tormented the life out of Mademoiselle Ronzière's cat, which Francine immediately noticed whereupon she asked her hypocritically by the way what do you think of her article, *ex abrupto*, without mentioning the name of its author, the schoolmistress was scarlet, then she added, I'm referring to Francine, I mean Mademoiselle Ronziere's article, talk about a tense atmosphere, it lasted for the rest of the luncheon after this sally, Francine back-pedalled a bit out of consideration for her aunt who hadn't invited old Lorpailleur for any great altruistic motives but for the reason we all know, but did *she* know it.

But did Francine know the reason for old Lorpailleur's presence at the manor this first Saturday in July, that's the whole point, Mademoiselle Moignon apparently maintained that Francine hadn't been there during the week, that it was just that Mademoiselle Ariane had hinted that she was coming to Amédée who hadn't seen a thing as he had been spending all his time down in the orangery where he was clearing the old croquet lawn, his employer had suddenly taken it into her head to want to see it made usable again, no one had used it since eighteen . . .

Amédée hadn't seen anyone nor had Marie it was her day off.

And that they apparently had a two-hour conversation in the former smoking-room, which hadn't been used since . . .

So that as the ladies didn't understand why the staff at the manor house had come to be so reduced, Mademoiselle Moignon began to give herself airs as she explained that the lady's maid had been dismissed on account of quite so that she was supposed to have, I'm not making it up, with Maurice the butler who had been away the whole month with his family, an intolerable injustice in the ladies' eyes, why wasn't he dismissed too the old satyr, Mademoiselle Moignon explained . . .

Because the former smoking-room which is the extension of the dining-room and whose window is at the back of the house . . .

Luncheon luncheon, Mademoiselle Ariane stood up and with an affable gesture took the curé's arm and walked over to the drawing-room door followed by Francine and the schoolmistress who was saying, encouraged by Francine who wanted to let her vent her spleen so as to make her malleable, that the article in question was very ill-informed, that Mademoiselle Ronzière hadn't said a word about the communal loan and had thus offended the subscribers of whom Monsieur Maillard was one, she had it from a reliable source, in a small community like ours you need so much diplomacy, the level of education being what it is, one can never take too much trouble over appearances, and that the allusion to whomever it was's witticism which was in the worst possible taste there was no denying it and from the pen of someone who professes to be a poet, by the way did you know that that little volume was remaindered by the publisher and when I say publisher, you know him, he'd do better to stick to you know what, there are no two ways about it, that'll make her sing a bit smaller, she was talking of old Ronzière if not in these words at least that was what she was getting at, that was it more or less, Francine was achieving her object, they were now crossing the drawing-room which was at its most effective the first time you saw it, old family hangings, old cabinets, big-bellied old copper kettles and all the rest of it with the portraits of Hyacinthe, Gaspard and Valère on the walls, all Knights of Malta or wherever, three dusty magi all mixed up with family photos framed in passe-partout, they came to the dining-room where Mademoiselle Ariane took her seat at the head of the table, the others followed her example and parked theirs after the curé had said a modest little grace.

In the dining-room Mademoiselle Ariane placed herself at the head of the table, the curé on her right, the school-mistress on her left, in other words facing one another each in the middle of one side, Mademoiselle Francine at the other end, the curé said grace and they sat down, Marie came in with the cheese soufflé, she went up to the mistress of the house who always helps herself first when all of a sudden Minouche in the artichokes . . . when all of a sudden Mademoiselle Ariane sees the artichokes stirring and then what does she do, nothing, she looks the other way and goes on helping herself but Francine who had followed her gaze goes pssht pssht, the two guests jump, Mademoiselle Ariane is highly displeased and drops the spoon into the soufflé or was it an eel matelote . . .

Marie came in with a cheese soufflé according to Made-moiselle Moignon, with an eel matelote according to the curé who had got to the second course and was just about to fill his plate when all of a sudden Mademoiselle Ariane seeing Minette said Nature, the curé Providence, old Lorpailleur opened her chicken's hole in order to swallow a mouthful and Francine went pssht pssht, which made him drop the spoon into the matelote, I'm referring to the curé, Marie said it doesn't matter and fished it out then went and put it on the sideboard and took another one which she put in the middle of the table beside the dish and then went out of the room while Mademoiselle Ariane who was very angry said young people or something of the sort, now the curé still according to Mademoiselle Moignon . . .

In short they'd got to the second course after the mess which was placed during the first the artichokes that is which one had no compunction about serving to one's intimates, they were as common as dirt that year, I'm referring to artichokes, they didn't let anything go to waste at Bonne-Mesure, Marie made the best of it with one of her special sauces, the curé glutton that he is had got it all over his napkin which he'd tucked under his collar, old Lorpailleur opened her chicken's hole just wide enough to scratch off the tip of the leaf which she then put down on her plate, whereupon Mademoiselle Ariane said don't stand on ceremony Mademoiselle, we're all friends here, put it there, pointing to the dish in the middle of the table, like the rest of us, look, and she encouraged her by putting her own leaf there but old Lorpailleur was hampered by her napkin which she'd tucked under her two arms, she had to keep her elbows in to stop it falling into her plate, in short after the first course, that was the point they'd reached.

What she didn't say, I'm referring to Mademoiselle Moignon, was that before the first course while they were waiting a minute or two for Marie, Francine who was breaking the bread had asked the curé to pour out the wine, he was a regular guest and the only male there and when I say male, now the curé had managed to spill some on the table-cloth while he was serving old Lorpailleur which had annoyed Mademoiselle Ariane, you'll never change, Abbé, alluding to the incident at Mass the previous Sunday, the curé had missed the altar-cruet the choir-boy had been handing him, it had fallen on to the ground and broken, which made him say humbly you see Mademoiselle Francine I'm no good for anything any more, the good Lord will forgive me, thinking of the incident on the Sunday, administering divine service so badly, to which Mademoiselle Ariane to make amends apparently added what *are* you thinking of, I was miles away, no no said the abbé you were right, we have to accept our afflictions, because he has rheumatism in his joints, which is apparently why old Lorpailleur said couldn't you take the cure at Rottard, I know a lady who was saved by it, it's true, the cure at Rottard that's what you need, then Marie came in with the soup-tureen, it was a cold consommé what with the heat that day, she filled the Wedgwood bowls herself on the sideboard and then handed them to each of the guests.

Or that before they left the terrace, putting his port glass down not on the table but to one side the curé had broken it and incurred Mademoiselle Ariane's remark, she had already been annoyed by Francine's attitude to Minette on account of what we've already mentioned, perhaps it was that, because there had been the first Saturday in June when it was very hot too, aperitif out of doors before luncheon, and Mademoiselle Moignon could have confused the occasions, it was excusable, she and Marie go over in detail every slightest thing that happens at the manor house which she then straightaway reports to the ladies.

But Francine, who detested the things her aunt grew in the dining-room window-box and thought artichokes and cacti extremely ugly was delighted to see Minette depositing her mess in the middle of them and in all probability only went pssht once the operation was completed, thus startling the cure who dropped the spoon into the sausages and that Mademoiselle her aunt probably wasn't looking at the cat but at her niece when she said Nature ... when she said young people ... in short a cacophony that would have made the ladies laugh if the incident had not immediately preceded the reference to the Ducreuxs.

For Mademoiselle Ariane who was waiting for the right moment to mention the Ducreuxs to see the respective reactions of the schoolmistress and the cure apparently took advantage of the latter's clumsiness to add, after they'd finished with the cure's outburst of modesty, do you know that Mademoiselle Doudin who was at the service maintains that the choirboy wasn't it Tourniquet may well have dropped the cruet on purpose, to which the cure replied why accuse a child, there's no harm in that boy, it was entirely my fault, the good Lord et cetera, but the name Doudin had been planted and that's where the tragedy begins, the aunt winked at the niece, the ball had been set rolling.

What she didn't say, I'm referring to Mademoiselle Ariane, was that after the service in question, as she was leaving with Francine and the ladies were already gossiping outside the church, Mademoiselle Doudin had come up to her and complaining of the great heat had asked her if she would mind if the following Sunday the little window behind the Virgin's altar were left open so that the air could flow between it and the window in the sacristy, Mademoiselle Ariane sat in the front row of the faithful, to which she replied oh no, nothing against it on the contrary, the heat was such that it had almost inconvenienced her, that's just what I foresaw said Mademoiselle Doudin, I'd opened it and Madame Serinet, butter wouldn't melt in her mouth, asked me to shut it again, she felt feverish, a thing she wouldn't have dared do if you'd been there, Mademoiselle Ariane had in point of fact not arrived so early as usual as she had wanted to see Amédée about that business of the croquet lawn.

So that after the service the ladies were all together outside the church commenting on the choir-boy's clumsiness, some saying that he had done it on purpose, others that he was upset by the heat, he was a highly-strung child, riddled with worms, then greeted Mademoiselle Ariane and Francine who were making their way to the baker's when Mademoiselle Moine came up to the lady of the manor and spoke to her in such a low voice that no one heard, Mademoiselle de Bonne-Mesure looked surprised, she took off her silk coat and held it at arm's length for a few seconds she was so intrigued at what she had been told and it was only when she got to the baker's that she apparently winked at her niece while Madame Ducreux who was coming in from the courtyard was entrusting little Frédéric to the shop-girl, look after him, I'll be back in a moment, so you see.

But Mademoiselle Moine wasn't convinced, she wasn't afraid of the schoolmistress, she's always said as much, and if it was her duty to approach Eliette's parents she wouldn't hesitate, it would be a point of honor, what's the good of going to mass and so on and so forth if you avoid the issue when it comes to saving a soul, she went as far as that, true she was in an exalted frame of mind but as the Father said everything is preferable to a lukewarm heart, now everything depended on the contrary on what he meant by lukewarm, Madame Monneau insisted, when it was a question of your neighbor a certain way of shutting your eyes seemed to her to be more christian than taking sides.

But the schoolmistress unclenched her chicken's hole at the second course under the effect of the white wine, which was what Francine had been expecting, and taking the cheese soufflé as a pretext started talking about her

childhood, the difficulties of that period, of her grandmother's severity, and ended up with an apologia for duty
at the same time relishing the fricassee of rabit flavored
with wild thyme which Marie had taken a lot of care over,
the curé adores it, he'd got it all over his napkin, we'd escaped the myxomatosis even though it had again started its
ravages in the district, how long would it last, Mademoiselle
Ariane admitted to a dead loss of a hundred thousand francs
the year the epidemic broke out, she trembled, and Francine
poured out some more white wine, because breeding is a
tradition at Bonne-Mesure which supplies all the markets
in the region, it is no negligible source of profit, like the
fresh-water fish, not to mention the vines of course, and
the cereals, the farmers were anticipating a good harvest
that year, and apropos of fish how was Etienne Bianle getting
on, she had no complaints about him though for the last
few weeks she had found him somewhat absent-minded,
was it the heat, or was it, a wink at the niece, the fact that
Magnin had renewed his connection with the Ducreuxs on
account of some work that was to be done in their yard, she
didn't know the details, that old business must certainly
have affected people's minds, what do you think about it
Abbé, but the abbé had his mouth full and went mm mm
hoping to escape the interrogation, now Francine was obser-
vant and the moment the ecclesiastic had sucked the last
bone dry and swallowed all the sauce apparently had another
go, what do you think about it, he didn't know, in all conscience he didn't know, the good Lord was the only judge,
how could we concentrate on the so-called responsibility of
just one person when we all by our weakness and cowardice
encouraged, the word is not too strong, things to go in the
way they did, he felt he himself was at fault, perhaps first
and foremost, you see Mademoiselle there is a want of saints
in our midst, that is what everyone should be aiming at,

saintliness I mean, what would a soul like Saint Francis have done in the circumstances or little sister Theresa, forgetting that these characters, Francine immediately pointed it out, had never been in similar circumstances, how do you know the curé had rejoined, how do you know, all human circumstances are alike and charity is eternal, something along those lines, in short impossible to get anything out of him but Francine didn't let go, she poured him out another glassful, Mademoiselle Ariane was really beginning to enjoy herself, which made her forget what she was after, people think her hard and very stubborn when she wants something but the most striking thing about her, it's congenital, is her princely indifference which gains the upper hand, there's no denying it, after a glass or two and she doesn't turn her nose up at it as you know.

And coming back to Etienne Bianle apropos of the eels, there were so many that year in the ponds that people were eating them with every conceivable sauce, Francine asked old Lorpailleur if she remembered a certain Vernes whom we used to see about but who'd disappeared since, used he not to frequent the Dumans at that period, broaching the question by way of a deliberate mistake, Ducreuxs said old Lorpailleur, the Ducreuxs at that period quite so, I thought it was the Dumans said Francine who are related through Madame Maillard to Mademoiselle Poussegrain, perhaps replied the schoolmistress, actually it all comes back to me now, Madame Maillard was a Pinson, by the way what happened to young Alfred, she was referring to the son who had gone abroad some ten years previously, trying to change the subject, but Francine didn't let go, she came back to the aforementioned Vernes, do you know anything, because she had heard from Henriette that old Lorpailleur on her way to the newspaper office had passed and greeted the accused, she happened to be in town, I'm referring to

Henriette, more precisely just outside the block next to a pork butcher who specializes in *andouillettes*, they are the only ones her mother will eat, this was her chance now or never to put the schoolmistress's good faith to the test, awkward silence for a few seconds then haven't seen him since says the latter but he hasn't disappeared, according to the telephonist at the *Fantoniard* he comes to see the editors, she just happened to mention it to me the other day, well well says Francine then everyone will end up working for the paper, but she'd got her proof, old Lorpailleur was lying just enough to get herself out of difficulties if danger threatened, Francine left it at that.

Or that Henriette Passetant from the pork butcher's may have caught sight of the said Vernes on his way to the paper and imagined that he met the schoolmistress there, she'd passed her, nothing easier, I mean to say than that she should give her imagination full rein, knowing what she did about Francine who maintained that the said Vernes who was to be seen in the avenue with the ladies . . .

Mademoiselle Ariane, wanting to put old Lorpailleur at her ease and not look as if she were pressing the point too far, left her floundering with her niece and repeated to the curé that she never remembered having seen so many eels in her ponds, there'd be a good yield this year, Etienne had taken on a young man from Hottencourt to help him, one Cossard, did he know anything about the family, I had no choice, he seems honest but you never know, Cossard Cossard replied the curé where have I heard that name, but he had a fish bone under his tongue right at the very back and he was trying to dislodge it without anybody noticing, in the end he just hooked it out with his finger, the good Lord will pardon me, there, on the edge of his plate, no doubt about it Mademoiselle Ariane was really enjoying herself, Cossard oh yes the father is a blacksmith by trade

95

unless I'm mixing him up just a moment, no that's it, Eugène Cossard, my mother knew him, for the curé is a local man but he couldn't remember the children, now he was mixing him up with the grandfather Cossard, the son i.e. the father of the young one was a market-gardener, Mademoiselle Francine who was listening with one ear pointed this out immediately to which the curé replied I'm no good for anything any more and so on, do have a little more matelote, they passed him the dish, he took another helping but it was only greed, he insisted, the good Lord et cetera, old Lorpailleur had got as far as young Pinson but didn't take a second helping saying that she'd already over-indulged, your cook is a treasure, and held her hand over her glass when Francine tried to fill it again, Mademoiselle Ariane who already had hers on the bell not thinking that the curé would have any more described a gracious parabola with it in order to take it off again without appearing to do so and pounced on a crumb on the tablecloth which she swept up to her mouth, they were all friends there, she didn't have any more either she'd had a surfeit of matelote, the curé was the only one eating then, Francine just to be polite had taken another spoonful of sauce saying in any case I think that Monsieur Vernes whether or not he has disappeared . . . in any case we shall hear more of Monsieur Vernes, then turning to old Lorpailleur, you ought to try and see him again, he was not without culture.

Or that old Lorpailleur had not been lying and that the Passetant kid . . .

And coming back to Etienne Bianle apropos of the eels Mademoiselle Ariane asked the schoolmistress if she remembered the ghastly accident that had happened to his brother, a child of two or three, or was it five or six, who had been run over by a truck it must have been ten years before, no though how stupid I am, weren't you in the

Argentine, to which the mistress replied my sister, you're mixing me up with my sister, but this was a trick on Mademoiselle de Bonne-Mesure's part, what a scatter-brain I am she murmured, how is she by the way, it seems a long time since I've had any news of her, that poor Doudin girl always used to tell me about her, the name had been planted, the ball had been set rolling, apropos did you know that the business of winding up the estate isn't quite going without a hitch, who was telling me the other day, I simply can't remember, second trap set for old Lorpailleur who had had a long conversation about it with Magnin who as it so happened had been on his way to the manor house that day and had wasted no time in reporting what the schoolmistress had said, the curé had finished guzzling and was belching silently behind his napkin, Mademoiselle Ariane rang the bell and at the same time looked somewhat fixedly at the accused, she was waiting for her to take the plunge, old Lorpailleur reclenched her chicken's hole as Marie came in, her reply didn't concern the lower orders.

Or that she replied just after the bell was rung, and Marie only came in immediately afterwards.

Third course or rather the cheese, local goat's cheese and blue Auvergne, Mademoiselle Ariane said to Marie we'll have our coffee on the terrace and to the schoolmistress will you have coffee, we have an excellent decaffeinized brand if that suits you better, the latter replied yes I'd rather have that, which made two with and two without, the curé being inclined to fall asleep after a meal, he'd got up to the choir-boy, there's absolutely no evil in the boy but as the Father says, better late than never or something of the sort, Francine passed him the cheese and asked him where the nickname Tourniquet came from and asked old Lorpailleur do you call him that at school, the schoolmistress said no we never allow nicknames, the parents might take exception and then when the inspector comes, you know what I mean such a bad impression, in short Mademoiselle Ariane poured out another glass for the curé and then one for herself, old Lorpailleur held her hand over her glass again and then pounced on a crumb on the tablecloth and swept it up to her chicken's hole . . .

The second cup of real coffee was for Francine who didn't like the decaffeinized stuff and she was so young, she didn't run any risk of not sleeping, so that the second cup of decaffeinized coffee naturally went to Mademoiselle Ariane, which indeed made four altogether.

As for Minette, on her way back from the kitchen-garden she jumped up at the window and then into the window-box where she deposited her mess without attracting any attention, the occasion when Mademoiselle Ariane had said Nature and Francine had gone pssht was the previous one, first Saturday in June, great heat, excusable error, we hadn't seen the like since . . . we'd never known anything like it, the harvest looked good but it might well be that on the other hand the ponds had less fish in them than Mademoiselle de Bonne-Mesure made out, it must have been the drought, they almost needed to call in a specialist in Amédée's opinion . . .

Sitting in her deck-chair daydreaming about the generosity of nature, such lovely weather, morning hymns, yes that was it, the day of the accident quite so Mademoiselle Cossard had wasted no time in reporting what the horrified ladies had said but the driver wasn't drunk, he got off with a suspended sentence, these things stay with you for ever no matter what, Etienne Bianle, yes, he nearly stayed there for ever too.

Mademoiselle Ariane, wanting to put old Lorpailleur at her ease and not look as if she were pressing the point too far, left her floundering with her niece, she helped herself to cheese and recommended the goat's to the curé who had the fine red face of a baby's behind that has been macerating in urine, with him it was white wine, a baby face, yes, almost touching on account of its blue eyes which couldn't have spent much time dreaming of romance, a thing which marks the windows of the soul, as the Father says, or if they ever had dreamed of it it was a long, long time ago, not a trace left, they had returned, I'm referring to the blue eyes in that little behind, to their vision of the feeding bottle, of mummy's titties, of everything that comprised the milky horizon of babes and sucklings, and said as he helped himself I see that Mademoiselle Marie hasn't lost her touch, it looks just right this cheese, and started eating it peasant-fashion with his fingers, mm it's good, a mouthful of bread, a mouthful of cheese, he'd got up to the point in his childhood when his grandmother and grandfather et cetera, he used to mind the nanny-goats, the good Lord had appeared to him up in the hills between two mouthfuls of cheese which he had in his pocket, the sun was rising among the rhododendrons and gentians et cetera, Mademoiselle Ariane had heard the story of this visitation a hundred times so she turned her attention to the conversation between her niece and old Lorpailleur, they'd got up the Passetant kid, it was quite true the little baggage, she'd turned poor Monnard's head at his age, that's where it had all started, just to think that she had him in her clutches to the point where he forgot his elementary duty, he was guilty there was no denying that but both of them being women were prepared to excuse him and lay all the blame on his partner, we'd never seen the like, he was going to have to give up his post as parish clerk, what's the procedure in such cases, does the council give him formal notice, so many things they didn't know, Mademoiselle Ariane chipped in at this juncture saying but why meddle in people's private lives, and under the influence of the white wine wouldn't you do the same ladies with such a fascinating man, she was going too far, people often forgave her her rather *outré* remarks identifying them with a certain seigneurial yes that's the word or shall we say libertine tradition of which she couldn't rid herself verbally being herself completely out of the running but here really no, on behalf of her guests Francine intervened to restore order, there's a limit to everything, Aunt, the curé felt obliged to say something but what, caught between two fires, dreading a sideways swipe from his hostess and having to take up the cudgels on behalf of the Church, morals, so on and so forth, as for old Lorpailleur, chicken's hole plus cork.

Dreading a sideways swipe from his hostess who in fact was enjoying herself tremendously but he wasn't supposed to accept this it seems that the curé first pushed his cheese into his left cheek and lowered his eyes, then began to concentrate, then raising them to Francine articulated the good Lord and all the rest of it, something of the order of we are all guilty he alone is the judge, which didn't fit the case at all because he seemed to be implying that Francine as well as old Lorpailleur and he himself had fornicated with poor Monnard, the schoolmistress said Monsieur the curé I'm shocked, what I mean is said the curé that our neighbor's sins which we judge so severely, he carried on doggedly putting his foot into it and forgetting his left cheek, it's such a nuisance when you have to do everything at the same time by means of the same canal, the words unleashed by our reason get blocked by the alimentary bolus, he decided to have a drink and swallow the lot, Mademoiselle was enjoying herself tremendously . . .

To have a drink and swallow the lot, which deprived him of everything at the same time, the cheese, the good Lord and all the rest, he said no more, his little eyes were either imploring the forgiveness of you know whom or had got left behind in the rhododendrons and nanny-goat's mess, luckily Mademoiselle Ariane had rung, Marie came in with the dessert, let me serve you said Mademoiselle Ariane to the ecclesiastic, she didn't want cream all over the table-cloth, the poor man held out his plate saying just a very little, a christian formula to disguise his gluttony et cetera et cetera.

Or that as Marie was about to ring the luncheon bell Francine emerged with her bike at the corner of the terrace and signed to her to wait, she had something to tell her, ssh with her finger, and went up to the cook, do you know whether Miquette Passetant has seen old Lorpailleur, now Marie knew a great deal about it but couldn't answer at a moment's notice, come and see me after luncheon, no though now will do, which would have meant that they went into the kitchen leaving the aunt and her guests to cool their heels, the guests helped themselves to some more port, a possible explanation of Mademoiselle Ariane's ribald mood from the start of the luncheon, the white wine alone not being . . .

The guests helped themselves to some more port but in the meantime Mademoiselle Ariane had got impatient and called Marie who apparently abandoned Francine and came running up to the terrace, what's she doing, have you seen her, yes, Mademoiselle is just coming but she's washing her hands and asked me to ask you to be so good as to wait just a few minutes, ah the younger generation Mademoiselle Ariane is then supposed to have said to the curé to which seeing Minouche in the hydrangeas she apparently added Nature, this version still according to Miquette Passetant but it has the advantage of reconciling . . .

In short, once Marie had explained things to Francine, she Francine is then supposed to have gone out on to the terrace to greet her aunt and apologize for being a little late, she had met Miquette, a wink at Mademoiselle Ariane, and couldn't just abandon her without asking after her mother, her poor aunt Doudin, re-wink, and the difficulties that had arisen over the winding up of the estate which everyone deplored but what could you do about it, to which Miquette replied that according to Madame Maillard a new fact had come to light but ssh I'll tell you about it another time, my respects to Mademoiselle your aunt, thanks very much said Mademoiselle Ariane drolly, shall we go in to luncheon, now Francine felt she would like just a little port, which delayed the bell even more, Marie was waiting at the corner of the terrace for a sign from her mistress, in short all this kind of overrated domestic tradition but it was probably necessary to go through with it all if they wanted to surprise impromptu the casual revelatory detail, something of the sort . . .

So yes, hardly was she on her English-type bike which she had mounted at half-past eleven in order to arrive at midday at the gate of the manor house which she intended to entrust, I'm referring to the bike, to Amédée the lodge-keeper so as not to arrive by bicycle at Mademoiselle de Bonne-Mesure's, than old Lorpailleur still according to Mademoiselle Moine saw some twenty yards away from her almost outside the baker's Miquette with Mademoiselle Cossard, a thing which had nothing surprising about it after what everyone knew of the difficulties over the inheritance, she could have gone on her way, she didn't, her curiosity had gained the upper hand, and taking as an impromptu pretext Magnin's building projects old Lorpailleur lowered her feet to the ground, leant her bike against the wall, took her gloves off and greeted the ladies then immediately adopting the appropriate attitude and indicating the baker's with her chin, you know they've decided to build says she, I thought I ought to let you know, they're going to Magnin thanks to Madame Monneau's machinations, she won't be able to take it with her, when you think that they had already contacted the Douves builders and everything, I'm not being spiteful but if anything were to go wrong it would serve them right, the ladies couldn't get over it, where and how had she heard the news, only yesterday Magnin had been saying the most atrocious things about the Ducreuxs, tell us, old Lorpailleur drew them aside into the mechanic's front yard and disclosed the fact that that very morning as she was on her way to school she had made a detour by way of the rue du Nid-de-Pie and what had she seen, old ma Passavoine in a huddle with Mortin who was tearing his hair, she lowers her feet to the ground, she leans her bike against the wall opposite and she goes straight to Verveine's, he was just opening his shop, he had already heard.

How to find out how ma Passavoine had was another matter but it could be that while she had been doing the cleaning the previous evening at the Dumans she had overheard a conversation and when I say overheard, and had wasted no time in passing it on to you know whom, wasn't it terrible, the ladies couldn't get over it, and that was how in a few minutes, five at the very most because she couldn't stay long, the schoolmistress had heard about the maneuver at which she was privately rejoicing as she had never been able to stand the Doudins, while at the same time going on saying to Miquette do you think you ought to, do you really think so, after all you are the only one who can judge, already ten past eleven, I shall be late at the manor, which was apparently what made Mademoiselle Cossard say when she'd gone well well so she's on visiting terms with the gentry now, whatever next, to which Miquette replied with some acumen she's only going there as an inferior to as you might say report on her activities, you know that the lady of the manor contributes to the upkeep of the school, an old tradition, and one thing leading to another a few hints about Francine who for some time had been rather off-hand to put it mildly, would there be something in the wind, you see what I mean, Monnard quite so just imagine.

And when the schoolmistress got to the gate she found it open, she got off her bike and pushed it up to Amédée's lodge with its well-kept flower beds full of mignonette or whatever, there she greeted Madame Amédée who lost no time in saying Mademoiselle Francine hasn't arrived yet, come in for a minute, I've something to tell you, it could have been in the course of this conversation, five minutes at the most, that the schoolmistress heard about the maneuver but no one could confirm this, Amédée was over at the croquet lawn and Madame Moine hadn't been able to wait, so that the conversation between Miquette and Mademoiselle Cossard could have been nothing but old Lorpailleur trying to be artful, I mean the fact of her claiming to pass it on straight from the horse's mouth to you know whom, or it could have been a dirty trick Miquette was playing on Mademoiselle Doudin who knew that old Lorpailleur was on her way to the manor, in short the schoolmistress comes out of the lodge pursing up her chicken's hole, goes up the drive which is in fact a gap in the beech wood which beeches give way on the right some hundred yards before the terrace to the rhododendron clump, terrific July heat, the old mansion comes into view with all its windows open to the half-past eleven sun.

It was possible that Mademoiselle Ariane who always did everything half an hour early so as to be punctual had taken up her position on the terrace with her needlework at eleven o'clock and then been inconvenienced by the sun or irritated by what she already knew about the Passetant kid . . .

But Mademoiselle Ariane who always did everything half an hour early so as to be punctual had gone to sit on the terrace at eleven o'clock, she would await her guests there, she had just given her last instructions to Marie who had first gone back to her kitchen and then taken up her position at the corner of the terrace in the resigned attitude we know so well, a nice picture of these two old bodies separated by convention and by fifty yards of raked gravel in front of the noble facade with its windows open et cetera, august silence, traditions, all the clichés you can think of on the subject, when suddenly Minouche deposits her quite so in you know what and makes Mademoiselle, Ariane roar with anger, clap her hands and go pssht, reserving her encomia on the subject of Nature for another time, class hypocrisy, she got up and went over to inspect the hydrangeas where she observed that the cat if she had not added anything to the compost so lovingly prepared by Amédée had at least not carelessly subtracted anything, meaning from the delicate stalks of the plants by breaking a shoot or a bud, you never know, she bent, then, over you know what and suddenly heard Marie shouting to Amédée to open the gate, which irritated her, Marie took liberties which while they might well be touching were none the less questionable, and then in her turn she called out to the cook to inform her that *primo* she had already told her a hundred times not to yell in her presence, *secundo* that Amédée was supposed to have opened the gate at ten o'clock and *tertio*, and this time it was a question, did he neglect his work, have you noticed anything, I'm beginning to doubt whether he really intends to clear the croquet lawn, tell me.

So there you are says she to Francine while she's telling

her about the gate incident, Mademoiselle was doing you know what, or if she didn't actually say it it came to the same thing, when I shouted to Amédée to go and open the gate, she came out like a whirlwind and told me *primo, secundo* and *tertio*, I shall never get used to Mademoiselle's moods, and she was crying, poor Marie, she was crying, which delayed the luncheon bell even longer, so that Francine, who had been present at other scenes, she knew it all by heart, went and rang the bell herself before greeting her aunt and the guests.

For Mademoiselle Ariane while she was waiting for the curé had gone to sit on the terrace with her needlework but being inconvenienced by the sun had gone over to the hydrangeas and put her chair in the shade, disturbing Minouche, so that the cat in order to avoid the pssht darted off into the kitchen garden from whence Amédée on his way back from the croquet lawn was going to open the gate, which explains why neither Marie nor Mademoiselle Ariane . . . in short the curé arrived before old Lorpailleur, it must have been eleven twenty-five, something like that, I can still see him coming up the drive, he had walked from Hottencourt, and wiping his forehead with his handkerchief as he came through the gate, a very characteristic gesture, lifting up his beret with one hand and his glasses with the other . . . or rather his beret and glasses with the same hand, the left one, so as to be able to wipe his forehead with his right one and use the other to greet . . . to greet with his head and his two hands since they all formed one unit as you might say Madame Amédée who was on her doorstep, she asked him if he had come from Crachon, he replied that he was going there that afternoon for the catechism class, ah your mignonette, but Madame Amédée who is hard of hearing must have heard Miquette because she immediately said she's just left didn't you meet her, now the curé must have thought she was speaking to her husband or else absent-minded as he is and always nervous when he comes to the manor house he didn't notice, he continued on his way up to the old mansion with all its windows open to the July sun.

Old Lorpailleur arrives, Madame Amédée asks her how it's possible that she didn't see the curé, with only five minutes between them it seems incredible to her, look, there he is just arriving at the terrace now, old Lorpailleur answers that she hadn't seen anyone, he must have come along the Hottencourt road in any case not along this one, had she a reason for not saying she'd seen him, according to Mademoiselle Cossard it would appear that she hadn't because she wasn't supposed to have any idea that the curé knew anything about it, unless the Passetant kid had pulled a fast one again and told her that the abbé had heard that very morning from his housekeeper, hardly likely, it was better to stick to probabilities, Mademoiselle Ariane sees them arriving then one after the other with five minutes between them and is amazed that they didn't meet on the road or at the very least at the gate, they say no, they sit down round the iron table on the wicker chairs and Marie who had been watching for them from the corner of the terrace comes and serves the port, the conversation starts with the heat, we haven't seen anything like it since, and with the absence of Mademoiselle Francine who is always so punctual, the aunt weighs her words and keeps them vague, she is counting on her niece's diplomacy to tackle the ticklish subject knowing that she herself is liable to get carried away and put her foot in it, and you Monsieur the curé do you think that just a finger of port is contra-indicated because of the heat, the curé apparently replied no but one thing leading to another that he approved of the young people of today who drink fruit juice and coca-cola, it seemed to him that

107

alcohol was not so popular with the workers these days, sport had done a great deal to liberate young people, the world was becoming healthier, Mademoiselle Ariane according to Francine in whom she confided apparently had it on the tip of her tongue to compare the sporting but irreligious younger generation of today with the other one, hers, that was religious but drank, an arbitrary view of the situation but pretty anti-clerical, she mustn't, she abstained and falling back on Minette apparently said it's odd, that cat is developing an obsession, seeing her going back into the hydrangeas, which was no less anti-clerical but had the advantage of beating about the bush if I may so put it.

That the curé, then, having put his beret and glasses on again apparently dawdled up the drive weighing up the situation, it was one thing or the other, either Mademoiselle de Bonne-Mesure was going to provoke him whereupon the schoolmistress would not fail to drop various hints aimed at you know whom, in which case he would have to be careful, very careful, he must not lose sight of the interests of the parish but he must stick to the point of view of the Church, or the other thing, in short he was dawdling, thinking up what he was going to say and didn't notice the rhododendron clump from which Minette apparently emerged at that precise moment having been disturbed in you know what and with a single leap landed in the kitchen-garden where Amédée who had come back from the gate was listening to Mademoiselle Ariane telling poor Marie off for what was in fact his fault, that's all there was to it.

Or rather, that old Lorpailleur who had come by bike like Francine could have followed the latter at quite some distance for an appreciable way, could have slowed down so as to give Francine time to get off her machine and push it up the drive, then gone in herself and having lingered only as long as was strictly necessary with Madame Amédée so as not to lose sight of the niece seen her go down the path on the right by the rhododendrons, immediately realizing that she was going to see Marie before greeting her aunt and the curé, an induction that was easy to grasp, she was not unaware of the relations between the cook and Mademoiselle Cossard whom she had just passed, Francine had missed her because she had come out, I'm referring to old Cossard, by the kitchen-garden, a low gate in the hedge, this intentionally, after she had heard Francine greet Amédée from a distance.

But Marie who didn't split hairs was telling her mistress again that Amédée was working just as he always had, that she hadn't noticed anything abnormal and that about the bell, she would ring it just as soon as the soufflé had risen, just too bad for Mademoiselle Francine, especially as the curé had his catechism class, not being artful enough to play on her displeasure with the niece who ought to have been there long before contrary to what old Cossard maintained seeing that she old Cossard was entirely responsible for Mademoiselle Ariane's irritation and the late arrival of the niece as it was through her that she had heard that old Lorpailleur was to be present.

Not artful enough no, poor Marie.

So that when old Cossard, on her way out of the kitchen-garden . . .

So that when Madame Amédée heard Francine greeting her husband from a distance she may well have said to old Cossard go through the kitchen-garden, the low gate, then the schoolmistress won't see you, she'll be here any any minute . . .

Or that Amédée himself . . .

She brought in the dessert, a creamy thing she had made herself, something of the vanilla-ice-gone-wrong variety, she was a bad cook, poor Marie, she was dirty and stupid and obstinate but these old servants take touching liberties with you and Mademoiselle Ariane probably kept her on out of regard for her mother or sister or aunt or else because she was so stingy and only paid her a ridiculous wage, Odette knows all about it, never a day goes by without Marie confiding in her, Madam Amédée's god-daughter, they are related in spite of the difference in age, the tragedy that day being that as Odette was away Marie had stupidly confided in old Cossard, yes that was where all the mischief had started and the ladies were amazed that with so little knowledge the old shrew could have talked at such length about what went on at the manor, they began to wonder, meanwhile Madame Ducreux who had got wind of something was saying to the young assistant you take over I'll be back in a moment but didn't go you know where, she joined her husband and Magnin in the yard and told them what was going on, what could they do, because Marie didn't know anything about it, the only person she ever saw was Odette and when Mademoiselle Ariane left the table and went out on to the terrace she made up her mind, she would go and see Madame Amédée, she'd find out.

So when luncheon was over Mademoiselle Ariane rang the bell and left the table, she took the arm of the ecclesiastic and followed by the two maiden ladies crossed the large drawing-room which when seen for the first time made an unforgettable impression, she stopped in front of Gaspard and said point-blank to the curé don't you think he has my nose or I his, certainly he replied, and perhaps even the mouth . . . when they got to the terrace she observed that the port hadn't been taken away and asked her niece to go and tell Marie but Francine very sweetly offered to do it herself, we are all friends here, and took the bottle and glasses away and then something like five minutes later brought the coffee, which displeased Mademoiselle Ariane, can't Marie do anything for herself she asked, if we make everything so easy for her she'll end up by doing nothing at all, Francine poured the coffee, two without for her aunt and old Lorpailleur, two with for herself and the curé, and sat down next to the schoolmistress, the sun was in her eyes so she turned her chair round a fraction which made it possible for her to see the drive, now during the five minutes she had been away old Lorpailleur had been talking about family picnics under the effect of the white wine and the sense of well-being engendered by her digestive processes taking place in a beautiful park under the shade of a century-old plane tree in aristocratic company, her life-long dream, Mademoiselle Ariane was surprised and didn't take the point up but when Francine had settled down again she repeated her remark to her, ah yes, picnics, my goodness me, doesn't that remind you of something, they might well be on the verge of a discovery, Francine's face was irradiated by a celestial smile and she said oh dear me yes how true picnics, we had so many with my parents and brothers and sisters, with you too Aunt don't you remember, wink at the aunt, all that's so long ago alas, but what a joy it was, each one was an adventure, our good people are carrying on the tradition I believe, Grance is full of people on Sundays, it's so healthy, and what charming pictures of family life, it develops the children's spirit of initiative they say, my goodness apropos of initiative that horrible business of the little Ducreux boy, do you remember, old Lorpailleur was caught like a rat in a trap.

Hopping, skipping and jumping among the meadow-sweet.

She's mad there's not the slightest doubt about it.

But is she a criminal, who's going to prove that.

That particular Sunday, the last in July, Mademoiselle Lorpailleur had gone off to the forest with her little pupils, a school outing as they call it, they had arranged to meet at the Oublies crossroads at half-past nine after Mass, it was such lovely weather or rather it was very hot, the children arrived in little white shirts, little blue blouses, little red skirts, little linen trousers, adorable, their hair nicely done by their mummies or else already untidy, with their little picnic bags on their backs, it was a great day, adventure, I can still see the Bianle twins, the girl and boy, arriving hand in hand, all the children were excited, the mistress had asked Mademoiselle Odette to come and help her, she would stay with her the whole day, you must have at least two people to keep a horde of little devils in order mustn't you, they were still waiting for the Magnin kid who lived at the other end of the rue de Broy, he was always late, to cut a long story short when he arrived they got going, first of all there was the crossroads to negotiate, the young ladies lined the children up two by two in a crocodile on the pavement and off we go merrily, Madame Monneau was watching them from her window, a pretty picture indeed, first they went down the rue des Casse-Tonnelles, some of the shop-keepers who were open on Sundays saw them go past, Madame Tripeau who was putting out her display even allowed them to take a couple of sweets each, thank you very much Madame said the mistress, say thank you to Madame Tripeau, all together now thank you Madame, and don't throw the paper on the pavement, naturally though with those little devils some of the papers did get thrown down, and off they go again up to number twelve which still existed at the time, there they forked left and went down the rue Ancienne where Monsieur Cruze who wasn't open that Sunday was walking his dog, such a funny dog, one black ear and one white one with a hideous pink nose, and as fat as a little pig, the children said doggy oh what a lovely doggy and they tried to stroke it but the young ladies said now now leave Monsieur Cruze alone as if he were the one the children were trying to stroke, it was true, she was simply dying to laugh poor Odette after her illness, simply dying to, she must certainly be excused for this little joke, next one of the children, a little girl, had her lace undone, the right foot, they all had to stop, Mademoiselle Lorpailleur took advantage of this to make a little rule, if one of them had a lace undone or something of the sort he was to ask Mademoiselle Odette, she would take him on one side and let the others go on so as not to keep stopping all the time and the stragglers would catch them up, is that quite clear, they went on until they got to the bus stop, the bus arrived, a bit of luck, and the driver happened to be Passavoine who is so obliging, he helped the children on and they almost all found seats, at that time on a Sunday the bus is to all intents and purposes empty, there were only three people, the young ladies stayed on the platform with the Bianle twins, little Henriette began to cry, she wanted to sit down, Passavoine had to deal with her and find her a seat with her brother who won't be parted from her, it caused quite a hullabaloo but he isn't the nervy type, in any case said the schoolmistress I wash my hands of them, find them seats if you like, and the three people looked indulgently at the little group, it reminded them of their youth especially as they were all pretty well past it, a lady and two old gentlemen, they weren't together, one of them was wearing a panama hat, I can still see it.

And so it went on until the Hottencourt stop, the first one because the mistress had decided that they would get into the forest as soon as possible by the les Vernes lane, the second stop carried them on too far, the children got off still helped by Passavoine, he was especially kind, was it because of the children or was it because of Odette who at that time, before her illness, was most appetizing, by the way Passavoine is still a fine figure of a man and I've heard that when it comes to quite so he's very much in evidence, isn't it admirable so many qualities combined in one man, not like that poor Magnin not to mention anyone else it seems he's no bigger than that and stupid into the bargain, can you imagine, well to cut a long story short they got off and straightaway took the les Vernes lane, they weren't in a crocodile any more, the young ladies let them form up in little groups or wander off on their own, relaxing their discipline because there was no traffic along this lane, the children were admiring the flowers and the little gardens on either side, this is a place that is mainly inhabited by retired civil servants and poor families, a few brats were watching the group go by and some even said hello to each other but less than you might have thought, children are actually very shy with each other at first, on the defensive, a bit like animals of different species when they find themselves face to face, they really are pretty slow to make contact, this was what the young ladies were discussing or let's say Odette who wasn't used to them and was therefore amazed and moralistic, new brooms sweep clean, they reached the end of the lane which is a cul-de-sac, it's officially listed as no throughfare but in fact it is continued by a path that passes gardens that get poorer and poorer with toolsheds in them until you get to the forest, at about three hundred yards from the bus stop that is, and here the mistress said right let's sit down on the grass, is anyone too hot, they all said me me, they wanted to take off their little shirts or blouses or whatever, the young ladies picked out three or four who were really perspiring and allowed them to undo their clothes for a moment while the sun was on them, the others wanted to do the same but the mistress said no we're going into the forest now and it won't be so hot there, I don't want anyone to have bronchitis or a cold or a sore throat tomorrow, so on and so forth, you may have a little to drink, has anyone got a water-bottle, several had, with coffee in or water that was already tepid, Odette half-filled a beaker and everyone drank from it in turn, they had decided to pool everything, children must be encouraged to be altruistic, what used to be called kind-hearted in our day, then they went into the forest, and this in two groups even though together, the mistress had decided on this so as to be on the safe side, you never know, she considered that it would make it easier for the children to re-assemble and as she had planned that they would play team games in the afternoon, this was a way of beginning from the beginning to inculcate the team spirit, teachers have these psycho psychi what do they call them ideas which have apparently been proved to have something in them, there was group A then with the mistress and group B with Odette and in fact the children were quite excited about it, they were quite bright-eyed about not being in the other group, except for the fact that the Bianle twins who had been allocated to B wanted to stay with the mistress, little Henriette had begun to cry, they had exchanged with the Voiret boy and the Magnin boy if my information is correct, there they are going into the forest then.

Or that from the very beginning, at the Oublies crossroads, Mademoiselle Lorpailleur had divided them into two groups, which would have been the cause of little Henriette's tears by which the mistress did not intend to be intimidated, that child took advantage of her great booby of a twin who indulged all her whims, she was already getting a psycho psychi complex which the mistress wanted to break, and that Mademoiselle Odette during the whole of the journey first in the rue des Casse-Tonnelles then in the bus then in the les Vernes lane had had constant trouble with the child and had been unjust to her little brother who simply couldn't help it, he automatically and you might even say viscerally took the side of his tyrannic twin, what a lot of problems already with the day only just begun, Mademoiselle Odette who is so conscientious as you know felt as if her head had become a factory long before they went into the forest, it must be added that the heat didn't make things any better and the little Bianle girl wasn't the only one who was suffering from it.

But what was creating difficulties was the fact that this was not the first school outing Mademoiselle Lorpailleur and her little pupils had been on, she had organized one at Easter in April and the children remembered certain details like the business of the groups A and B which instead of simplifying matters complicated them, the mistress couldn't remember who had been in one or the other and as the children either hadn't all been there at Easter or wanted to change groups this time you couldn't leave it to their initiative to divide up as they had before for instance, apart from the little ruck-sacks some of which were too full but hadn't hurt their little collar-bones in the spring because of the woollies covering them but which when they had got no farther than the rue Ancienne had already given rise to complaints and ex-changes, one going to a stronger boy, one being carried by Odette herself, she wasn't used to it, she didn't know that children must arrange things among themselves according to psycho psychi principles and the mistress didn't want to show her up in front of the pupils.

They had met at the crossroads at half-past nine, the mistress was counting them as they arrived with Monette Dondard who had been so kind as to agree to accompany her for the day, it was still cold, the kids arrived all muffled up with their picnic bags on their backs, I can still see little Odile Mortin at the corner of the rue de Broy, she was so slender, with her brother Frédéric they were holding hands, they were each wearing a thick red woolly cap with a pom-

pom, the mistress and Monette were saying my goodness isn't it cold, if only the sun would break through, and it was at this moment as the little Mortins were crossing between the studs that a truck coming from the rue Neuve suddenly braked, only just missing the children, there were no policemen about, the young ladies were shattered, the road-hog carried straight on, wasn't it disgraceful, Monette rushed over and took the children's hands and Mademoiselle Lorpailleur kept on repeating a drunkard another drunkard, when shall we rid ourselves of that turbulent breed, Madame Dumans who was passing stopped, she asked her where she was going with her class, she answered to the forest to pick primroses, the day is beginning badly, did you see that drunkard, she wound her veil around her neck, there was an icy little wind, if only the sun, and the troop set off up the rue des Casse-Tonnelles as far as the corner, the shop-keepers saw them going by, it was a Thursday, the Thursday before Easter to be precise, so Tripeaus' stores next to the grocer's which is run by the husband had already got their display of toys and plastic goods out, the children stopped, they coveted everything, Monette had to drag them away, they were blocking the pavement, two old men, I can still see them, were grumbling as they tried to get past, they had just got off the Douves bus which stops outside the chemist's while the little troop was going to turn right into the rue Ancienne and then take the Hottencourt road, Cruze who was chatting to Madame Monneau in his shop recognized Monette whom he hadn't seen since her return, he was offended, is that little creature going to give herself airs now, when you think that her mother used to go out charring for mine et cetera.

Then they went into the forest which is not yet very dense at that point, the young ladies intended to go down the path which comes up at right angles on the left to get to the big

117

clearing where they were going to have their picnic but whether it was that they weren't used to it and that the appearance of the wood was so different from what it was in the spring they couldn't find the path and for a whole hour drove the little party on almost at random, they were still roughly going in the right direction, Odette had been a guide captain in her youth and knew how to use the sun to get her bearings, they did in fact get to the clearing at something like half-past twelve, the children were thirsty, put your bags down and sit on the grass, the mistress automatically counts their lunch-bags, one was missing, the one belonging to the Bianle twin, he had so he said given it to the Voiret boy who had given his own to someone else but when, did you still have it when we stopped just before we came into the forest, did you put it down somewhere try and remember, he couldn't remember, let's count the bags again, does anyone remember having seen Jean-Pierre's bag on the ground, no one had seen it, but what did you do come on now, you're not an idiot are you, didn't you know that you had one bag and your sister another, that everyone had a bag, the child was on the verge of tears and said that he had picked up his little sister's bag, she was tired, how could we not have noticed that the little girl was walking without a bag, the young ladies were quite put out, right said the mistress I'll go back the way we came, start the picnic without me, but Odette said no I'll go, I'll be back in half an hour at the very most, it must have been left behind at our first stop, we ought to count them every time, and she went back while the children were unpacking their food and Mademoiselle Lorpailleur was getting them to pool everything in the middle, they were going to share it.

So as Madame Monneau said you can quite see that Odette wasn't on good terms with the schoolmistress at that time, their relations had been strained before that, well before that, and the day she went to see her godmother didn't make matters any better, it was the first Saturday in July, I know that from Mademoiselle Cossard, in other words a good three months after the Easter outing, so you see, but Cruze wasn't so sure, he said that he had recognized Odette, after all I'm not mad, I was talking to someone or other and I saw the children go by in charge of the young ladies, Madame Tripeau even gave them some sweets, it was a Thursday, he brought out his note book, look I'm not mad ... while Monette who had quarrelled with old Lorpailleur a long time before went into the baker's and said to Madame Ducreux ... it must have been half-past eleven ... this was many years later ... many months are you sure ... in any case well after the invitation to Mademoiselle Ariane's, well after ...

A fortnight at the outside, how could he have remembered that idiot of a chemist with his note-book, he's never shown it to anyone so far as I am aware, I'd give a lot to have a look through it, how could she have been so naive as to believe that he wrote everything down in it, it was a trick, a plot, Madame Dondard was worried about her daughter, the knowing airs she gives herself, and mumbled poor thing, we'd never seen the like, and if only it was airs she gave herself but alas, alas ...

Were unpacking their food under the eye of the mistress who was getting them to pool everything in the middle so as to share it, they were going to start their picnic as Mademoiselle Lorpailleur didn't dare wait for Monette who had gone to look for the bag because that bitter little wind had sprung up again, she didn't want anyone getting a sore throat or bronchitis, so on and so forth, they would eat fairly quickly and then organize a game to prevent them catching a chill and in fact half an hour later Monette came back with the bag, what luck, all the children shouted bravo, children are so sweet, their little hearts and brains are so spontaneous, a bit like animals of a different species, you don't know what's going on inside them but then all of a sudden they do something impulsive that gives you new confidence in humanity, isn't that so, the young ladies were laughing, they were so pleased, I can still see the schoolmistress winding her veil round her neck and saying none of this is going to get you to eat your lunch my dear and here's that nasty wind again, come on now we kept you an egg and some of Monsieur Bouboule's pâté, Monsieur Bouboule was the nickname of the pork butcher, in her joy the mistress was forgetting her principles, never any nicknames et cetera, to cut a long story short Monette started toying with the food while the children under the eye of the mistress piled all the papers up in the middle and shut their bags and then put them tidily under a tree, all right then just for once we'll make a bonfire with the paper, the children clapped their hands, that's what real joy is, the joy you share with innocent creatures.

Then they played at policemen and robbers, they were already divided into two sides, group A would be the policemen and group B the robbers, but the very little girls would play another game that was rather more up their street, ring-a-ring-o'-roses, things like that, and they wanted to pick primroses too, there were lots everywhere, Monette would look after them, five or six amongst whom was little Henriette still as tyrannical as ever, she wouldn't let her brother leave her, he wanted to be a policeman, he was going to cry, what should they do, must they lay down the law again and cause a scene, Monette had the idea of nominating him chief of the girls to keep him with his sister, he would organize and run their games, he was all for it, whilst the mistress kept her eye on the others, whatever you do don't go far away, no one is to hide any further than two trees away from the clearing, do you understand, then all the little lot got going and shouting and laughing, not forgetting the adorable little tantrums, the tears and the grazed knees even though there ought to have been less danger on the moss but the Magnin boy and the Dumans boy and also Mademoiselle Moine's nephew what's his name managed to graze themselves by falling over an old stump or a rock for instance, there are some immediately after the clearing, which was one more thing for the mistress to worry about, she had to disinfect the places and put that red stuff on them, nevertheless she didn't want to shirk this responsibility by forbidding any violent games that use up children's energy, we must give her credit for that, she has strong views when it comes to pedagogy, ah yes that's the word I was looking for, while the little girls were adorably miaowing away at their little songs and counting-out chants, it was so charming, or picking little flowers, there were bluebells and anemones too, while the young ladies still keeping their eyes on them were confiding their professional secrets to each other, or rather Mademoiselle Lorpailleur was confiding hers to Monette who showed a natural aptitude, she was at the age which differs with different temperaments when the maternal instinct is so it would seem pure and unadulterated ... free from how to put it, they don't see the connection ... in short Monette was still at that stage although she was in her fifteenth year which could have caused people to reflect on the case of Mademoiselle Lorpailleur who was getting on for forty at the time, was she still ... you might well have reflected on it but it was of no interest really given the physical appearance of the person in question, after a certain degree of ugliness the observer looks the other way, she's an old maid and that's all there is to it, you'd have to be depraved or have morbid leanings towards the psycho psychi to have any interest in her.

121

So that after an hour or two the children, I'm speaking about the bigger ones, were perspiring, the heat had become stifling, the young ladies decided to stop the games, in any case the tantrums were becoming more frequent, the mistress called them all together, assembly, their little faces all red and out of breath, adorable, their clothes all untidy et cetera, now children let's have a little rest, we're going to pick up our bags and walk as far as the hill, the days are so long in July that Mademoiselle Lorpailleur had agreed with Odette that they would go as far as the miraculous statue where from the lay point of view she could tell the inspector that the view is superb, a little lesson in regional geography for the children, she was thus killing two birds with one stone in considering the christian families who would be grateful to her and Odette who had mystical leanings at the time, she herself being quite simply against religion.

And what the ladies found interesting in all this, I'm referring to Mademoiselle Ariane and Francine, was in noticing the exact moment when old Lorpailleur would contradict herself or hesitate or appear to be less at her ease, however she continued without the slightest hint of embarrassment with her evocation of the picnic which little by little with every detail she described seemed to become totally remote from the tragedy in question and even to blur its outlines completely, absolutely no connection, so that with the schoolmistress well it was either one thing or the other . . .

And what interest Marie, and the reason she was going to see Madame Amédée, she had just gone round behind the house but Francine from where she was sitting had seen her cross the drive, was to find out whether or not old Cossard before she left had thrown out any hints about the fact that the god-daughter, Odette that is, whom she was going to question knowing that she wouldn't say anything . . . or rather to find out whether Mademoiselle Francine had said

122

anything to Amédée contrary to what she had stated I waved to him from a distance or then ... in short the curé at three o'clock got up to take his leave, he was so sorry, he'd hardly digested his luncheon, the shade under the big plane tree was so pleasant and the ladies so gracious, I'm referring to the aunt and the niece, real christians, there was a sort of emanation that came from them and from their conversation, he was not mistaken, he was a confessor and psychologist, it was all very well for him to tell himself when he was with working men for instance that he was amongst his brothers and that that was where true charity was to be found, he had to pinch himself a bit in order to believe it when he was as today in the company of beautiful ladies, education and tradition are what make the most beautiful souls, he had opened his heart to Mademoiselle Ronzière in this connection, she knew a great deal about his holy thoughts, she compared them to those of Saint Francis de Sales who as you know was an aristocrat, if the curé Maillard wasn't one he at least had this of one et cetera, right, he lifts it up from his armchair, he stands up, Mademoiselle Ariane remains seated, Francine and old Lorpailleur stand up and it's all charming goodbyes, encouragements, smiles and unctuousness on all sides, then Francine accompanies her pastor to the gate and they start off down the drive.

When they've got their bags up on their backs again, they were light now, everyone could look after his own, the little troop started off up the path leading to the hill, in a north-westerly direction that is, very pretty, with branches that brush against you, the children were pulling leaves off and Odette asked the mistress if they should let them wasn't this encouraging their destructive instincts, she didn't feel it was the same thing when they were picking a bunch of flowers, she was quite right the mistress told her but you can't instill too many ideas at the same time into their little brains, do we know what goes on in them, we shall be having to lay down the law soon enough when the children start getting tired and not wanting to walk any farther or pretending to be tired so as to stop for a moment, in short you had to ration your interventions, the young ladies had dropped back a bit so as to be able to chat but they soon came to a crossing of the ways, there was another path at an acute angle to the one they were going up and the children in front called out which one shall we take, I'll go said Mademoiselle Lorpailleur, I'll stay in front and lead them, you stay at the back and see that we don't lose any *en route*, watch little Henriette, she's supposed to carry her own bag, I completely emptied it, if she starts sulking be firm but don't raise your voice, explain to her that she's a big girl now and that she must set an example, and she went on ahead to lead the children in the right direction, they asked her but where does the other path go, it went towards Agapa, the children would have liked to go there but the mistress replied what an idea, it's much too far, we'll go there next year, it's a lovely town you'll see with a river, what's the name of the river Dominique come on now, he didn't know, he ought to have known, regional geography, Mireille was the one who knew, the Manu she said, that was right, and she went on to say that she had been to Agapa once with her parents, there was a shop full of toys and a *pâtisserie* where she had had a *mille-feuilles*, she had been just a little girl at the time, she had wanted one for her doll to eat too, she remembered it very well.

And thus a little question to this one and that just to keep track of their ideas and make sure their minds were alert, to avoid any tendencies towards passivity, the mistress deserved a good deal of credit when you come to think about it, teachers don't count the cost of their efforts, they give of their best don't they, how tired she must have been at the end of the day but also it can't be denied that it's an acquired habit and what may seem admirable to someone like Odette may not be so any more in reality, what you might call the schoolmarm spirit had got the upper hand, the mechanism functions almost without any conscious intervention, Mademoiselle Lorpailleur may well have been thinking of something quite different and in fact when Philippe Voiret who was walking beside her asked what is that tree she didn't answer, he repeated his question, she said what, what tree, but you know that one come on now, this was certainly the mechanism in action, it's a beech tree, what were you doing during the lesson last week, how do you spell beech, the Dumans boy gave the right answer, very good, and what species are to be found in our region and in particular in the Forest of Grance, who can tell me, little Magnin said beeches M'selle, yes and what else, fir trees said Jacquot, no said the mistress fir trees are usually to be found on high ground, what else come on now, and little Yolande said oak trees I think, that's right, oak trees, how do you spell oak, then Philippe Voiret trying to be clever said ah yes I thought it was oaks, why didn't you say so then, because I wasn't sure, while Odette bringing up the rear was saying to herself all these children, thirty or so, what a great responsibility, would she be equal to it if she were to adopt this career, to find yourself at the end of the day with a child missing, my goodness my goodness, she counted them again, she couldn't manage it, what if one of them were to stray ever so slightly to left or right suddenly interested in a flower or a bird or I don't know what, he wanders off, he gets lost in the wood, he calls out but it's too late ...

He had wandered away from her, she thought he was with his father and when he called out she didn't know if it was Daddy or Mummy, there's an echo in this part of the wood, she ran like a madwoman ...

And wasn't the picnic bag a warning, how could Mademoiselle Lorpailleur be so relaxed, asking them questions about spelling, rather casual wasn't it, did she really like children, she would never trust her own, I'm talking about Odette, to anyone, how could you tell whether that person was really what you thought him or her, the business of the division of the estate with her sister, after the mother's death in the Argentine or wherever she'd heard about that, it was pretty sordid, and all the pills and medicines they'd found everywhere and the attitude of the mistress which had apparently changed towards everyone after she had moved and the black veil she's been wearing since since ... she had confided after the event in her friend Antoinette to whom she told everything or more or less, the school outing had made her think, what a responsibility, no fault to be found with Mademoiselle Lorpailleur but you never know, she had suddenly said to herself what if she was an amoral character or in league with I don't know, kidnappers perhaps, I'm exaggerating of course but only so as to give you some idea, is she really what we think, Antoinette reassured her, she was laughing, you'll never change, if we had to be suspicious of everyone where would that get us, what about you do I really know exactly what you're like, we haven't been friends for more than five years so you see.

Hopping, skipping and jumping ...

Saying that during this picnic after she'd seen her husband's attitude, how passive he was, how casual, hadn't he let her go and fetch the picnic basket herself, she hadn't enjoyed herself in the slightest, in the first place the fatigue, and then the thought that her little boy could have got lost and ... my goodness my goodness it made her tremble, and then on top of it all her husband who looked as if he couldn't care less, who couldn't in fact have cared less, eating his ham and at the same time laughing and joking and

126

scratching his thigh, she could still see him, and then yawning and wanting to have another nap which in any case he did have, was he amoral, would he even have suffered if the child ... she didn't dare pronounce the phrase poor woman but when she was confiding in Madame Dumans she came back to it, did she really know him, was he what she thought him, what if she had married a monster can you imagine, to which Madame Dumans who as you know never gets excited replied you're exaggerating, you're too highly-strung, how do you know your husband couldn't care less, he was probably terribly upset but wanted to give you back your self-confidence, to calm your nerves and so may well have pretended to be indifferent, he could well have been forcing himself to keep cool, men aren't women you know and when women start passing judgment on them ... but her friend started all over again yes but the picnic basket, even so he let me go and fetch it is no matter how tired I was, she always brought everything back to herself.

The little party in the undergrowth still kept going, red and blue and twittering, would they be there soon, it's still a long way, come on children come on be brave, you'll see there's a place where you can get refreshments and I'll buy you a lemonade, the very little ones were beginning to lag behind, little Delphine and particularly Henriette who was such an awkward child, Odette had already told her three times that she was a big girl now, it didn't pay dividends any more, she was whining and her brother was carrying her bag again in spite of it being forbidden, Odette was turning a blind eye, the little pest had nevertheless made her point, when all of a sudden the beech trees began to get farther apart and they saw the hill and the path leading up to it, the mistress said stop, we'll have a rest, the children wanted a drink but she said no, in half an hour or three-quarters of an hour at the outside we shall be at the refreshment place, you'll see what a lovely view, little Auguste asked whether you could see the Holy Virgin from here, she said no but you see that clump of trees up at the top, the statue is in the middle, what about the refreshment bar asked Delphine, on the other side a little lower down, the Voiret boy asked whether they had coca-cola he liked that better, so to give them a bit of a fillip for the climb Mademoiselle Lorpailleur said who would rather have a coca-cola put your hands up, they all put them up, she said to Odette you see I really do belong to my generation, we used to drink lemonade in my day, do you like coca-cola, personally I think it tastes of chemicals, then they set off again and in the sun this time, it wouldn't do for it to go on for too long, at one moment while they were still on their way up their path crossed a road and a truck that was coming down rather quickly . . .

At one moment while they were still on their way up their path crossed a road and the children saw a man going past with his child, the mother was following them with a basket, the mistress who knew them said good afternoon goodness me isn't it hot, the man said yes but the lady looked tired, she was quite red, the children asked who are they, you're too inquisitive the mistress replied, cross quickly, they crossed and went on climbing, this time little Henriette didn't want to go any farther and Odette started carrying her on her shoulders, Mademoiselle Lorpailleur said that she would tire herself out but Odette before her illness was a strong girl, don't worry she said we'll be there in ten minutes, the path had become stony, there were pale blue chicory flowers growing along the verge and in the grass on either side a sort of summer dandelion smaller than the other ones and with longer stalks and also other vaguely mauvish flowers still according to Odette which she didn't recognize, the sun was beating down, the young ladies were walking together bringing up the rear again and saying I hope to goodness none of

them gets sunstroke, they had made the children put something on their heads if they didn't have a beret then some
little item of clothing or even a napkin or a handkerchief, it
was rather quaint, as for Mademoiselle Lorpailleur she
couldn't bear her hat with the crêpe on any more, she'd put
it in her rucksack and on her head a white muslin scarf,
Odette told her it made her look younger, was she just trying
to be nice, but she poor thing was lumbered with little
Henriette and she was really getting hotter and hotter, four
or five of the bigger ones were getting too far ahead, the
mistress called out to them to wait, they were excited at the
idea of the refreshment bar.

And Madame Voiret when her child came back that evening with his bag bursting with primroses and bluebells said
they're very nice but where are we going to put them, there's
only the washing-up bowl and the bidet, we'll see what we'll
do with them tomorrow, go and wash your hands and come
to supper, your father's already in the kitchen, it was nearly
eight o'clock, she was afraid that the child who was rather
delicate might have caught a chill and when he had sat
down she quickly rubbed his forehead with eau de cologne,
he had had a cold the week before, the father said you can
do that later it stinks, because he was already eating his
soup, he's quick-tempered as you know and hates having to
wait for his meals, and little Philippe told them all about his
day, that the mistress had stood them a coca-cola, that
Mademoiselle Monette had carried Henriette Bianle on her
shoulders and that her brother had lost his bag but that
they'd found it again, next time they would be going to
Agapa, the mistress had said so, and when he'd finished his
mummy said off to bed quickly now, you've got to go to the
Good Friday service tomorrow, I promised the curé you
would.

And Madame Voiret when her child came home that

evening with a lot of summer dandelions and mauve flowers that she didn't recognize . . .

Right, still according to Madame Voiret they finally got to the top and the mistress who from the lay point of view couldn't have made the Holy Virgin their goal simply said look here's the famous miraculous statue and down there that's the roof of the refreshment bar, let's go down, the children ran on, Odette confided to Mademoiselle Lorpailleur that she would very much have liked to meditate in front of the statue, oh but do said the mistress, in a way it was for your benefit that I brought them here, go back quickly, they were only about thirty yards past it, I'll look after the children and we'll come back and join you to look at the panorama, then you'll have all the trouble said Odette, we'll see about that go on now, so Odette went back to the shrine, a few people were praying there, she knelt down on one of the steps to ask for guidance about whether she should eventually adopt a teaching career, the statue is a replica of the one at Lourdes and the view it contemplates is indeed very extensive, far beyond Rottard the spa, how beautiful the landscape was and what a noble spirit must have inspired the people who made that spot a place of meditation, just as the Greeks still according to Odette chose the most beautiful site in any given region for their temples, Odette's girl friend was astounded at her culture, yes that was the career for her, the kneeling girl stayed there thus thinking several thoughts at once, though at the same time feeling somewhat worried at all the responsibility the mistress had taken on, she could see the children running about all over the place and making a noise, they were annoying the holiday-makers, she oughtn't to be here, she got up and went and rejoined the party, Mademoiselle Lorpailleur had her work cut out dealing with them, I can still see them she said to her girl friend with their coca-colas, instead of sitting down quietly they kept moving about in and out of the tables ... or else that the mistress had them well in hand, she had made them sit down not on the terrace but in the meadow at the far end of it and they weren't in the least annoying the holiday-makers ... or that it was someone else who said that Odette had told her about all this and about what she felt about prayer as well as about the different things that had occurred to distract her attention, while her girl friend knew nothing ... in short when the children had quenched their thirst the mistress collected them up to go back to the panorama.

Or that the business of meditation, of her reflections on culture and on her career were just one of old Lorpailleur's tricks because she wanted to make Odette appear in a bad light in the eyes of you know whom or at least didn't believe a word of it, jealous as she is, and maybe ten years later she was still pursing up her chicken's hole when referring to Odette's qualities which she had discovered that day, purposely confusing the summer outing with the Easter one, in other words insinuating to the Dumans family that Monette was a liar, can you imagine such wickedness.

Publicly flogged.

In short after they had passed the little troop the family that Mademoiselle Lorpailleur knew went a bit further down the road and then the father apparently suggested that they should take the short cut on the left that went down through the forest, parallel or nearly so to the path the children were taking, the mother was already tired and would have preferred to stay on the road but how could she oppose her husband's wish, he's a man who needs to use up his energy, who needs freedom and adventure, shut up as he is all day in his workshop, she followed him then, he had picked the little boy up and put him on his shoulders and gee-up gee-gee they were off at a gallop to the forest, the poor

131

mother was very happy but so tired, so tired, she put her
basket down on the ground and sat on a rock to watch them
playing and it was only when her husband got to the first
trees that she reluctantly decided to get up again, this was
the last time she would bring a picnic basket, what a ridiculous idea, but she wasn't used to it, she hadn't even
liked them when she was a girl, picnics, she'd preferred to
have her meals at home with her feet under the table, a real
home-bird, her husband had asked her to try now and then,
how could she oppose his wish, he's a man who needs . . .
she couldn't say no, it was good for the child too but she
would never bring a basket again, it was inevitable, as she
hadn't been a guide-captain when she was a girl she was
what you might call a novice in this domain, in short her
first experience of it was a fatigue such as she had never
previously known, she was rather a fat woman, a bit flabby
but very nice poor thing, a niece of Magnin the builder he
brought her up, both her parents died young, she had been
married to Simon Bianle for six years at the time I'm speaking of, a brother that is of Antoine the father of the twins,
that was why the mistress had not only said good afternoon
to them but pointed out at a distance their nephew and
niece who were following with Odette, some people might
have been surprised that they didn't stop to kiss them but
what with the heat and knowing they were in good hands
they had gone on, and when her husband saw her so far
behind he had called out something but she hadn't heard
what, there's an echo at that place that blurs all the sounds,
he waited for her under a tree but she would have preferred
him to come back and carry her basket, that's what she told
Madame Dumans or Madame Moineau.

You can just imagine the geography lesson in front of the
panorama, the children weren't listening any more, they had
perked up at the refreshment bar, the mistress was wasting

her breath and she was standing too near the shrine so she was irritating the people meditating there, it's a well-known fact that believers prefer their little tête-a-tête or what they take to be such with the Sacred to the acceptance of Human contingencies which latter are at least not illusory, still according to Odette who has thought deeply on the subject, since future teachers, I'm speaking about the best among them, are predisposed to speculation, but she didn't dare say as much to the mistress who had finally got cross, she raised her voice contrary to her principles in order to collect the children up and lecture them she said to Odette come on let's go home, we won't get any more out of them, I suggest we go by the road, it's only fifty yards away, and avoid the forest, it'll be easier even though a little longer but it doesn't get dark until half-past nine, we have plenty of time, so they drove their flock on in that direction and that's where the tragedy begins . . .

Now Mademoiselle Ariane just when they were getting to the crux of the matter suddenly began to lose interest, another example of the temperament that tends to be indifferent to the lower orders or shall we say to any other preoccupations than its own, in spite of her efforts her attention had wandered, she saw Minette in the hydrangeas and murmured Nature and all the rest of it, as the curé was no longer there to call her to order she spread herself on the subject, this suited old Lorpailleur but it didn't at all suit Francine who stood up and said I'm going over to the croquet lawn to see what Amédée is doing, this was a clever move on her part because Mademoiselle Ariane was in fact afraid that he hadn't really been putting his mind to it, she asked her niece to be firm, if some of it hadn't been done properly she was to make him do it again but Francine as we may well imagine the minute she got into the kitchen-garden went over towards the keeper's lodge, Marie was already there, she must have known in any case and she told Madame Amédée as much the moment she arrived, she couldn't get anything out of the schoolmistress who was artful enough to go off at a tangent and get lost in all the insignificant details of that day, that wasn't the solution, they would catch her out some other way, to which Marie replied you won't catch her out with our gossip and tittle-tattle, Monsieur Cruze is the one to help you or Monsieur Monnard or even Latirail the schoolmaster who has done a lot on his own to reconstitute the affair, he's got some documents, ask Madame Moineau, I didn't come here to talk about that with Madame Amédée, we were discussing cherry jam, weren't we Madame, old mother Amédée agreed, liar said Francine, liar, she was beside herself, you're not going to tell me that . . .

An echo in the forest near the place where the path that leads up the hill comes out, Blimbraz the *garde champêtre* heard some muffled cries but how can he be made responsible for every little noise especially on a Sunday, even so he apparently told his wife that evening that he had heard a child's voice round about four o'clock, why did he say that, he'd heard plenty of others, it seems that there are coincidences between chance and the conscious or let's say the unconscious mind of the most humble people, meeting points, thingummies what do they call them, with clairvoyants and witches for instance, it's not a myth, they record events which they haven't taken part in, it's the same with simple-minded people like the roadman, there wasn't the slightest reason why he should have noticed let alone remembered that child's voice in the forest.

For according to Monette the little party apparently met the family in question not outside the forest but actually inside it near the clearing where there is a sort of echo that blurs the sounds and the child's disappearance should be

134

traced back to that moment, as while Mademoiselle Lorpailleur and Odette were exchanging a few words with the family the children were scattering to the right and to the left, how was it that she didn't count them again as they went out of the forest, Madame Bianle remembered having left her husband and the young ladies for a moment and gone and asked her nephew where his little friend was, the kid apparently replied behind that tree over there, he couldn't wait, they won't be cross with him, which had made his aunt laugh.

In actual fact Francine apparently arrived at the manor quite some time before the visitors, she had had time to change, to see Marie and then with Mademoiselle Ariane to go round the kitchen-garden which is next to the cherry orchard which was magnificent that year, morellos mostly which ripen in July, they had already made jam with the white-hearts, now they would have to tackle the others as Marie said, the ladies had their eye on a new market for the greater part of the fruit, Morier was only offering a ridiculous price in view of the glut, there was so it seemed a firm in Douves that they should get in touch with, would you like me to deal with them for you asked Francine, her aunt apparently said yes and then seeing Minette et cetera, what a misleading attitude, you might have thought that even her own interests were foreign to her, and yet Francine had learnt to her cost if you can put it that way that in some years her aunt had displayed ferocious energy in the conduct of her business affairs, were her fits of indifference to be attributed to the seigniorial disposition or quite simply to her artistic temperament, this side of her nature too had manifested itself in her youth seeing that she had had a passion for Rodin, she used to organize meetings of every kind of painter at the manor house and she herself drew and had tried her hand at sculpture, a few plaster casts in the large

drawing-room testified to this, these had escaped the holo-
caust of the destructive frenzy that had come over her when
she was about forty, she had never again touched a pencil or
anything of the sort but Nature, what a thing it is, isn't it,
could you ignore it in the circumstances, so that Francine
connected in her own mind as she was telling her girl friend
the unpredictable reactions of artists with those of aristocrats, there was food for thought there, then as they were
coming back along the drive the ladies apparently saw Marie
at her post on her chair at the corner of the terrace, which
displeased Mademoiselle Ariane, it was only a quarter-past
eleven or something of the sort, she apparently said in her
half-seigniorial half-artistic outspoken way she doesn't do a
damned thing any more, if her bloody meal's ready she
could start polishing her copper couldn't she, Francine interrupted her gently to remind her how old Marie was, she was
getting on for seventy at the time, these old retainers, in
short that didn't stop Mademoiselle de Bonne-Mesure being
delighted to jerk the cook out of her somnolence by calling
to her bring us the port.

Or that Francine may have offered to go herself, which
would have made her aunt say can't she do anything for
herself and all the rest of it, to cut a long story short once
the port was on the table and a couple of fingers already in
the glasses, of port that is, they then apparently heard the
crss crss of the gravel, they turned towards the drive and
there he was, he's limping worse than ever, it was in fact
obvious that the curé who was arriving did indeed look as if
he was having some difficulty in walking, which would have
made Francine and not old Lorpailleur say once he was
sitting down why don't you consider taking the cure at Rottard.

Then old Lorpailleur arrives, then dining-roomwards.

But she couldn't remember, I'm referring to Francine,
where to place the allusion to the altar-cruet and the choir-

136

boy, was it during the aperitif, was it during the meal, because she had forgotten as she said to her girl friend that part of the conversation or was it another subject they were discussing when after Mademoiselle Ariane had complained about the way the preacher spoke the curé had replied something like he's a holy man, the children love him, because they had just heard ... or perhaps they had only heard later and it was years after that Mademoiselle Ariane had brought the subject up again and added apropos of the Father I told you so I told you so, meaning by that that the way of speaking she hadn't liked had made her smell what you might call an unconscious rat which justified her ten years later in giving them to understand that she had not been so wrong in mistrusting the preacher, to cut a long story short one evening during the course of the Mission Madame Moineau was going home very late from the sewing-bee and she heard someone panting in a hedge, she was frightened but she suddenly recognized in the clear night the Father in the act of quite so young Tourniquet, that's where the love of children had led him, he hadn't heard her in the heat of the moment that seems to be the appropriate expression, she tiptoed away and the moment she got home she rang up several of the ladies to raise the alarm, what should they do, tell the curé, the police, so on and so forth, it was a delicate problem vis-à-vis the diocese, they all agreed that they would tell no one but the curé and that not till the next day though as early as possible but when the latter then remained completely incredulous Madame Moineau was shocked, are you sure he kept saying, in all conscience could you swear to it on the cross of Our Lord, in any case the Mission ends tomorrow, the Father has to leave us during the evening, I'll do whatever has to be done in relation to the diocese, don't say a word to anyone, but the harm had been done and plenty of words were already being said as you

137

may well imagine, yes it must have been years after that apropos of an altar-cruet that was broken by a choir-boy who was no longer Tourniquet Mademoiselle Ariane in her outspoken way again brought up the scene of the quite so behind the hedge adding I told you so I told you so, and it was this that made old Lorpailleur purse up her chicken's hole and sit there silent and shocked, which apparently caused Francine to say do you think you should bring that terrible thing up again Aunt, there's a limit to everything, this last expression not apropos of anything else, she didn't remember, I'm referring to Francine, but quite simply apropos of the scandal in question.

Present in the smallest manifestations of nature.

As for what happened to the Father, no one ever knew, the thing was hushed up and Tourniquet went off to serve his apprenticeship shortly afterwards, which was very convenient ... or else that they had heard that the preacher had friends in high places, a terrifying sort of mafia both lay and religious so it would seem, how could the government and the Holy See tolerate such goings-on, it was high time in this day and age that these things were eradicated from our society and so on.

And that coming back to the mafia, on its lowest rung among others was Lorduz the gendarme whom Monsieur Monnard had surprised one day in the station urinal in the act of quite so with a railway employee, Monnard hadn't said anything about it until ten years later when Lorduz had been moved to another region, in any case he had got married in the meantime, do you realize.

And that still on this subject or let's say on a parallel one Monette after her religious mania had I don't know how to put it with the Doudin girl who was so ugly you recollect her don't you, well yes quite so, and they even used for their thises and thats so it seems an instrument with so it seems, isn't it terrible, can you imagine, it looks as if everything happens in our region even though it is so pure, so close to the good Lord with its lovely country and soft sky, Mademoiselle I don't know who any more whom you always see communicating of a Sunday, you remember was shocked, thinking back to these horrors she was shocked, you can understand her.

The curé was most embarrassed by Mademoiselle de Bonne-Mesure's remarks, he couldn't see where to stick Providence in amongst all that and considering the matter as he chewed his eel or whatever it was he finally said Nature it's true isn't it she has her aberrations, Mademoiselle Ariane cut him short, ha ha you're coming round, Abbé, Nature, Nature you say, that's an atheist's word, you see how we always come back to it, to which the abbé subtly replied yes that may well be but what do you make of the Redemption.

Or apropos of these manifestations that it was the gendarme Topard and Lorette Magnin, personally names you know . . .

In short the curé once the schoolmistress was out of the way still stayed for a good hour with the ladies, they were so attentive, education endows people with the unique quality of good manners, you feel at your ease, you don't notice the time passing, she'd come to the end of her reminiscences about the Easter outing which hadn't turned out quite so well as she had hoped since little Sylvie had had indigestion, she kept feeling hot and cold all over, Mademoiselle Monette had offered to take her home by bus from the refreshment bar, the stop isn't very far away, I'm referring to the Agapa one, and she herself the mistress that is had brought the little party back on her own, what a responsibility, Francine agreed, she said that she had been tempted some time ago to adopt a pedagogic career for her father as everyone knew had lost all his money and she had had to choose a career but she had decided to become a secretary, though she nevertheless still had thoughts about teaching et cetera, during which time Mademoiselle Ariane was first of all stifling her yawns and then vaguely dropping off but in such a refined manner shutting her eyes but going on tapping on the arm of her armchair when suddenly there's a noise in the hydrangeas, she opens her eyes again, Minette and so on, so that the schoolmistress had all the time in the world to talk about her neighbor's cat of whom she was very fond, such an intelligent creature you really did ought to see it according to Madame Moineau who can speak in a very common fashion, forgetting, I'm referring to old Lorpailleur, that everyone was aware that she tormented the animal, something along those lines, but it was soon half-past four, my goodness Mesdames how impolite I am, she stood up and took her leave accompanied to the gate by Francine who was giving her the line about how wonderful Amédée and his wife were, these faithful retainers, and who carried her amiability so far as to ask the schoolmistress's permission to attend one of her classes one day, whichever one you prefer, which flattered old Lorpailleur more than I can say but the conversation began to drag a bit, Madame Dumans, who couldn't in the least understand what attraction the mistress had for these society people, you know what she's like, she likes to make a show of having communist or at least liberal opinions, stifled her yawns at first and then didn't stifle them any more so that Mademoiselle Lorpailleur cut it short and said goodbye very coldly, she was casting her pearls before swine.

As you may well imagine Latirail the boys' teacher who professes the same ideas as the Dumans family i.e. anti-clerical to the core was looking forward to exposing the scandal to the light of day, it was a unique opportunity, the dog-collar brigade, eh, they make such a song and dance about their Missions, they indoctrinate the common man and then they go behind a hedge and quite so our children, it must be brought out into the open, it must be used to attack the church as a whole, he was chewing it over in his mind without however quite daring to write about it in his rag yet, the consequences for him in his capacities both as journalist and civil servant could be awkward not to say deadly, he was chewing the matter over and at the same time looking for proofs, he had interrogated Madame Moineau at least twenty times, what time was it, how far was she from the couple excuse the expression, what position was the preacher in, and Tourniquet, that was it all right, there were no two ways about it but they had to go further than that, make enquiries about the Father, move in those circles, clerical ones I mean, he was chewing it over, he remembered that one of his school friends had been to a theological college and was a curé somewhere in the region or then again there's that frightful clique of laymen who spend their time hanging round the bishop, the various associations, the church army and so on, something must be done, repeating over and over again to anyone who was prepared to listen, we can't leave things as they are, fine hands our children are in.

Or that this sordid business didn't happen until well after Latirail had left and that he had been told about it by his successor, who was he now, and had come back and renewed his contacts with a good many people and in particular the Dumans, at all events he did come back for several days you remember ... or was it later, years later, when it wasn't a question of the Father any more but of the Duchemin inheritance ... this didn't suit old Lorpailleur who in the zeal she showed in reconstituting the tragedy was leaving no stone unturned in her efforts to implicate Latirail.

Magnin however on his way back from discussing the

141

estimate with Ducreux had called in to see old man Moineau, his watch needed repairing and it seems that it was just as he was going into the shop that he caught sight of old Lorpailleur talking to Monnard at the corner of the rue Neuve, this was so unexpected that he apparently stopped short in the doorway to watch them and Moineau apparently said what's going on, left his counter and observed the event as well, it must have been five o'clock, something like that, was that the day of her visit to Bonne-Mesure, that she couldn't remember, which was annoying in view of what Marie had said to Mademoiselle Francine, you remember, Monnard could tell you, the two cronies apparently stood there watching for a good ten minutes, it could only have been something quite out of the ordinary that they were discussing as Monnard hadn't been speaking to old Lorpailleur for a good ten years, were they insulting each other, no they had shaken hands as they parted, here was something to add fresh fuel to the ladies' conversations, was it plausible to look for the cause of this event in the fact that the child who had been drowned had almost been a pupil of Monnard's, Monnard at that time used to coach backward children but it was quite some months after the accident even though in one sense everyone had been reminded of it by the terrible business of little Frédéric being run over, they commented on the tragedy, they made comparisons, they brought the conversation back to the other one, what could be more natural, nevertheless she wondered, I'm referring to Lorette, whether it was a valid hypothesis, another figment of my imagination she said, it'll drive me mad, because even though she liked to make out that she couldn't care less she was in fact much attached to the family of the little boy who was drowned and her sense of justice was in revolt, how could Blimbraz who was always passing the ponds at those unwonted hours and who had actually heard someone calling out not immediately have tried to find out where the cries were coming from.

Hopping, skipping and jumping.

But it was rather late in the day to be still torturing oneself years later, she had said months, it was years, some ten years, and when they went to visit her in the asylum because she had in actual fact gone mad it gave you the shivers the way she gabbled out her monologue, a monologue in which she mentioned all the names of that time, all the details, it was as if the years between had never existed, it was as if what takes place in people's consciousnesses can emerge just like that as fresh as a daisy years after, it's just happened, it's happening now, it's just about to happen ... because she was going back in time a good decade to say the least and situating the event at the time of her youth when she used to go skipping about among the meadow-sweet ...

Poor Lorette there's another one who has paid dearly for her artistic temperament, she used to do such pretty drawings and she went in for modelling too, her mother kept everything in her drawing-room, all over the house, yes indeed, quite prostrate after that attack in July what year was it again do you remember, she never really got over it that's to say she had her ups and downs but in the end they had to put her away, yes, that's right our little Lorette, she was much too straightforward by nature, how that unfortunate business of the inheritance weighed on her, as if she could have done anything about it the poor innocent.

Or that she died then and there, trapped by the truck outside the chemist's shop but it was a Sunday and Cruze was out picnicking with the Dumans that was why they weren't able to give her any first aid which though it wouldn't have done any good would at least have salved their consciences, I'm referring primarily to those of her sister and her mother as the accident happened quite some time before Madame Lorpailleur's death, certain details such as for instance the fact that the driver was Polish plunged you right back into the atmosphere, everyone remembered it so that they began to wonder whether the mistress had worn mourning since that moment or only since her mother's death, very likely it was since the accident.

For when it comes to being mad the Lorpailleur sister, the other one, that was what she was all right, she ought to have been put away long before but people can be just gently round the bend or they can be raving mad, she had taken the former path, Lorette remembered that distinctly, Henriette to the unobservant eye and for the space of let's say five minutes could have appeared normal but then after that thanks a lot, I mean after the five minutes, she would start laughing to herself or making gestures in the street so that you didn't know where to look, some people are sensitive and Lorette was one of them, yes she was terribly upset, she quickly crossed the road and either went and had a pastry or to confide in her girl friend that little what was her name again, they were always together it had even set some tongues wagging, to cut a long story short Magnin like the good sort he was used to listen without turning a hair unless of course he wasn't listening at all, some people have the knack of looking as though they're paying attention, she wished she had too, she said, it makes everything so much simpler.

As for the asylum where people were advised not to go and visit her, with its strait-jacket, cold showers, so on and so forth, this was pure invention on Lorette's part even though she was an educated girl, she had wanted to be a nurse and had already passed one exam before her illness, she remembered the terms and that made an impression.

Lying in the road, the kids in a circle at a distance, poor thing how could she have done that.

A funeral like everyone else's, like mine, like yours, with flowers and wreaths, it was a Tuesday then, terrible heat, I can still see the mother dragging herself along on her daughter's arm, she was enormous, she had an illness, legs as fat as thighs right down to the ankles, she wore long dresses to hide them but the swelling showed below, so sad, with the brother and sister-in-law, she was the one who had caused so much trouble about her mother's estate, what was it actually that made us laugh so much or am I mixing it up with the Duchemin estate, in short where the rue Neuve crosses the rue des Casse-Tonnelles a truck coming down like a lunatic nearly cut off the tail of the procession that's to say the school children in the charge of Lorette, I can still see her deathly pale clasping the Ducreux kid in her arms, the driver didn't stop.

But that the women's gossip, she mistrusted it and preferred to glean her information from the men who are reputed not to talk so much but that's not true, they talk more calmly, as to whether what they say is truer or not that's another matter, they didn't want to disappoint her, they left her her illusions, she must have questioned poor Magnin at least twenty times and he good-naturedly answered the first thing that came into his head probably but what difference did that make, she felt she was getting somewhere, that she had practically achieved her object, I'm referring to Mademoiselle Lozière, it was Lozière wasn't it, she was going to bring out a series of documented articles with supporting evidence, she had permission from the newspaper given the antiquity of the facts, all they asked was that she put people's initials instead of their names and that amused her . . . or else perhaps not the newspaper, a little monograph, something of that sort, with initials to add spice to it, she had certainly not changed and in any case this would be more interesting than the volume of poetry you know the one I mean, all the copies were remaindered, you

145

can understand the publisher, I always say these hack-writers you must leave them their illusions, poor thing what would she have left if she didn't have them, that's true, an old mother to clean up, life had never offered her anything that wasn't pointless and insipid and when I say insipid, gathering primroses in spring time the only pretty ring time, childish pleasures which with the passing of the years begin to turn sour, she is responsible for the catechism class at Christmas too, she hears the children recite their poems and sing their songs, she decorates the parish hall always with the same streamers even if the greenery isn't the same, the ladies lend their flower-pot covers and their busy lizzies, what else, the annual jumble-sale to organize, the stalls where you find the same lace and the same doll-cushions, the tombola never gets rid of the lot, in short books are as you might say her escape and her Saturday article in the *Fantoniard* . . .

There was one thing in her existence though, her passion for Monnard the parish clerk, that had gone sour on her too, poor old carcass that nothing had ever been able to make blossom, she smelt of moth-balls in a cradle so that her little poems and her little articles all have more or less the same smell, yes let's leave her her illusions, she happened that day to be on the Quai des Moulins where the rue du Bouc joins it but she only saw the truck afterwards when the driver had already put his foot down and was disappearing fast, this didn't stop her commenting on the event though, not that that was of any importance . . . or that she was in the rue du Bouc outside the chemist's and did see the truck tearing down the road but not the accident that happened round the corner, in other words on the Quai des Moulins, she questioned several witnesses the next day, she went to the Swan café as she preferred men who according to her say more in less words, this didn't stop her questioning poor Mortin the builder's cousin at least twenty times, there's another one who has been amusing himself for years by reconstructing the tragedy, what a lot of idle people there are around our parts, he has run a guest house since he became a widower, let's put it that his house was too big so he took in paying guests and that as he'd kept his maid on she does the cooking for the said ladies and gentlemen, Mademoiselle Lozière had all the time in the world to question the owner as she lodges there, The Lilacs it's called, the guest house, like the road it's in, le chemin des Lilas, there's only one left though at the corner of the rue Piéro, so yes they more or less wrote the article in question together a fact of which Mortin is no little proud, he told Monnard still according to Magnin that Mademoiselle Lozière was incapable of seeing things synthetically, everything she writes is always submerged in a mass of detail, it's confused and childish, it takes a man to make any sort of sense out of it all, does that mean to say that he revises all her articles, not impossible, but in that case given the end result he too presumably writes like an old maid but I rather think I have told you ... or was that apropos of someone else, to cut a long story short that's the sort of food for thought or whatever that we get from the *Fantoniard* ... it seems to me ...

Monsieur Mortin she said my goodness that takes you back doesn't it, Alexandre his christian name was, you remember the guest house he started after his wife died, she was against it while she was alive, may her ashes rest in peace, such a refined guest house, no one but aristocrats or at least people of our class, educated people, a retired professor what was his name, a lady from the Argentine, much-travelled people, quite a lot of money he charged them but it was worth it, with that exquisite garden in front of the house, it was number twelve rue des Lauriers, twelve or fourteen, she had known Marie the cook well, a cousin of Mademoiselle Rosette who died not so long ago half-mad so

147

it seems, they had to have her put away, she was an incomparable cook, the whole district used to talk about the meals at the guest house, some of the residents the Crottets for instance used to invite their friends there on Sundays, you remember Monsieur and Madame Crottet, she was so refined in the English manner, he was always looking for his handkerchief of pince-nez, well Monsieur Mortin was still very aristocratic in spite of his function if it may so be called, he went out every morning around eleven o'clock to take his dog for a walk, I can still see it, it was a wire-haired fox-terrier called Fonfon or Ronron, he was wearing a tie and everything whereas while his wife was alive he was always tremendously hard up, he wore a terribly shiny bum-freezer for years, at last he was comfortably off, Monsieur Monnard knew him well, he used to tell him between ourselves I've started to live again since my poor Jeanne died, we had nothing left can you imagine, if she hadn't died I should have had to sell the house but why was she so against the idea of a guest house, that's the old bourgeois spirit for you, never lose caste, keep up appearances, how stupid don't you agree.

Well it was this same Mortin that she was referring to apropos of the Duchemin inheritance, he had had inside information about the unscrupulous behaviour of you know whom about the shares in the Argentine or wherever, the thing had grown to such proportions because of his vague relationship with the deceased woman, people even said that the daughter, not the school teacher the other one . . .

This same Mortin that she was referring to apropos of the accident, he had seen it all from his window, it must have been before eleven o'clock then and if there was any fault to find with the examining magistrate it was precisely the fact that he had not interrogated him but you know how it is, among society people . . .

Or his vague relationship with Madame Moineau, a cousin on the wrong side of the sheets so it seems, which would explain old Lorpailleur's frequent allusions to the guest house being a *pension de famille,* in short Mortin who had nothing to do but take his dog for a walk knew a great deal about you know whom and even so it seems had proof of it which he is supposed to have shown to Mademoiselle Lozière, just as Sinture the postmaster was reputed not to have been a stranger to certain indiscretions committed in the post, keeping certain letters back just long enough to steam them open so it seems but all that is such a long time ago, I only mention it so as not to forget, and she went on and on, sowing such doubt about that unfortunate business that no one came out of it unscathed, it was a mafia, a general conspiracy, it was a disgrace to our region, a condemnation of all humanity, poor Rosette she will have paid dearly for her ... she will have paid dearly for her ...

Or that it was this Mortin and not the builder that she was referring to apropos of the Father, he was an old acquaintance of his, he had stayed there for nothing during the Mission, that relieved the curé who only just had the wherewithal, the scandal in question had rubbed off on to Mortin, tell me who your friends are ... but his life was so remote from all our tittle-tattle that it probably didn't worry him, his guests took his side, educated people don't take the slightest notice of the opinion of the vulgar masses and in any case the preacher's conversation was so exquisite, the ladies were mad about it and were contemplating inviting him again just to annoy the rabble but at this time i.e. shortly after his secret had been discovered it was very much in the ecclesiastic's interest to be forgotten and according to Mademoiselle Lozière he went into retreat by order of his superior, in short everyone doesn't see things in the same way, far from it.

None of which prevents the most fascinating part of the story being the situation of Mademoiselle Lozière, her arse turned out to be between two stools excuse the expression, widely read on Saturdays by the ladies,I'm referring to those of our class, and widely appreciated at the guest house for her culture, she didn't know which side to take and she chose the wrong one that's to say to be shocked with both sides let me explain, with the Moneau clique to rebel against the morals of the church and with the other one against the barbarity of the villagers.

And that Monsieur de Broy who was a great friend of Mortin's in spite of the difference in their circumstances was a great help in this business for he had invited the Father to his place during the Mission and the lord of the manor had appreciated the priest's refinement or that according to some other people he had known him for years and it was he who had arranged for the preacher to stay at the guest house, the manor house was too far from the village, to cut a long story short this nobleman is a relation of Mademoiselle Ariane and when the scandal broke they again saw a good deal of one another, it was the occasion of some splendid evenings either at Bonne-Mesure or at Broy, all the gentry, my goodness she said and all that still exists, when you've been mixing with no one but the plebs for some time you forget the very notion, she was forgetting her common sense too, she started scheming, I'm referring to old Lorpailleur, to induce Mortin to get her the entrée to the manor house but I ask you what interest could Monsieur de Broy possibly have in making her acquaintance.

It's also possible that she may just have hinted at it to Mademoiselle Ariane on the first Saturday in July but it was a delicate matter ... or that she may have found a pretext in the fact that the child of the Broy farmers who was her pupil had got out of hand or that she thought he seemed unhappy and over-sensitive, after she had made some in-quiries it turned out that his parents beat him but as they refused to come and see her she had to deal with it in some other way, the simplest was to get in touch with the father's employer in other words Monsieur de Broy.

But she had heard that Monsieur de Broy out of pure friendship sometimes used to go to the guest house not to have a meal there but just quite simply to have a drink with his old friend Mortin, some of the ladies had caught a glimpse of him or had even been introduced to him, this might be a way for old Lorpailleur to approach him, she made inquiries of Mademoiselle Lozière, was it possible to find out when the lord of the manor was going to visit his friend well no it wasn't possible, he only put in the most sporadic of appearances and Mortin obviously didn't inform his guests of them in advance, but she wouldn't take no for an answer and suggested to Mademoiselle Lozière that she telephone her next time he came, she could get there in ten minutes if she hurried, to which the other woman replied but my dear what makes you think that they will join us either in the drawing-room or in the garden, Monsieur Mortin may well see his friend in his own apartments, he isn't reduced to our company as yet, nevertheless she agreed given the great friendship she had had with her mother . . .

Which more or less came to the same thing as saying that the whole of the psycho psychi life of our little society might well rest on one or two very vague phrases, a few remarks about anybody or anything invented by two or three people at the outside which may well unconsciously have set the general tone for years to come of the conversations or rather of the behavior of our compatriots, yes it certainly was odd, this network of gossip and absurd remarks had conditioned our existence to such an extent that no stranger coming to live in our midst could have resisted it for long and that if he had come to follow the trade of let's say baker he would inevitably have branched off into that of child-killer for instance, without his having been in the least responsible, which would explain among other things why our hack writers who set out to be critics or novelists don't get any further than writing serial stories or meteorological reports, which also includes the people who compile poetry anthologies, such was Mortin's opinion, should we believe him and in particular on the subject of irresponsibility, she thought that would be doing him too much honor, I'm referring to Lorette, to start with let's just try and find out who it is she added but I ask you what does that matter, whether there was an explanation or not we would still be trapped in the same hornets' nest ...

For Lorette with her sensitivity and desire for knowledge or was it Monette would have gone through fire and water in the interests of the truth or of what she imagined to be the truth, she wouldn't have hesitated, she wouldn't have considered her own interests, she would have become involved quite so.

Or that Verveine with his desire to hurt people may have invented the story about Mortin rewriting Mademoiselle Lozière's articles but it came to the same thing, the first necessity was to find out who it was, that was supposed to be why old Lorpailleur decided to turn up at the chemin des Lauriers one fine July Thursday though she had taken the precaution of informing her colleague who was reputed to have jibbed at first but when threatened asked Marie to lay an extra place.

Old Lorpailleur arrives, Mademoiselle Lozière asks her how it can be that she didn't see Mortin, he was in the garden, she had told him she was coming, he had been surprised but courteous in view of the great friendship ... the respect he professes for Education, something along those lines, she replies that the only person she has seen is the gardener Irénée with whom she exchanged a few words about his son, he wasn't working well at school, when suddenly Madame Irénée comes out from behind a bush where she had been weeding giving her husband a helping hand and starts complaining about her arms, her legs, her whole organism in general, nothing to do with the intervention of the mistress who begins to wonder whether the woman is mad or what, to cut a long story short a few minutes' impatience for old Lorpailleur and then raising her head or turning it absent-mindedly she catches sight of Mortin's back at the corner of the terrace it looks as if he is trying to avoid her, she is extremely displeased, extremely, takes her leave of the Irénées and goes into the house where old Lozière is all sweetness and charm and introduces her to the guests did she even see them though, her displeasure was increasing, the teaching profession has its legitimate claims however none of the persons present had any children, nieces at the very most, which she supposed would explain their indifference towards her never imagining that her ugliness . . . which would explain their indifference towards her but this the newcomer didn't see in her displeasure, in short she parks it on a chair and finds herself facing her colleague at a little table for two, there are a few others apart from the host's table where the smirking residents are sitting, amongst them an ancient old dame, ancient but made up like a marchioness and with dyed hair, wearing a flowered dress that was ridiculous at her age, they called her Madame Apostolos or as near as makes no difference, she was whispering this and that through her dentures which were in continual danger of falling into her plate, very amiable with her neighbors she was but more interested in what she was eating, let's say it was soup or if it was hors-d'oeuvres she didn't take any radishes or anything else that was difficult to chew, she helped herself to tomatoes and hard-boiled eggs in mayonnaise, even so you could see her poor jaws working and her tongue foraging around under her noodle-crusher, with on her right Monsieur Crottet or as near as makes no difference, personally people's names you know, on his right was his wife who is so refined, a blouse of écru lace with a high neck, a person in her sixties, very pale, her hair frizzed at the temples who was pretending not to look at what she was eating and reminiscing about her travels, you could hardly hear anyone but her so to speak, she preferred to address her remarks to the couple opposite her, very simple people who looked a bit lost and were still apt to blush even though they were in their fifties, so touching, the ideal public for mother Crottet and for a lot of other people that you know, with on her right Mortin at the end of the table that is, with on his right the wife of the couple and then the husband who must have been a representative, something of the sort, you could tell it from his tie can you imagine and from the way he unfolded his napkin, a lot of little details so well observed . . .

Or if what she was telling us about the host's table referred to another day, in fact the one when Monsieur de Broy actually was there, not in the least important, the lord of the manor arrives at the gate and the gardener who happened to be there opens it for him, the gentleman slips a coin into his hand and then seeing the wife coming out from behind a bush he instinctively steps back a pace however she had been weeding and greets him, he walks up to the house and goes in without ringing, the dining-room door is open, he sees the guests at luncheon and not being able to do otherwise he goes in and says how do you do to them, what an idea arriving so late, he apologizes, Mortin should be coming down from his room to luncheon any second now, please don't bother says he I'll go up, I would like to have a

word with him, please don't bother, for one of the gentlemen was already on his feet ready to go and tell Mortin,
Monsieur de Broy goes up to the first floor, knocks at his
friend's door and goes into his room, what he had to say to
him was about Monnard or Dondard, she couldn't quite
hear, she was cleaning the adjoining room, I'm referring to
the maid, in any case it was a name ending in ard, then for
about ten minutes they were talking about the *Fantoniard*
unless the whole conversation had been about the paper, in
the meantime Mortin had come out of his room and called
out to the assembled company from a distance please don't
wait for me, which would have meant that old Lorpailleur
wasn't at the guest house that day as Mademoiselle Lozière
hadn't been able to let her know so late, everyone was
already at table, but there was nevertheless a sort of coinci-
dence seeing that the schoolmistress works for the paper,
unless Mademoiselle Lozière had invented the whole business
about old Lorpailleur wanting to be introduced to Monsieur
de Broy because she could just as well have gone to the
manor as she had the farmer's son as a pretext.

Old Lorpailleur arrives, she rings at the gate, Araignée the
gate-keeper comes and opens it for her, she says that Monsieur de Broy is expecting her and asks the man to look after
her machine as she doesn't want to appear at the manor
house on a bicycle, the gate-keeper says the Monsieur has in
fact told him that she was expected, she has only to go
straight up the drive, his wife at that moment comes out
from behind a bush and asks the school teacher if it isn't on
account of the farmers' son, the Vernets, if that isn't why she
has come, the school teacher replies evasively that she has
the interests of all her pupils at heart so there is no reason
why she should neglect the Vernet boy, it's just a pity that
his parents won't put themselves to the trouble of coming to
the school, I knew it says the woman, I thought as much, just

imagine only yesterday I happened to be near the farm and I heard the child screaming, they beat him, isn't it a disgrace, yes I thought as much, that's why you came, the school teacher registers amazement, says she doesn't know anything about that she has simply come to ask Monsieur de Broy's advice about the future apprenticeship of the child who doesn't seem to her to be strong enough for agricultural work, something of the sort, she says either too much or too little, the gate-keepers get a bit suspicious, this goose is giving herself airs, what's she up to, when you think that her mother used to go out charring, a woman like us, carry on straight up the drive they repeat, he will be waiting for you on the terrace.

She leans her bike against the wall of the lodge, purses up her chicken's hole and sets off up the beech-lined drive, a couple of hundred yards of fine gravel, the old mansion comes into view with all its windows open to the eleven o'clock sun, the rhododendron clump on the left, the little path that disappears into the wood, a cat comes out of the clump et cetera, the great heat has made her perspire, she hasn't had time to get her breath back, her blouse must be stained under the arms, it makes white halos against the black, she puts on her silk coat that she'd brought just in case, which is a bit ridiculous in this heat but it's just as well to look respectable all the more so as she ... well yes in actual fact perspiration does smell rather strong, her nose had furtively approached her armpit, a bad habit, she turns round to see if anyone has seen her but the lodge is a long way away and the gate-keepers have gone in, she winds her crêpe round her neck and arrives at the terrace, Monsieur de Broy who was sitting there with some friends stands up when he sees her coming and takes a few steps in her direction, he is a man in his fifties, tall, athletic, very casually dressed in a navy blue polo-necked shirt with white linen trousers, his face is still young and what a smile, you couldn't imagine such courtesy in your wildest dreams, very beautiful teeth, she wonders in her innocence whether he is going to kiss her hand like they do in novels and she has already removed her glove but the jovial squire just shakes it, how brave you are in this heat, thank you for bothering about the child, I have some friends here but don't let that worry you, we'll have a quiet talk on our own somewhere, they go up to the group to whom he is going to introduce her when judge of her amazement, whom does she see among the guests, there are four of them, the Father in person, what does that mean, introductions, first of all the ecclesiastic, he says suavely that he surely knows her, was she not already the school teacher some ten years previously at the time of the Mission, she says yes I was, but you'll have a drink with us won't you says the squire, she says all those look rather strong but she would like just a finger of port and she plonks it down on a wicker chair, the Father starts talking to her and mentions the word mission again, her own this time, with the children, it's a true vocation, the good Lord et cetera, they must be getting restive with this heat but what a good thing isn't it that the school breaks up in a few days, she says that in fact she can no longer control them, the other gentlemen put in a word here and there and after a moment the squire says come with me Mademoiselle, we have some serious matters to discuss, and takes her over to the French window leading into the drawing-room, they go on . . .

The drawing-room, they go in, family portraits, hangings, tapestries, old Lorpailleur . . . Monsieur de Broy sits her down in an armchair under a portrait, he draws the school-mistress's attention to it and says amusingly, don't you think he's like me, the same nose isn't it, and now to our business, tête-à-tête conversation about the farmer's son, or at least that's what Latirail supposed, he has no scruples even about inquiring into what goes on at Broy, even so he can't know everything, in any case old Lorpailleur came out again after half an hour or perhaps three-quarters with the lord of the manor who had courteously asked her to stay to luncheon knowing that her sister was expecting her, she replied no thank you, it would have been a pleasure but I am lunching with my family, what a shame says he, another time I hope, they go back to the others and the schoolmistress takes her leave very flattered by the fact that they all stand up in her honor, there's nothing like high society, when she's in the drive accompanied by Monsieur de Broy she sees the cat again, the squire says Minouche et cetera guessing that the school teacher must have seen the animal depositing its mess in the rhododendrons which Araignée had just hoed but the mistress doesn't take any notice, she really seems anxious about the Vernet boy and says once again then I shall take the liberty of counting on your support if need be, it's really serious, he repeats yes, she can count on him, and then they're outside the gate-keeper's lodge and he comes out to open the gate . . .

His valet had told him that the schoolmistress went to her sister's on Tuesdays that was why he had invited her on that day and anyway she would never agree to take pot luck if he might so term it with the gentlemen.

Or if she had excused herself from her family meal on the off chance and had actually accepted, they come out of the drawing-room, they go and join the guests and Monsieur de Broy courteously suggests that she stay and take pot luck with them, she accepts saying that that would be a great honor but I shouldn't like to put you out, the lord of the manor says but not in the least, a wink to the gentlemen, it is we who shall be honored, she plonks it down again on the wicker chair and the conversation flags, she is the only one who isn't irritated, luncheon at Broy, she's been dreaming of

158

nothing else for years, the Father makes another effort and asks after her mother who is dead, she replies she's dead, he says my goodness how sad, I remember her so well, such a pious, devoted woman, I have such a happy memory of her and he goes on and how is your sister but in a very little voice in case she might be dead too, fortunately no, old Lorpailleur answers that she's very well, she doesn't dare ask the preacher what he's doing there and she hardly dares think about the scandal of ten years ago, she begins to doubt it, such a dignified man can only be of great moral worth, she tells herself that there must have been a conspiracy against him, slander and so on, meanwhile the other gentlemen start talking amongst themselves again, about horses, following the lead of the lord of the manor who doesn't want everyone to be bored to death by his gaffe, he has decided on a relaxed attitude to put them all at their ease but the Father is annoyed with him, he has a shrewd idea that he's the one that's going to be the gull throughout the meal, the only one to have to keep up a conversation with this pain in the neck.

Now since old Lorpailleur arrived not at eleven o'clock but at half-past eleven as she had been delayed by the crowd round the truck Monsieur de Broy who had promised his friends that contrary to their usual practice they should lunch at midday as this suited them better feels obliged after a few minutes to invite old Lorpailleur and she accepts so that the conversation hasn't time to hang fire, they finish their aperitifs, just a finger of port for the intruder, the butler is already at his post at the corner of the terrace waiting for five to to ring the bell, the school teacher observes all these old-fashioned domestic details with delight and there it goes, ding ding, they get up and walk towards the French window into the drawing-room, the lord of the manor laughingly excuses himself for being in a polo-necked shirt and then offers his arm to old Lorpailleur as if she were a duchess and goes into the house with her followed by the other gentlemen who are winking at each other, they are promising themselves that they'll have a good laugh during the meal.

Just imagine old Lorpailleur arriving hatted, crêped, titivated and all in the sweltering heat, the gentlemen in polo-necked shirts and linen trousers all except the Jesuit of course, she apologizes for being late, just imagine I was delayed by an accident, I was passing the baker's when suddenly a truck came careering down the hill et cetera, Lorduz was preparing his report and I couldn't leave as I had been a witness, these drunkards isn't it a disgrace, the danger they represent, she was still trembling with emotion and started going into detail, Dumans, Magnin the builder and Monsieur Cruze had been there, in short they listen to her out of politeness Monsieur de Broy takes advantage of the moment when she's searching for the name of one of the witnesses to suggest that a finger of port might make her feel better, she accepts and when she has finished her story it's nearly ten to, the lord of the manor no longer has time to take her aside about the Vernet business and offers her pot luck, impossible to do otherwise, she accepts as she has cancelled her lunch with her sister on the off chance, in short the butler at five to rings the bell and they go into the house ... description of the large drawing-room, family portraits, hangings, tapestries, furniture of three successive centuries, in one corner there's even a choir-stall that dates from the middle ages and comes from a monastery where Flaminien de Broy was Prior, very strange history this piece of furniture which shouldn't really be there, it was stolen during the Revolution when the monastery was sacked and then found again quite by chance by the descendant in an antique shop, the Broy arms are carved on the front, isn't it

160

amusing, the squire casually points this out to the school teacher as they pass and then they go into the dining-room it's very much in the grand style, old Lorpailleur is fascinated, she's too hot but she keeps her hat on, they sit down to table and the butler immediately brings in a cold consommé or some artichokes, they were as common as dirt that year but they were all friends there, the estate produces a great deal and supplies the local markets, enumeration of the various products grown with details of the various business concerns who are their clients, the days and hours set aside for the carriers, the system of accountancy et cetera.

The squire places the school teacher on his right and then says sit anywhere you like, gentlemen, we don't want to stand on ceremony, but he pushes the ecclesiastic round to the right of old Lorpailleur, he has to sit down and starts asking after the mistress's mother et cetera, at one moment a young gentleman opposite lets the spoon slide down into the dish of eels that a manservant is handing him and this breaks the ice as they say, the others laugh and conversation comes more easily, in any case the butler is pouring out white wine almost continuously on the instructions of . . .

The butler said he had never seen a meal like it, just the sight of Monsieur coming in with the madwoman in black on his arm had made him guffaw, just imagine what she looked like that village woman pursing her mouth up like a chicken's hole trying to look refined, her hat with its crêpe thing wound round her neck in this heat, her silk coat to hide the perspiration stains, her black stockings on her goat's legs and her red hand holding her imitation box-calf handbag, a thing that came from the Tripeaus' general stores, he had served the hors d'oeuvres and then Monsieur had immediately said we won't stand on ceremony today, just leave the dishes on the table will you and we'll help ourselves, Mademoiselle will certainly excuse us, these gentlemen have an

161

important engagement soon, that will save time, and he invited old Lorpailleur to help herself, it was raw vegetables from the garden and cold fish in this heat, trout in aspic and salmon mayonnaise, take a proper helping he said, here try this just to please me, adopting a familiar tone which was designed to put them all at their ease and match the gentlemen's get-up, they were in polo-necked shirts and linen trousers all except the Father of course, at one moment one of the young gentlemen is supposed to have let the spoon slide down into the mayonnaise which apparently made the others laugh and the atmosphere less tense, it made the butler sick to see them controlling themselves on account of that old cat, when you think that her mother went out charring, what on earth had made Monsieur ask her to stay to luncheon, he apparently inquired into the matter after the event and discovered the secret, the accident had apparently not happened at eleven o'clock but at ten and old Lorpailleur had contrived her late appearance so as to force Monsieur to invite her to luncheon, if he'd only known in time he'd have found a way to snub the old pest in front of them all by some little detail of etiquette that she wasn't aware of and which he would have made her observe as for instance . . . or that someone had told him that old Lorpailleur had left home late or had dawdled on the way so as to get herself invited, which she is supposed to have confided to the person in question who in a spirit of vengeance apparently hurried off to the manor house and not being able to ask for Monsieur de Broy told the butler, which he apparently took advantage of during the meal to make her observe the detail in question, as for instance to replace her knife on the knife-rest every time she left it on her plate or to change her fork when she confused the fish service with the other one, something of that sort, Latirail couldn't remember exactly what the butler had told him.

In short, after asking after her mother the Father went on to ask after her sister, such a pious woman and so devoted, hadn't she gone to live in the Argentine, old Lorpailleur answered him and Monsieur de Broy took advantage of this to steer the conversation round to this country which he knew, the school teacher was able to put in a word here and there as she had corresponded with her sister over a period of years or else she may apropos of an accident which one of the gentlemen brought up in conversation have told them about the one that happened to little Frédéric, one of her pupils who was drowned, it was so sad, it was about ten years ago but you never really get over it whatever people say ... or that Monsieur de Broy apropos of his friend Mortin whose name had just been mentioned by the ecclesiastic may have spoken about this person, an old friend whom the gentlemen knew well, as a matter of fact he should have been here today but he couldn't manage it, then about the guest house and one thing leading to another about the guests, in particular a lady called Apostolos or as near as makes no difference who was so amusing, he had had a glimpse of her not long before, a subject totally lacking in interest but which gave old Lorpailleur a chance to say something, or about Mademoiselle Ariane whose name may well have been mentioned by the schoolmistress herself, am I being too inquisitive if I ask you whether you are related, certainly not he replied, we are cousins four times removed but her nobility dates from the fourteenth century whereas ours dates from the thirteenth, after old Lorpailleur had mentioned her visit to Bonne-Mesure that is, yes that must be it, she was expatiating on it complacently, she was all but referring to her as the dear soul, not taking anyone in as you may well imagine, the gentlemen knew what was what.

The lady of the manor had invited her the previous Saturday with Monsieur le curé, it was such lovely weather, she had admired the century-old beeches bordering the drive and the rhododendron clumps and the beautiful mansion with all its windows open to the July sun, what a charming person Mademoiselle Ariane was, so simple, and Mademoiselle Francine, so well-mannered, she had always enjoyed their company, implying that she often saw them but deceiving, I repeat, no one, Mademoiselle Ariane had told her cousin just a few days previously apropos of the Lorpailleur luncheon that she had laughed so much seeing her arrive rigged out in such a fashion in that heat and that anyway she had been inconvenienced all through the meal by the odor of perspiration that emanated from this village woman, suggesting that they might get the chemist to inform her that such things as deodorants as they call them exist these days, don't you think that would be amusing my dear cousin, and he nodded his assent, which made him laugh inwardly when he thought back to it that day because at table he had very soon perceived this odor in his neighbor and had indicated it to the gentlemen by surreptitiously holding his nose while appearing to be pinching it absentmindedly, the butler whenever he passed behind her mimed the same gesture and each time nearly made the young gentlemen watching him choke with laughter.

And one thing leading to another still according to the butler apropos of something quite different from the presence of the Father at table, perhaps apropos of the young people who left the district the moment they had finished their schooling, someone tactlessly brought up the name of Tourniquet or was it on purpose, in short old Lorpailleur blushed to the roots of her hair and didn't dare look at the preacher any more but he very calmly said that he remembered the child and asked what had become of him, no one had any answer, but without a shade of embarrassment, that ignoble story could only have been invented, the school teacher pulled herself together, Monsieur de Broy made her help herself to some more matelote or gibelotte, and yet the atmosphere at the meal was not relaxed, no one was being natural, the conversation kept lagging, which wasn't of the slightest importance seeing that the gentlemen had other cats in their bags than hers as you might say, they were getting rid of a chore and as the moment was approaching when the two young gentlemen had to take their leave Monsieur de Broy told the butler against all etiquette to serve the coffee at the table and once again made his excuses to Mademoiselle, then they got up and went out and the butler didn't hear what followed or said he didn't.

For Madame Apostolos in spite of her ludicrous appearance is the only one in the guest house who has any common sense or any fun in her, now she knows the butler well and she questioned him at length about the luncheon at Broy, she wanted to hear it all several times over so as eventually to be in a position to snub the old prude whom she detests, that's how she apparently heard of her late arrival and the obligation under which Monsieur de Broy found himself to ask old Lorpailleur to stay whereas she made out that she had been invited, and other details of no great importance but which completely modify the tone of the conversation at luncheon.

But old Lorpailleur could only have been seen at the guest house with Odette on the day of the concert given by the little pupils of Mademoiselle Lozière who gives classes in diction, she is very old poor thing and absolutely penniless, the schoolmistress and the curé between them have sent her four or five children to whom she teaches Lamartine, then she has three young ladies from the choral society of whom Miquette is one who want to continue their studies, it's a sign of the times it seems, to cut a long story short Monsieur Mortin lends them for the occasion a room which is a sort of annex at the back of the guest house, the former owner didn't finish it and it is used as a store-room, they clear it out the day before and decorate it with old ribbons and paper flowers that the ladies keep from one year to the next, they bring the piano in and all the chairs they can find, it begins to look like a concert hall, Monsieur Monnard said that he'd been there that year, he'd arrived at exactly half-past three but nothing was ready, the guests were taking their seats after paying an entrance fee which goes to Mademoiselle Lozière, that's as it should be, he went to say how do you do to Mortin and the ladies and gentlemen, they were gossiping, they were smirking, this concert was a great pleasure, the ladies had dressed up and the gentlemen were smoking Mortin's cigars, he turns this occasion more or less into the guest house party and he also offers refreshments in the interval, in short it still didn't begin, they could hear Mademoiselle Lozière behind the curtain giving her instructions and the sound of preparations, comings and goings, in any case not all the audience were there yet, at one moment Madame Apostolos had a bit of a spat with old Crottet about a chair that was out of line she maintained that she could see better that way but old Crottet said that she was blocking everyone's view, she made her put her chair back where it came from and the ladies agreed with her because they are jealous of Apostolos who is the one who is most intimate with Mortin in view of her breeding and her sense of fun, it sometimes happens that they both stay up talking in the proprietor's apartment until something like two in the morning.

The other spectators they were waiting for were the ladies from the village like old Moineau and old Magnin and some old bachelors, Irénée was throwing his weight about in the hall, he called out to a maiden lady in a blue muslin frock and spectacles who was supposed to be selling programs, hurry up said he it's going to begin and the person started selling the typewritten programs bound in cardboard with a postcard stuck on, an autumn landscape, which her pupils had made, it was priced at one franc, very pretty, everyone bought one except an old gentleman who ever since half-past three had been argufying with the lady who was selling the entrance tickets, he finally bought one of the cheapest in the back row and then insinuated himself into the front row, this caused more arguments but Mortin said it's not in the least important, it still didn't begin, at one moment Irénée went up to Monnard and whispered into his ear, Monnard didn't seem to understand, Mortin went up to him and he too said something in a low voice, Monnard shrugged his shoulders and Irénée went behind the curtain where Mademoiselle Lozière said please thank him very much, that will be perfect, everyone heard and turned to look at Monnard and wondered what they had asked him, had he given some money or what, they thought it was extremely kind of him to come, such a cultured man, everyone felt flattered, The Walnuts was no ordinary guest house, it had intellectual entertainments, you opened the program and you saw the heading private concert by the pupils of Mademoiselle Lozière member of the Poetry Society and after that the different items of the performance were numbered, number one a poetical pilgrimage, author Mademoiselle Lozière, played by Mademoiselle Francine Magnin, Mademoiselle Mireille Moineau, Mademoiselle Solange Dumans and Mademoiselle Miquette Ducreux, number two a sentimental pilgrimage, author Mademoiselle Lozière, played by Mademoiselle Solange Dumans, Mademoiselle Francine Magnin, Monsieur Irénée and little Mireille Moineau, number three a tribute ... or was number one a sentimental pilgrimage played by Mademoiselle Miquette Ducreux, Mademoiselle Solange Dumans, Mademoiselle Francine Magnin, Monsieur Irénée and little Mireille Moineau and number two a poetical pilgrimage played by Mademoiselle Francine Magnin, Mademoiselle Mireille Moineau, Mademoiselle Solange Dumans and Mademoiselle Miquette Ducreux, number three a tribute to the glorious dead by Professor Duchemin, Chevalier of the Legion of Honor, he could have been the gentleman in the first row, people looked at him but he didn't look round, number four the Sleeping Beauty a poetical essay by Mademoiselle Lozière played by Monsieur Irénée in the role of the Poet and the author in the role of the Muse, Mademoiselle Mireille Moineau in the role of History, Mesdemoiselles Solange Dumans and Miquette Ducreux in the role of Youth, Mademoiselle Francine Magnin in the role of France, with at the bottom of the program at the piano Mademoiselle Lozière, the ladies said what a first-class program, what an effort, Mademoiselle Lozière is very deserving, it still didn't begin, the gentleman in the front row got up and went to re-argufy with the person at the entrance, he couldn't find her, he asked Irénée if he had seen her, it was very important, Madame Apostolos said that ill-bred old fellow, if he's the Legion of Honor I'm not looking forward to his talk, the ladies hushed her up.

Then ma Magnin and ma Moineau arrived in their capacity of pupils' mothers and they said that they were entitled to sit in the front row, Mortin tried to get them to see that it was a delicate situation, everyone was seated but they threatened to withdraw their daughters from the show, they had to move the Legion of Honor, it made him feel very small, he took himself off to the back and one of the guest house ladies who was very angry brought a chair up herself and put it down in the front row tucked away in the corner, Madame Crottet considered this the height of vulgarity but Madame Apostolos stood up for the intruder as we might have expected, it still didn't begin.

There were some paintings by Mademoiselle Lozière on

the walls but everyone had seen them dozens of times before, our poetess was also a gifted painter and she had yet another surprise for us up her sleeve that day, Monsieur Monnard looked at the paintings and said to old Crottet that they had a remarkably sensitive quality, she replied that's what I always say, Mademoiselle Lozière is a great artist, you'll see what a success the concert will be, Irénée was bringing up chairs for some other ladies who were just arriving, they were beginning to feel hot but no one complained, they were gossiping, they were in festive mood, the Legion of Honor tried to come up closer into the second row but the seat was being kept for a little girl or a little old woman who hadn't arrived yet, he had to go to the back again, they were sure now that he wasn't the lecturer and they were wondering where the real one was, hadn't arrived yet probably, it couldn't be Monsieur Monnard since the program specified Professor Duchemin, unless he was using a pseudonym to talk about the glorious dead, in short people were questioning one another, it still didn't begin, Mortin was behind the curtain and the maiden lady in spectacles took advantage of it to sell her last programs, you were allowed to choose, Madame Magnin would have liked a landscape with a river but it was already sold, she said I asked Francine to keep it for me, she's a feather-brain, and then they heard the three knocks but the curtains weren't pulled, they parted just enough to let little Mireille through, she was dressed up as a communicant, they heard afterwards that it was her mother's wedding dress, but the child has put on so much weight in the last two years that she filled it out widthwise, embellished with roses and carnations that she'd embroidered on it herself, she's full of ideas, she had a rose in her hair kept in place by a gold ribbon, first she announced that this was a private concert by the pupils of Mademoiselle Lozière under the honorary presidency of Monsieur Monnard the Clerk to the Parish Council, that was why Mademoiselle Lozière had sent Irénée to whisper something in his ear, it was honorary, then she read from the program the first number sentimental pilgrimage with all the names then she said that she was solitude by Mademoiselle Lozière and she read from a book a poem by the author that was stuck in it to make people think it was printed said Madame Moineau but perhaps it was an anthology, to cut a long story short a rather melancholy piece, it was Autumn with weeping willows and the twilight casting its spell on you, the curtains hadn't closed properly and the child who is intelligent tried two or three times to put them right with her foot.

Then she bowed and pushed the curtains to right and left, the runners don't work any more, and the audience saw the surprise it was Miquette dressed up as a ballerina lying on the floor or rather with one leg very bent at the knee and the other leg stretched out with her head on that knee and her arms outstretched, she was wearing a sweet little satin skirt in crushed strawberry pink the same as her bodice and she got up slowing, raising her arms, this was the invocation recited by Mademoiselle Lozière at the piano but you couldn't see her, it was like a prayer coming from somewhere else, she stayed behind the curtain, to a melody by Chopin, Miquette moved this way and that two or three times raising her arms and legs in a gracious fashion, pity she already has such fat thighs and you could see her yellow feet, she was taking great care not to catch them in the carpet, in short she was dancing in a new way so it seems to soft music, so Mademoiselle Lozière was gifted in that direction too, a real artist, as for the yellow feet Madame Magnin who is unkind said afterwards to Madame Ducreux that they ought to have put ballet shoes on her or ankle socks but it seems that Mademoiselle Lozière's theory is all against it, the harmony of the body is what's wanted, next Miquette went to the back of the stage and pulled a little curtain which revealed a landscape by Mademoiselle Lozière it was like as you might say a window on to nature then she lay down again as she had at the beginning and that was when ... that's to say that before she had got up little Mireille had sat down on a bench against the piano and she shut her book to intimate to the audience that solitude makes us dream and Miquette got up, it was after that that she lay down again, and that was when Solange Dumans and Francine Magnin came on reciting Lamartine, Mademoiselle Lozière had just announced it, they recited in turn while the pianist played very softly, it was still Chopin.

At one moment they went over to the bogus window and this corresponded exactly to the poem, the autumn landscape was revealed, Mademoiselle Lozière really did know her job and they pointed out the trees to each other then they turned round and went and sat on a bench opposite Mireille and they read another book, they were turning its pages over while they recited a poem on love also by Lamartine, it really was ingenious, as if they were reading it from the book for the first time, then Miquette stood up in what was left of the space and that was when Irénée came on, nobody realized that he was about to give the first performance of a poem by Mademoiselle Lozière on autumn solitude, they all clapped and he sang how to say not so very well but it was touching that he had made the effort, he is attracted to the things of the spirit, he walked up and down as he sang because Mademoiselle Lozière's theory is movement, there were six verses, after the song Miquette made two or three more movements and then went to draw the little curtain, that meant that solitude is shut in on itself and at the last note she nearly lost her balance, Solange caught her in time, it was the end of the first number, people clapped a lot, they said that Mademoiselle Lozière had all the gifts and it was true.

Madame Crottet turned round to Monsieur Monnard and said what did I tell you, isn't it exquisite, and he agreed, everyone was getting expansive, that fellow Lamartine after all he certainly knew how to express the things of the heart, the ladies wondered whether he had been unhappy, how many lady-loves had he had, if their own suitors had spoken to them in poetry when they were courting they would have been different today, there was nothing more beautiful than poetry and this particular poetry was so how could they put it so modern, you had to make an effort to realize that it was written a hundred years ago or more or less, how many in fact, what century was it, Madame Apostolos what a wit said that he must have been a gay dog, a womanizer, that was the only sort she liked, Odette was really shocked and old Lorpailleur pursed up her chicken's hole, a pleasant little hubbub arose in the hall but Mortin said that the interval would be after number two, don't let us disturb the artistes, silence fell again and the curtain gave way to little Mireille who had draped a blue veil over her shoulders, she was Poetry now and she recited a rather melancholy poem on solitude by Mademoiselle Lozière, it was autumn with . . . or twilight . . . something of that sort, she hadn't got a book this time and when she'd finished she pushed the curtains to the left and right and they saw Miquette in the same costume sitting across the bench, one leg very far forward and the other bent, her left arm stretched out over the back of the bench, it was autumn lassitude, she stood up and made two or three movements but she didn't go and open the little curtain and Mademoiselle Lozière at the piano was reciting Lamartine and accompanying herself then Miquette went over to the right and curtseyed to invite

Solange and Francine to come on, they came on reciting the stanzas to the beloved, they replied to each other, that was ingenious too because there was the voice of the lover and that of his chosen one, you understood the dialogue better than with one voice and they showed each other a bust of Lamartine on the piano as if to say there is the genius who is inspiring us, there is the ideal lover, then little Mireille went and picked up a bouquet of leaves that she had made out of wrapping paper, she's very clever with her hands, she laid it on the floor in front of the bust and then Solange and Francine recited the stanzas to autumn or the homage to Lamartine, in short a long poem on twilight by Mademoiselle Lozière whilst Miquette was circling round them raising her arms and legs then she went and sat down beside Mireille and they both swayed gracefully to left and right to intimate to the audience that the wind was blowing amidst the autumn leaves but Irénée didn't appear this time and finally Mademoiselle Lozière played a Chopin ballade with brio as Monsieur Monnard said.

People clapped even more and Mademoiselle Lozière came out from behind the curtain to bow, the program said that both her town and stage hats were by Brivance, but according to Madame Monneau they must have been several seasons old, they gave them to her free gratis and for nothing, in any case the guest house residents have never known her to have more than two hats, the white one she was wearing that day and the black one she wears in the winter, in short the first half was over and Mortin announced the interval, they would find refreshments in the garden, the audience got up and went to drink their fruit juice and beer for the gentlemen, goodness it was hot, why shouldn't they have the show in the garden next year asked Madame Dumans, to which Mireille replied but Madame because of the curtain, it wouldn't be a real show, because

173

the actors had joined the rest of them and it was so exciting, Irénée as well, people were congratulating them, the girls were all made up, it looked funny but they explained that don't you see on the stage you have to otherwise your face looks so pale even so they'd been a bit heavy-handed especially little Mireille who even looked too red on the stage, in the garden she looked like one of the painted figures in an Aunt Sally, a first communicant who's gone to the bad, Mademoiselle Lozière was sitting down near the refreshment table surrounded by the ladies, it was her day, her triumph, the girls help me so much in my work she was saying modestly, they are so gifted, but Monsieur Monnard murmured that the show revealed a truly noble inspiration, poetry is the supreme art, he recognized her talent in each line because he read the *Fantoniard* on Saturdays but he quoted a line by Lamartine as an example and Mademoiselle Lozière said you flatter me, he didn't know where to look.

Old Lorpailleur was holding forth to our poetess with a few side-glances at Monsieur Monnard, he was the one she was hoping to fascinate by her excellent command of language, would that our little ones might be photographed says she amidst your beautiful setting, and Odette who was more down to earth was talking to a lady about the absolute necessity of parent-teacher meetings, she was getting a bee in her bonnet about it, it dated from the time when she believed in her vocation, the other ladies were talking to Miquette, no one had known that Mademoiselle Lozière gave her dancing lessons, was she a real dancing teacher and Miquette replied that when she was young she had studied with the famous Ida Duran for many years, she had wanted to be a ballerina but she had come down on the side of painting after an illness and then poetry and journalism because it's very difficult to earn your living from paintings,

the ladies wondered if dancing was good for you and Miquette replied it's very good as a sort of gymnastic for the
harmony of the body, even so she hadn't got all that much
thinner and that was when Madame Dumans made her
remark about the yellow feet to Madame Ducreux, I can still
see her, or was it Madame Magnin or after the lecture . . .
in short people were gossiping and drinking their fruit juice,
the bogus Legion of Honor had found the ticket lady again
and was re-argufying, they couldn't hear what he was saying,
the maiden lady in blue had only one more program to sell
and Madame Apostolos was fussing about the lecturer,
which one could he be, when all of a sudden Professor
Duchemin appeared at the gate, Mortin went over to him,
he was an old man in a bum-freezer in this heat, they
wasted no time in offering him some refreshment and the
ladies all wanted to shake hands with him, his sight wasn't
all it had been and he kept on saying delighted, delighted,
nevertheless Monsieur and Madame Crottet managed to get
him on one side and he talked to them about a cousin of
theirs whom he had known well, the poetess Louise d'Isimance who was a Bottu as everyone knows, he loved poetry,
which explained why Mademoiselle Lozière had the honor
. . . or rather why he had the honor to give this talk on the
glorious dead, everyone was proud to have a professor, he
went to say how do you do to Mademoiselle Lozière and she
said my old friend, my dear old friend, how very kind of you
to do us the honor . . . or that our little artistic circle had
the honor, to cut a long story short the interval was nearly
over, Mortin politely asked the audience to resume their
seats.

The professor went up on to the stage and stayed in front
of the curtain where they had put a chair and a table with a
jug and a glass, Mademoiselle Lozière had been categorical
in her instructions that they weren't to forget that, lecturers

tend to have dry throats and the professor had a very delicate one, in any case he didn't speak very loudly and Mortin
asked everybody to come up as close to the front as possible,
that had occasioned more scenes, the bogus Legion had
taken advantage of it to install himself in the front row and
Madame Apostolos had called him a gigolo in a loud voice,
to cut a long story short after the professor had sat down he
took his specs out of his top pocket where there was a
handkerchief that was sticking out too far, he pushed it back
down again and you could see the Legion of Honor on the
lapel of his jacket, then he gave them a little introduction
and told them that the dead of the nineteen-fourteen to
eighteen war were ever-present in his memory, heroism was
eternal and France's heart was still bleeding that was why
the honor of having been a soldier was a recompense for him
in his old age and we all knew that patriotism was the
highest moral value of the spirit . . . that heroism was the
spirit in which there breathed the moral value of those who
have the honor to have been soldiers and patriots, long live
France, people clapped a lot and Irénée was already crying
because he had been wounded somewhere or other by a
shell, to cut a long story short the professor started reading
his lecture from his notes, it was about the Chemin des
Dames and the trenches on the Marne with Clemenceau and
other well-known generals, it all took place so it seemed in
taxis and balloons, the whole of France was dying for the
honor of having been the eldest daughter of the Church, for
the clergy were chaplains in those days, he gave them a lot
of details about how the hungry populations got by and
about the Red Cross which filled the Belgian hospitals so as
to delay the advance on Paris, the Marshal was the right
hand of the Dreyfus affair in holding out against the es-
pionage that was continually threatening our brave and
gallant private soldiers but even so the Jerries retreated and

General Magnin decorated on the field of battle the men who were killed in action and the nurses who married them, he himself had a cousin who was married to one of these saints recruited by the allied armies, you could read about it in the American papers of the time, in short the audience realized that this battle had been a page of history as he said but maybe it was going on a bit too long, they were finally beginning to mix up the various maneuvers, the ladies were too hot and Mortin got the air circulating by opening the kitchen door just when the orator was saying and now for my conclusions, something political in which he foresaw the second world war and he finished by repeating long live France.

People clapped a lot and Mortin went up to the professor to help him down, he pressed both his hands and thanked him warmly, everyone was impressed and people were wondering what he was a professor of, it seemed that he was retired but had been a professor of nineteen-fourteen, something of the sort, the audience looked as if it wanted to relax, slight hubbub and little laughs from the ladies, the heat was becoming stifling because Madame Crottet had got them to shut the kitchen door again as she was in a draught but Mortin announced that they were going to continue as time was limited, there would be more refreshments after the show, would everyone please bear with them, so then it was number four the Sleeping Beauty a poetic essay by the author, the curtains had been pulled from behind, they hadn't noticed, and this time Mademoiselle Lozière at the piano was visible, she had taken off her hat and her head was enveloped in Mireille's blue veil which was hanging down over her shoulders and the back of her chair, she was the Muse, then, Irénée was sitting on the bench with a book, he was the Poet, the Muse started playing Chopin in the moonlight, they had put out all the lights except a little blue

177

lamp on the piano, Irénée threw his head back to intimate to the audience that he was looking at the clouds and at one moment the Muse started reciting, first with a very soft accompaniment and later with nothing, it was the stanzas to autumn then the Poet replied and suddenly the ceiling light came on again and Youth appeared, it was Solange Dumans and Miquette Ducreux holding hands and lifting their legs, a dance about love which ended with dead leaves because they were each holding a bit of the bouquet and they dropped some of the leaves, very poetic, Solange had the same costume in yellow, her thighs aren't so fat but you could see her knickers, they made two or three movements while the Muse was changing from one poem to another, it was the story of the epics with Roland and Duguesclin and Joan of Arc, the Poet lowered his head over his book and from time to time he tried to catch hold of Solange or Miquette to intimate to the audience that his youth was leaving him then the two of them re-opened the little curtain in front of the landscape which the Poet contemplated for a long time, he was falling back on Nature while the ballerinas slowly crouched down to right and left, shutting their eyes, until the moment when the Muse began to play some very loud chords and History entered, it was Mireille Moineau with a gray veil over her communion dress, she was holding a book and she started to answer the Muse and at the same time pretended to push Solange and Miquette away from her, you understood that History was the opposite of heedless youth, next the Poet stood up and threw his book onto the ground, History gave a little jump backwards and shut her eyes like Solange and Miquette had after they pulled the curtain then the Muse recited 'Twilight' by Mademoiselle Lozièr in a voice that got sadder and sadder as if she were going to cry, roughly what she was saying was that autumn's inspiration was about to be conquered by the privates in the nineteen-fourteen

178

war, they understood that solitude was immoral, it was re-
placed by patriotism, in fact France did appear, it was
Francine Magnin enveloped in the Tricolor flag, she made
the gesture of obliterating the three who were sleeping,
nothing existed any longer but the Country, the Poet stood
to attention and the Muse played the Marseillaise first verse
on the piano then France recited unaccompanied Victory by
Mademoiselle Lozière, again the history of the trenches and
the dead but not so long this time with at the end trumpets
announcing the eternity of the People, next very loudly the
rest of the Marseillaise with the pedals, the Legion of Honor
was crying, the bogus one too, Monsieur Monnard too and
Irénéé too in spite of his being an actor, it was very moving
but afterwards people began to wonder who the Sleeping
Beauty was, whether it was Youth or History or even France
who had been woken up by the pedals, in short people
clapped a lot but perhaps not enough because they were all
sweating and they went out to drink their fruit juice.

They met in the garden, Mademoiselle Lozière was con-
gratulated like anything by the ladies, all the gifts she had,
and so modest just like a real artist said the president who
started off again about noble inspiration, Professor Duchemin had less of a crowd round him as he was less
well-known or perhaps people were afraid that he too would
start all over again, if he'd been a professor of the trenches
that was all he had to say, nevertheless Mortin was looking
after him, he advised him to put his bum-freezer on again
because old men catch cold particularly when it's hot, the
professor was pink with pleasure and said that he'd never
had such a good audience, the bogus Legionnaire was sink-
ing beers with Irénéé who was patting Miquette on the
behind as if she'd been his grand-daughter, he was taking
advantage of the fact that she was still dressed as a ballerina
but Madame her mother saw what was going on and pulled

Miquette away by the arm saying come and explain to Mademoiselle Lorpailleur how you are taught to dance, the other ladies were talking to the actresses and asking them how they could remember it all, it seemed it was a knack that was facilitated by the rhymes, the girls explained for example that *langueur* rhymes with *douceur* and that's what you might call a landmark, even so they admitted that they had gone wrong one or twice, had people realized, but nobody had heard, there was another thing that was bothering little Mireille and that was that she had studied the role of France but just the week before it had been given to Francine who is taller, that was why she hadn't . . . or was it Solange who was supposed to have played France and Mireille Youth, in short there had been a change that was why the little girl had been so disappointed because she had had to read her part instead of reciting it by heart but her mother Madame Ducreux that is, no, Madame Moineau pulled her by the sleeve and said come and explain to Mademoiselle . . . in short it was at this moment that they heard that the communion dress was a wedding dress she had put on so much weight in the last two years, Madame Apostolos was having a bit of a spat with old Crottet now that no one was bothering them, she was saying that she would never again subject herself to that airless room it was enough to make you ill, you and your mania about draughts you make everyone uncomfortable, ask Monsieur Monnard if he wasn't inconvenienced, gentlemen wear more clothes but you only think about yourself, she was furious.

Or that Mademoiselle Lozière being a royalist would never have dressed France in the Tricolor, the Magnin child was in white and the only allusion to the regime was the Muse's blue scarf and Miquette's strawberry-coloured costume, very subtle, as for the pictures on the walls and the landscape behind the curtain they weren't by Mademoiselle Lozière who may well have all the talents but not that of the painter you can take my word for that, everything that's hung here is by Monsieur Vérassou, such a refined man, he was a guest some ten years ago and he succumbed to cancer he wasn't even fifty, just like Irénée caressing Miquette, it didn't make sense, the mischief-maker was that horrible skinflint who had insinuated himself into the front row, it seems they inquired about him afterwards, one Jolivot who used to be an intimate friend of Mademoiselle Lozière's but with whom she hadn't been on speaking terms for the last twenty years, he has so little sense of shame that he comes to every concert, she completely ignores him and leaves him to sink his beer, before you assert such things you might verify your facts, and what was more neither the poem on victory nor the one on twilight nor even the stanzas to autumn were by Mademoiselle Lozière who may well have all the talents but not that of the poet you can take my word for that, they were by the little old woman who hadn't been able to be present as she had been tied to her wheel-chair ever since eighteen seventy-three or as near as makes no difference, a real artist she was but so humble that she let old Lozière correct her poetry and then she has the cheek to put her name to it, couldn't something be done about it, it's a violation of authorship what's it called now, psycho psychi property, it seems that there's a society in Paris for that sort of thing but you know what Parisians are, swine all the lot of them, no point in getting in touch with them, they might ask Lorduz or Topard how to go about it.

Or that Mademoiselle Lozière, seeing young Pinson, a friend of Mortin's, hovering round Miquette whom he was ask-ing whether the art of dancing was difficult, whether she was going on to study at the Conservatoire, what famous ballerina she preferred, may have said, I'm referring to Mademoiselle Lozière, to several of the ladies do you think that there will be a marriage there, wouldn't that be nice, such a refined young

man, my little Miquette would be so happy et cetera, a completely unfounded pious hope given that ... in short she was
barking up the wrong tree because young Pinson was just
being polite, he's not interested, he's a friend of Mortin's and
of Monsieur de Broy, he has never talked of marriage or
anything of the sort, so she kept saying to the ladies, that
young Pinson what's his first name again that's right Edouard
don't you think it might come to a marriage with our
Miquette, why didn't we think about it before, she was still
under the influence of the fruit juice and the marvellous
excitement of the matinée, she was seeing everything through
rose-coloured spectacles, she wanted to marry everybody off,
a remarkable phenomenon with old maiden ladies, like an *a
posteriori* necessity if I may so put it to fill the gap they have
suffered from, and the ladies were saying yes indeed he's so
charming, you ought to mention it to Monsieur Mortin or
rather Madame Apostolos ought to but it would be enough
for us to ask her for her to refuse, how should we go about it,
someone must open Monsieur Mortin's eyes, he must use his
influence with the young man, it's the ideal match for such a
sensitive child, it made you wonder the way every one of the
ladies even the married ones were hot on the trail, what secret
hogwash were they mashing in their sentimental buckets that
they wanted to make the poor children copulate come what
may.

Or that young Pinson hadn't been at the matinée and that
the remarks about his marriage had been made another day
during a meal at the guest house in fact it did sometimes happen that the young man out of the kindness of his heart came
to say how do you do to the guests but he never ate with them,
Mortin either invited him into his private apartment or gave
him dinner in town.

So that he might have come across Miquette then one day
when there was a rehearsal and having no alternative have said

something to her about dancing and that Madame Crottet or Madame Apostolos may have noticed the young people either in the corridor or in the hall, which would have been the reason why one of them the day of the concert said but why isn't young Pinson here, he seemed to be interested in our Miquette, and then started weighing up the possibilities of a marriage in view of this defection, it was all very tricky.

Or that quite simply this conversation hadn't been passed on by Marie but by Monsieur de Broy's butler who adores gossip, that young Pinson and Mortin had happened to be at the manor house a short time before with some friends, that there had been a very amusing atmosphere that day, the talk had been rather free, and that one of the gentlemen had started imitating one of the guest house ladies who was anxious to marry Edouard off to that frightful pudding of the name of Miquette, details and dumb show in illustration which bordered on the indecent, that was much more likely.

Well yes then the day the Father was at Broy one of the young gentlemen was indeed Pinson but without his friend Mortin and the conversation which was very gay since in actual fact old Lorpailleur wasn't there apparently came round to the Tourniquet affair which Edouard hadn't heard about, it had happened ten years previously with copious details bordering on indecency but the gentlemen are so amusing, nothing shocks them, it's an education to listen to their remarks unless you are a bigoted old woman or a schoolmistress of course.

Because it isn't absolutely excluded that the second young man at Monsieur de Broy's that day may have been Mademoiselle Moine's nephew, and so to say that they were all aristocrats would be wrong, personally it wouldn't surprise me if he was the one the butler was referring to when he was talking about one of them not knowing how to eat fish and using the wrong knife and fork, a thing he apparently drew his attention to in a nasty way by changing his knives and forks every time he made a mistake, he can't stomach the fact that his master is interested in this boy who is not only ill-bred but stupid as well, young Pinson doesn't think very highly of him either, and she went on about the evening that had followed that lovely party at the guest house, Mortin and his friend Edouard had been invited to Broy to help them digest as the lord of the manor said the purgative of the concert, it's really very unkind of him to talk like that about something that elicited so much niceness, youthfulness, and devotion but he is pitiless.

Well yes then the day of the luncheon at Bonne-Mesure Mademoiselle Ariane had already heard about old Lorpailleur's misadventure, she had been shown out by the butler, the tactless creature had turned up at the manor house shortly before midday to so she said talk to Monsieur de Broy about an urgent matter, the lord of the manor doesn't receive before luncheon and the servant had no alternative but to . . . or that Monsieur de Broy had been called away at the last minute and not had time to let the school teacher know so had told his butler to make his excuses for him, in short she was furious, which had amused the squire no end, yes Mademoiselle Ariane did know about it because she was seeing a lot of her cousin at this time because of the affair in question, she apparently asked Francine to steer the conversation diplomatically round to the lord of the manor to see the schoolmistress's reaction, which Francine had done the moment she arrived by simply saying ah, I didn't quite understand you on the telephone, Aunt, I thought our cousin was to have been one of the party, and then turning to the chicken's hole do you know him, he's a charming man and so amusing, so amusing, old Lorpailleur is then supposed to have adopted a surprised look and said that she didn't know Monsieur de Broy, she may possibly have seen him once or twice in his car or in town, she had never even been curious enough to go and look at his beautiful mansion, it dates back to the sixteenth century does it not or the seventeenth, then turning to Mademoiselle Ariane, is Bonne-Mesure older or of the same period. I don't remember the characteristics of the styles, I'm getting so rusty it's unforgiveable, Mademoiselle Ariane apparently replied that Bonne-Mesure was what they called a fortified manor house, it had been completely restored if not rebuilt in the eighteenth century, that the only remaining part of the former construction was the back of the house, a tower that had been razed to the ground and incorporated in part of the seventeenth century building work and the fifteenth century moat that had never been filled in, she offered to show it to the schoolmistress, wink in the direction of the niece, would you care to see it, we have time before luncheon, Monsieur the curé isn't here yet, and she apparently got up and led old Lorpailleur round to the back of the manor, they crossed the drive and then turned right and went along the path by the moat which had been turned into a sloping lawn with ivy and clumps of impatiens, this side of the house was the side on which the sun set and was in any case very much overshadowed by the beech trees, you know how impatiens hate the sun et cetera.

Or else that the main facade of Bonne-Mesure had only been partially restored if not rebuilt in the eighteenth century, there was still one seventeenth century wing or some seventeenth century building work though goodness knows which incorporated in a more recent construction of the beginning of the nineteenth century, was it a veranda or an extra story, something pretty horrible in the taste of the period, confusing it, I'm referring to Lorette, with what she may have seen somewhere else at Malatraîne for instance since Broy is all of a piece unless . . . in any case the girl doesn't know anything about it.

185

Old Lorpailleur arrives, she says straight off that she's never known such heat, there'd been nothing like it since eighteen seventy-three, it was in the paper, then in the course of the conversation that the day before or two days before she had been to our poetess's concert to hear her little pupils, a most commendable effort she makes this dedicated person but obviously how could she put it, obviously it isn't all perfect, she would have been only too pleased to offer to help her at rehearsals but you know how it is, her school takes all her time, her corrections to do at home, keeping in touch with the governors, in short she had spent a charming afternoon at the guest house, Monsieur Mortin is so kind, he provides refreshments for all those good people, whereupon Mademoiselle apparently avowed her great friendship with Madame Apostolos, such a distinguished person, amazement of the schoolmistress, she thanks heaven that she hasn't said anything nasty about that lady, she continues about Monsieur Mortin's kindness and that of his young nephew, he is his nephew isn't he, such a distinguished young man and Professor Duchemin was there too, he spoke about the atrocities of the nineteen-fourteen war and the heroism of our private soldiers, we must always keep them in the forefront of our memories, and turning to Mademoiselle Ariane, was your brother not killed on the field of battle for in fact ... or was it her father or her cousin, Mademoiselle Ariane came to her aid and said my brother yes that's right, the general.

And still apropos of the concert that Mademoiselle Thing was supposed to have told the schoolmistress she was preparing for the following year, a grand description of the Bonne-Mesure manor in verse, descriptions were so refreshing, and another of the Forest of Grance and a third of Madame Magnin's poultry-yard which she can see from her window, she would dress her little pupils up for the recitation, one as

186

a seventeenth or eighteenth century lady, which century is it exactly, the other in leaves and the other as a chicken, rather like in that play by Rostand do you remember what was it called now, in short she was so enthusiastic, so young for her age, people wondered where she got her freshness from, you needed to know what they meant by that though, in any case Mademoiselle Ariane knew all about it, the poetess had told her about her project and even asked permission to allude to the owner's ancestry in some of her lines about the manor, how tactful, they had got to this point when the curé appeared, limping up the drive, Francine immediately got up and went to meet him and Mademoiselle de Bonne-Mesure took advantage of this to ask old Lorpailleur what she thought . . .

As to the Tourniquet affair it had long since given place to that of young Pinson, the lad of rural extraction who frequented the aristocrats, he had broken with his family and didn't live in our midst any more, a room in town paid for by you know whom, talk about immorality and it kept turning the knife in the wounds as you might say of our bog-trotters, they hadn't forgotten the dreadful scandal ten years before of little Frédéric who had been violated in the woods by a sex-maniac who they thought one thing leading to another might have had some dealings with you know whom, it had upset the whole district that business but the child had got over it quite all right, at least that's what the poor mother said even though no one went to see, when he'd finished his apprenticeship the young man went to live in Paris where they lost sight of him.

Little Frédéric, it was Frédéric wasn't it, had gone out of the yard all by himself, he'd been making mud pies, it must have been half-past twelve, somewhere around there, he had crossed the road and then gone up the rue Ancienne . . . or if he wasn't making mud pies as he was already getting on for eight years old he was playing at something else but alone, that was where his parents went wrong, the danger of the only child, in short he went up the road without attracting anyone's attention, took the little path that leads to Malatraîne and then the fork into the forest where he got lost, he called out Mummy or Daddy being a bit backward for his age, was it Mummy or Daddy, there's an echo et cetera, then saw a gentleman behind a tree who ... well a gentleman who said would you like some sweets, the child said yes and then, then ...

Or little Jean-Claude, the fifth or sixth, the day of the picnic with his parents, the family had set off on foot at about ten o'clock, the father needs exercise after spending the whole week in his workshop and as for kids it doesn't do them any harm to walk, they arrived at the forest about midday and got settled, first of all they quenched their thirst from their gourds which contained lemonade or tepid water, the father's one was filled with wine and each child would be entitled to one mouthful during the picnic, the mother unpacked the bags and started handing round the hard-boiled eggs and ham sandwiches, she was so pleased poor woman and so tired, she doesn't go out much and a picnic is a real joy, she suddenly seemed to be discovering her children and was telling this one that he had grown, that one that he had nice hands, she even found something pleasant to say to her husband, what a lovely day they were having there but the children were still hungry, it's incredible what these little stomachs can tuck away when they're in the open air, she looked for the cheese in Jean-Claude's bag, it wasn't there, nor in Marie-Claire's, my goodness I hope I haven't forgotten it but no no, I'm sure I put it in one of the bags, it must be in yours darling, and in fact it was, but sweating all over and stinking, I'm referring to the cheese, but the children threw themselves on to it and it was the bread that was in short supply so that the father finally told the children that that was quite enough whining and carrying on thank you, the next one to start grumbling again will go without his supper when we get home, go and play, don't go too far away, your mother's tired, because he was beginning to feel sleepy, that was when the children scattered in the wood and they organized a game of cops and robbers, there were five of them playing, two cops and three robbers, little Louis, it was Louis wasn't it, was only three and he had to have a rest and that's where the tragedy begins, little Jean-Claude the fourth or fifth that is who was a robber went further than the first trees in the clearing against his father's strict instructions and he went down a path that led deep into the forest he ran at first and then he couldn't find the path any more and then he walked for a very long time not having the slightest sense of time or direction, so that he found himself all by himself and very far away, he began to feel frightened, he called out et cetera, until the moment when he caught sight of a gentleman behind a tree who ... well a gentleman who asked him et cetera but you see what sort of sweets they were what a shocking thing, how is it that this sort of monstrosity hasn't disappeared from our planet, really it's enough to make you despair of the Holy See, something of the sort.

For the poor mother who is a Duchemin through her grandmother and therefore related to the lecturer was at the concert ten years later with the ladies commenting on the lecture and on atrocities in general and apparently suddenly thought back to her little boy who was grown-up now and in Paris, never any news, she wondered perhaps you never know in her heart of hearts not even formulating the question, it was so vague, whether the tragedy hadn't had an influence on her child's character, comparing his case with what Madame Moineau had just said to her about Tourniquet but they had no means of knowing anything about that either they could only make suppositions, the fact is that she remained silent, suddenly absorbed in her thoughts, she didn't say another word until she left, Madame Erard who is so sensitive even apparently said to Madame Apostolos that poor woman looked very sad, who was she, Madame Apostolos didn't know because the mother hadn't dared to go and say how do you do to her relation the lecturer and as he is short-sighted he hadn't seen her in the hall.

Old Lorpailleur arrives, the curé is already there, Francine too, Minouche has just deposited her mess and is escaping into the kitchen-garden, Francine gets up and goes to meet the schoolmistress, the latter is in a terrible state and says that a truck et cetera, really fate is very cruel to the poor Ducreuxs, after their little Jean-Claude ten years ago and you know what happened to him now it's their little Louis, will he pull through, they've rushed him to hospital, Mademoiselle Ariane is no less upset than the curé and Francine, she make old Lorpailleur sit down and one thing leading to another, a finger of port helping her to pull herself together, they talk about atrocities in general, what times we live in, Mademoiselle de Bonne-Mesure however says something disconcerting and so unexpected having children you see where that leads people, the curé is shocked, how can you say such a thing, the good Lord et cetera, old Lorpailleur purses up her chicken's hole and Francine is the only one who acts reasonably, she takes as a pretext the fact that it's going to be half an hour before the bell goes, couldn't they show the guests the back of the manor the north facade that is where Amédée has just planted some clumps of impatiens, the plant that can't stand the sun, on the sloping lawn where the old moat was, what do you think, that would give us something else to think about, for

190

Marie contrary to her usual custom had apparently not taken up her post at the corner of the terrace, Francine had been to the kitchen some time before and found the poor woman in a terrible state, she'd burnt the soufflé, she was starting another one, such a thing had never happened to her before, she added, I can still hear her, it's no good getting old, Mademoiselle, you lose your touch, you lose your patience, you lose your head, something of the sort, Francine apparently reasoned with her or reassured her, these things happen, don't worry dear Marie, we'll wait as long as is necessary, just today Monsieur the curé hasn't got his catechism class, they finished last Saturday, the holidays have begun, and then joined the guests and took them round to the back of the house, Mademoiselle Ariane on the curé's arm like old acquaintances and old Lorpailleur going into ecstasies about the sixteenth or seventeenth century architectural details incorporated in more recent parts, a veranda or an extra story in the deplorable taste of the period, she mixed the styles up, I'm getting so rusty it's unforgiveable, implying that the fact of being so used to her school curriculum which had nothing to do with the history of art made her forget some of the elementary things, this to put them off the scent because there was no reason at all why this rustic even though she had some of her rough corners knocked off by her psycho psychi studies should ever have had the slightest notion of the subtleties of style.

Or that poor Mortin who never stopped saying to his friend de Broy that he hadn't succeeded in making his way in life, he was in despair, completely crushed the day of the concert because he had caught a glimpse of some sort of relation between Mademoiselle Loeillère's products and his own, his forgotten writings having something in common with the lamentable pastiches of our poetess, everything became merged in the limbo of abortion, a thing we were

191

unaware of at the time, I mean his despair, as Monsieur Mortin always seemed to us to be so self-confident, so distinguished, so completely outside the hurly-burly of literature and furthermore we didn't know that he had once been one of its adepts if not representatives.

And in that connection, I'm referring to the luncheon at Broy, young Pinson perhaps after the Father's allusion to the destiny of youth and the flight of time, he's so conventional, may have brought up the subject of our parish clerk who is always so distinguished, so self-confident, who as we had heard, was it from Mademoiselle Loeillère but in that case how could we not be on our guard, had had his literary pretentions too, which made quite a good few in our village, and gone on making jokes in somewhat bad taste about it because he was including with all the other lot his friend Mortin who was not there that day, which Monsieur de Broy apparently picked him up on rather sharply contrary to his usual habit of haughty indifference, there was a sensitive side to this blasé aristocrat then which his guests discovered with amazement all the more so as it was revealed apropos of a friendship, they wouldn't have imagined that this nobleman whatever may have been the affection he felt for his old comrade, they had been in the same regiment, harbored any sort of respect for the absent man's literary tendencies or pity for his lack of success, in short all the clichés you can think of on the subject.

Next, next well that the truck driver after he had nearly run the child over was apparently aware of his state of intoxication and stopped at the side of the road a few yards away from the forest maybe on the Malatraîne side, had a bit of a nap in his machine first, woke up round about two o'clock and as he didn't have any deliveries to make that afternoon treated himself to the luxury of a walk in the forest, seeing that he was fond of mushrooms or simply of taking a constitutional as they say, he apparently happened to be not far from the clearing at the moment when the family in question were finishing their picnic, the children were just about to disperse, little Jean-Claude ... this disquieting truck driver with disquieting tendencies towards drunkenness and you know what, anything is possible since the sex-maniac was never caught, he's still at large and that's where the tragedy begins because ten years later the child had become a young man and when he had finished his apprenticeship had gone off to Paris for reasons which his parents hadn't been able to understand and since then they had had no news, there was food for thought there.

So yes, while Mademoiselle Ariane's guests were at the back of manor house going into ecstasies about the beauty of the flower-beds Francine gave them the slip and went into the kitchen to interrogate Marie about you know whom, had she really seen young Pinson in an embarrassing situation to put it mildly, had he recognized her and above all who could the child with him have been, this to reassure the poor mother who had every reason to be upset but she swore to the servant that she wouldn't breathe a word in front of old Lorpailleur, whom do you take me for, this lamentable affair will go no further than us, always supposing of course that you were the only witness, are you certain that Madame Magnin didn't see anything, and Marie repeated that she was certain, her companion on the walk was a long way behind picking ferns, she had even hurt her fingers, their stalks cut like glass you know, good said Francine, good.

And so it went on for days on end, reminding you of such disturbing details for instance the heat of a Sunday in July coming out into the square after Mass, Mademoiselle Ariane taking off her silk coat and the truck passing at that moment with the words *Transports Pégin* written on its tarpaulin in big letters whereas it hadn't passed either at the same place or on the same day or in the same year but with so much art in her evocations, so much truth in her analyses, so much knowledge of our reactions and of the psycho psychi climate of our village over a period of many years, as if she had fashioned us after the manner of her little pupils, so that no one ten years later would have been capable of distinguishing the true from the false the reason being that everything was accurate only it was wrongly put together, a feeling that had never actually happened, I can still hear her in the visitors' room of the asylum that smelt of floor-polish, she was sitting by the window and occasionally turned her head towards the garden whose lawn was embellished by a clump of impatiens.

And so it went on for days on end, inventing details that were so untrue that they made you quite impatient as for instance Odette Magnin leaving home at eight o'clock and raising her head to greet Madame Maillard at her window, now Madame Maillard lived in a basement and had been dead ten years when Odette came back from the Argentine, and trying to get you to believe that at this moment old Lorpailleur's class was going by on the opposite pavement, out for a walk with their teacher, whereas given the position of the school in relation to the Malatraîne road it would never have occurred to anyone to take the children through the town, in short such lack of judgment, such ignorance of the places and facts as well as of the reactions of us bourgeois with our ingrained habits that it was impossible even ten years later not to be able to distinguish the true from the false and not to feel indignant at her insincerity, I can still hear her in the little sitting-room that smelt of mothballs, it overlooked the garden et cetera.

So that on the day in question . . .

As if the fact of being in the asylum excused *ipso facto* . . .

Good said Mademoiselle Ariane, good, I'll make a note of

it, hearing that Araignée didn't want to deal with the croquet lawn, Francine dared to confess to her aunt that the
gardener was tired of her unpredictability, she had called in
at the lodge on her way and found Madame Araignée in
tears, after thirty years of service her husband was refusing
to go on, but what's got into him she kept saying, what's got
into him, and when Francine insisted she finally told her
after a great deal of periphrasis that Mademoiselle well was
how could she put it, odd yes, what will become of us,
just imagine he's already made inquiries in the district, it
seemed there was a gamekeeper's job going at Chatruse but
she didn't want it at any price, it was weighing on his mind,
she didn't recognize him, whatever you do don't say anything
to Mademoiselle, whatever will she think, I'm so miserable,
so that Francine could think of nothing better to do than to
pass it on to her aunt straight from the horse's mouth, she
was irascible but not necessarily intimidating, to tell her
something straight out was much better than beating about
the bush and in fact Mademoiselle Ariane was not annoyed,
she would know how to deal with it don't you worry, just
flatter the imbecile a little, ah yes apropos of the impatiens
for instance, that would be enough to calm him down, and
as for the croquet lawn well we'll talk about that next year,
what do we want with a croquet lawn, it's true that I'm odd,
all this before the guests arrived of course, it must have been
twenty-five past eleven, Marie had lost her head and put the
soufflé in the oven as if it were midday, which explains why
she had to make another one half an hour later, as for
Minouche she was preparing . . .

Or if the soufflé had already been in the oven since eleven
o'clock as Marie had thought it was midday, it would all
depend on the time when she was supposed to ring the bell
that day, time is so precious at Bonne-Mesure, which would
mean that Mademoiselle Ariane knew that the curé hadn't

got to take his catechism class, they could lunch at the usual hour at half-past twelve that is and not at twelve as on every first Saturday in the month, all this is very tricky.

Well yes write it down, write it down, on the day in question Mortin was outside the chemist's, what time could that have been, eight o'clock something of the sort, he had got up earlier than usual, don't interrupt me, and when he got to the chemist's he was amazed that Verveine had not yet raised his corrugated metal shutter that you push up with a hooked stick and pull down in the same way in the evenings, on the other hand the baker's opposite was open and he could see the baker's wife behind her counter with her knitting seeing how little rush there was at this hour, she was finishing a little garment for her child who was still in baby clothes and how, little William or Guillaume who was born well after the tragedy in question, about ten years, the poor creatures didn't want any more children you can understand them and then one fine evening instinct got the upper hand again to such good effect that the bun was in the oven and nothing could get it out again, they hang on to life these little things, he went to term all right this kid, a big boy they called William or Guillaume as I said, the christening was a fort-night later, what's more Mademoiselle Lorpailleur was the godmother, those were the days when she was on visiting terms with the Ducreuxs but later when the child went to school it was different, the baker's wife was one of the most virulently against the schoolmistress, she wanted to sign petitions, things of that sort, it needed all the diplomacy of our parish clerk to dissuade her, in fact who was he, Magnin quite so, such a distinguished man, he got on well with Ducreux, they used to go hunting together all through the autumn, don't you remember, it's a long time ago all that, people went hunting and shooting, and before that boating on the river, how young we were, in short all the clichés you can think of on the subject.

Was amazed then that Verveine wasn't down, it must have been at least half-past eight by now, when suddenly Madame Moineau went into the baker's followed a few seconds later by Loulette Passepied who had only arrived back the day before from the colonies or was it from a protectorate, in short a genuine event, people hardly ever travelled in those days, one fine July morning, the swallows are singing themselves hoarse round the church tower, the street is coming to life, the women are sweeping the pavement outside their front doors, the men are on their way to the fields or the factory, don't interrupt me, and then here's Mortin scratching his head and wondering whether his eyes aren't deceiving him, he has suddenly found himself taken back in imagination, but so irresistibly, so forcibly, to ten years previously when people were grieving over the tragedy in question, that poor child who had fallen in the river and whom they had tried to revive on the bank with the firemen, so on and so forth, I can still see them . . .

Or that ten years before at the same time Mortin had happened to be outside the chemist's just as the child was coming out of his parents' yard all by himself and had wondered why the mother wasn't keeping an eye on him but not being responsible either for the education of parents or the safety of children apparently and that's where the tragedy begins decided to mind his own business, in any case it seems he only saw him for a few seconds just before the bend in the rue Neuve and then didn't give him another thought until late that evening when the whole village was wondering in anguish who could have done it, but no one strange to say had seen the child go out except Mortin that is who reputedly only admitted to it ten years later to his intimate friends and is supposed to have

197

excused himself in his own eyes by the fact that at that hour of the morning he had other fish to fry as they say, that was the whole point, why had he got up early, but even so and even ten years later he still felt a sort of remorse, it would only have taken him three minutes to run after the child and restore him to his mother.

It was the year of the Mission, the Father had just appeared in the parish, everyone thought him so distinguished except perhaps Mademoiselle Ariane who detected in him an air of how could she describe it, would it be affectation, would it be haughtiness, in short an ambiguous air, what they call a funny look, which she repeated to her niece who didn't agree with her but didn't contradict her, it was of such minimal importance in comparison with the interest that the preacher had immediately shown in the children, the good Lord's own creatures, little allotments in which the good seed must be sown, a magnificent sermon on the future of humanity which depend on each and every one of us, we were all responsible et cetera, and he took the trouble, he cut short his private prayer time to take the trouble to go for walks in the village and approach the young people with so much kindness, getting their confidence, talking to them about their studies, about their parents and about charity, which he called fraternity so as to remain within their comprehension, encouraging them to join the youth club, to organize themselves, to help each other, all that sort of thing, which we thought so intelligent in an ecclesiastic, he's a man who is really with it, he's a saint, a whatever you liked to call him.

And ten years later Mortin was apparently wondering whether he hadn't seen the Father coming out of the church after the first Mass and walking with that spiritual air of his in the rue Neuve, greeting the ladies, asking after their children, joining in the games which the little ones were starting to play in the backyards in such beautiful July weather in the good Lord's sun, playing leap-frog why not, he was so down to earth, yes Mortin was apparently wondering ten years later whether he hadn't caught himself thinking at the time that the ecclesiastic however devoted to children he might be was maybe laying it on a bit too thickly, but being suspicious of himself as well and of his old-fashioned behavior it seems that he finally persuaded himself that the priest had moved with the times and that he was right, youth must come first.

Or that when Mademoiselle Moignon, it was Moignon wasn't it, as she was going out apparently saw Mortin on the watch outside the chemist's, why on the watch, because how could she put it, because he was staring in the direction of the rue Neuve, she apparently wondered what was going on and was so intrigued that she too hung around until Mortin disappeared round the bend in the rue de Broy, what was he watching for, but she was too far away to follow him and went into the baker's and said to Madame Ducreux Monsieur Mortin has a funny look about him, I've just seen him disappearing in the direction of the rue Ancienne, he looked as if he was tailing someone as they say, it was a Sunday yes, the street was still deserted, our people get up late that day, to which the baker's wife apparently replied you'll certainly never change and laughed as she put the money for a well-baked French loaf in the till, I don't mind if you give me a burnt one even, it's so much better for the stomach, because Mademoiselle Moignon had an ulcer or something of the sort.

But Judge Paillard to set his mind at rest was looking up an old file and found that a certain Vernes or Vernet had in fact been convicted ten years previously for a disgusting moral offence, he called his wife and said that's it all right, an indecent assault on a child, still according to Machette who was their maid at the time and who was a great one for

199

keeping her eyes and ears open, but Madame Maillard apparently said what on earth are you talking about, nothing to do with the child who was drowned, in any case the Vernes or Vernet fellow left the district after he had served his sentence, don't you remember we heard about him from who was it now who had come back from the Argentine or wherever, but the judge wasn't convinced, it looked as if it was exactly the same thing, this was the sort of offense that people were only too likely to repeat, and went on thumbing through the file and taking notes, he had made up his mind to inform the powers that be of his suspicions, one thing was in his favor though, which excused his lack of memory I mean, and that was that the affair had either not come under his jurisdiction or had been heard before his nomination.

Because at the passport photo place just opposite the law-courts when the Vernet fellow, a postal worker, called there one morning there were quite a few people either waiting for the machine to go gling gling or for their series to come up, more precisely they first of all paid three francs fifty and waited their turn to be invited to sit in the armchair by a lady in a white overall like they wear in hospitals, take off your overcoat and sit down, they parked it one after the other, look over here, bring your knees over to this side, don't blink, hold it, gling gling six times running, that's all, next please, then waited for their series to come up ready developed out of the crooked hole, who's this one now, another lady in white scooped up the photos and glanced at the distressed clients, it's you, she cut the strip up and put the individual photos into a little bag which the accused with an apologetic smile took and carried outside with him where he looked at his face which the inexpensive processing had completely mangled but the poor have no alternative, so yes, Vernet was one of them and was staring at them, people may well have wondered whether there wasn't something at the back of his mind, whether he wasn't trying to find some resemblance, and when it was his turn to sit in the chair it seems he wanted to keep his coat on and turn his collar up, to make himself look somewhat less ghastly then the other faces he'd glimpsed on paper but the lady told him no take it off, so he sat down and started smiling at the birdie with the same idea in mind but the lady again said no, no passport smiles, gling gling, and when he went out with his packet he saw it, there he was for all posterity with his eternal convict's face, he went to have a drink at the Swan and Cyrille the barman apparently said to him ...

And Cyrille apparently said to the roadman I wonder why Vernet had a passport photo taken, there's something fishy there, referring to what he had seen in the paper the day before, the police the law, so on and so forth, don't you think he looks a bit off, he looks at you as if you'd just sold him a peck of rotten apples and his way of speaking to you as if as if ...

But someone in the forest as night was falling, was it a man or a woman you couldn't tell, was walking round and round a beech tree looking for something it seemed, feeling the ground then suddenly ...

Or that when Serinet was murdered they apparently found in the wood a child's woolly which obviously didn't belong to the dead man, the widow had confirmed this at the inquiry, the examining magistrate was extremely worried, as if the crime had grafted another one on to itself, now at the time there had been no question of any child disappearing or being drowned or strangled, a thing Mortin was to remember ten years later when we had already forgotten three quarters of the affair, yes actually that little red woolly, what had they decided about it, and he made up his mind to ask Paillard to have another look at the file to set his mind at rest.

And the shadow, it was a shadow now, insinuated itself

among the trees, crossed the clearing, went along the sunken path that leads to the road at the top and disappeared round the bend behind the wall of that tumble-down house what was it called now which when we were children had caused us as well as the old people so much distress, it gave you goose flesh as if the whole unsolved question became mysterious but that very fact or on the contrary with the passing of the years just a simple news item that you find in an old paper, who was it though, that name rings a bell, such were Mortin's thoughts, don't interrupt me, what he might have thought, you never know.

When all of a sudden the roadman apparently saw it running on to the road just where the sunken path comes out and disappearing behind the tumble-down house, was it a man or a woman you couldn't tell, someone young in any case to be able to run so fast, the doubt about the person's sex came from the fact that that very afternoon he had passed Machette and her girl friend both wearing trousers going towards Malatraîne, very amusing it had been at the time talking about it to the roadman, he saw the devil in this present-day sartorial confusion, now talking about Machette it's my considered opinion that he knew a great deal more about her than he was letting on as he had been observing her closely since she came back from her travels and nobody could hold that against him when she was putting on such a free and easy not to say extravagant act, he apparently knew that practically every day in the July of the year in question she went to the old house in Malatraîne that had belonged to her mother's family and from which you could see the vicinity of the refreshment bar and consequently of the miraculous statue.

Was apparently told by the girl friend in question that on the day of the school outing, not the Easter one, the July one, it wasn't old Lorpailleur who was in charge of the children, she had got two pupil-teachers to take her place, girls whom neither Machette nor her girl friend knew, they had even wondered where on earth the mistress could have dug them up, from the town probably, but they apparently didn't know, I'm referring to the roadman and the two girls, why the schoolmistress had got them to take her place, so that everything that the ladies or goodness knows who had thought up had been a fabrication, it was quite certain that there was nothing definite to be discovered about what happened that day and God knows whether . . .

It was quite certain that there was nothing definite to be discovered about what happened that day unless they interrogated all sorts of other people, ah yes what about the people who kept the refreshment bar, always supposing of course that what the girl friend had said hadn't also been a fabrication, what sort of a hornets' nest good God.

Or that the refreshment bar people had in fact been interrogated and had answered that yes the schoolmistress had indeed been there with the children but that she had suddenly had to leave them as she had telephoned her mother who was not well, she had entrusted the little group to Louisette who had accompanied her and who would be responsible for the return journey, doubly apprehensive, then, I'm referring to old Lorpailleur, she kept on giving the young pupil-teacher hundreds of instructions before finally catching the four o'clock bus, they remembered that, and the same evening the old mother died, during the night that is, after which Louisette was apparently responsible for the class for a week, the time for the funeral and the formalities, with the aid of a second pupil-teacher, and that this was presumably where the confusion came from, the two girls seen a second time with the children because it seems that the refreshment bar people had been categorical, Louisette on the day in question had been the only one to see the children home.

The shadow in the forest, an unidentified shadow, the

voice that came from no one knows where and which was equally unidentified, a sort of feeling of distress or shall we say uneasiness which is supposed to have gained ground, the confusion of the rumors, the hearsay, the theories and all those years in the way, the details which were quite irrelevant to the facts but which seemed to arise out of people's sick consciences and probably had something to do with some other facts and were brought in to prove the point, which falsified one's recollections . . .

Don't interrupt me.

Write it down.

It'll all come out in the end.

For Mademoiselle Ariane's dinner on that famous Saturday Marie apparently suggested to her mistress that they should have the meal out of doors, such lovely weather, it wouldn't be the first time that they had had a meal under the big plane tree and the table looked so beautiful in the evening with its two polished paraffin lamps, they gave out a light that was almost tender, it was better than candlelight, candles could always blow out and if they didn't then they were continually flickering, which is unpleasant, the lady of the manor apparently agreed, that would be delightful but don't forget to put the rug from the small drawing-room by my chair, there's a draught sometimes even though it never seems to bother anyone but me, no one has ever complained about it, thus admitting that she was getting old, because she had been as strong as a horse all her life, and Marie's suggestion might be thought surprising as domestics don't usually like serving meals out of doors in view of the distances to be covered between the table and the kitchen but it must be said that at Bonne-Mesure from the large dining-room to the kitchen stove the distance was even greater and there were three doors not to say four to open, which made the service complicated and which explained why when she was on her own Mademoiselle Ariane had her meals served in the small drawing-room, and she knew that Francine adored dining out of doors, she was so fond of her niece, too bad if it didn't suit old Lorpailleur, as for the curé he wouldn't say a word, so long as his plate was full he was content.

Old Lorpailleur arrives, she apparently got off her machine the other side of the main gate which had been left open in honor of the guests as Araignée shut it at seven o'clock winter and summer alike, pushed her machine and leant it against the wall of the lodge, Madame Araignée who was at that moment in the kitchen-garden saw her and gave her permission to do so, old Lorpailleur wanting to be friendly stayed and had a little chat with her, just a few minutes, it wasn't ten to eight yet, somewhere in that region, the question of the lodge-keepers' little boy came up automatically seeing that she was his teacher but she didn't want to dwell on the subject because you couldn't hope to find anyone more narrow-minded than his parents and she made up her mind to open her heart to Mademoiselle de Bonne-Mesure about him unless there is some confusion here with the child of the Broy farmer and his wife, in short just a few minutes, then apparently started to walk up the drive admiring the century-old beeches bordering it, hat with its crêpe, black dress, black gloves, black woolly over her arm just in case, tarted up like nobody's business in this heat after being in mourning for ten years, it's enough to disgust you with both the quick and the dead, then on her right apparently noticed a cat sneaking into the rhododendrons which cat was none other than Mouchette, looked at her watch and seemed to be calculating that she would arrive at precisely eight o'clock at the terrace where from afar she could see Mademoiselle Ariane sitting on her wicker chair, apparently she very graciously gave her a little wave when she was some fifty yards away, how do you how do you do, a familiar gesture which was the last thing old Lorpailleur expected seeing that she had maybe spoken to the lady of the manor four times in her whole life, what was Mademoiselle Ariane expecting to get out of this invitation, but the honor was so great that the schoolmistress decided to overlook this shadow if indeed it was one and was only thinking of how she would boast about it to the ladies, if indeed again.

To cut a long story short she arrives at the terrace and goes up to Mademoiselle Ariane who is waiting for her under the big plane tree or rather who gets up or has already got up to come and meet her in spite of her age, she's so well-bred, aping a genuine familiarity which has the further advantage of dispensing one from subsequent ceremonies in other words expenses, Marie had been told to produce a very simple dinner, a question of adjusting one's style, she's looking out for the schoolmistress from the terrace and as soon as she catches sight of her at the bottom of the drive she goes into action and meets her just on the far side of the rhododendron clump from the manor, so that when Mouchette takes refuge there and old Lorpailleur jumps Mademoiselle Ariane carries on quite naturally with a question that breaks the ice, have you a cat, they're such affectionate creatures, and takes the schoolmistress's arm, no need for any ceremony between us, old Lorpailleur couldn't be more flattered.

In short she gets up to the terrace and goes over to Mademoiselle Ariane who has just come out of the drawing-room as if by chance, they meet under the big plane tree and sit down without any ceremony, how is your mother, tell me about your sister but first of all isn't it a beautiful evening, you have no objection to dining out of doors I imagine, such lovely weather shall we wait for Monsieur the curé for the port, what do you think, still exquisitely gracious and flattering old Lorpailleur who can only reply by all means let us wait for him, because port is expensive, so they sit down at a little table on which Marie has put four glasses and the decanter not far from the big one which is already laid, Monsieur the curé is so fond of it she adds, I'm referring to the hostess, it would really not be quite the thing, little laugh, for ladies on their own, in short she simpers exquisitely and puts all the blame on her servant who really worships there's no other word for it her pastor, so that the schoolmistress is pretty well forced to pretend that she never indulges, I'm referring to the port, and the lady of the manor is then able to conclude exquisitely but you will take just a finger just to please me but here is Monsieur the curé I believe, they both turn round and in fact the curé is limping on to the terrace, Mademoiselle Ariane gets up and takes a few steps in his direction, well Abbé what do you think of this beautiful evening . . .

But as the curé arrived on the arm of Mademoiselle the niece Mademoiselle the aunt didn't have to get up to welcome him, the ecclesiastic mumbles a few polite words and apologizes for arriving so late but Providence had caused him to meet Mademoiselle Francine at the gate and this act of grace was well worth the . . . the . . . sit down Abbé you will certainly take a finger of port, it was at this point that Francine apparently asked her aunt to excuse her for a second, she needed to change her little skirt or her little blouse or her little God knows what, she didn't go into detail but simply asked permission to go up to Mademoiselle Ariane's room, and then the rest of it.

Immersed in something else, don't write that down, the tragedy is brewing elsewhere, how to effect the transition, the question was put right at the beginning, answer it only gradually and imperceptibly.

You will certainly take a finger of port, Mademoiselle Francine pours it out and they sip the nectar that Mademoiselle Ariane says she had from her brother some ten years ago when he used to cultivate his vineyards, he used to exchange part of his wine for spirits he did it through that firm what was it called do you remember darling, Francine doesn't remember, it's such a pity that his widow, her sister-in-law that is, has rather neglected the cultivation of her land, she is going to stay with her the following week, which explains why it was impossible for her to be at home to Monsieur the curé as usual next Saturday which is in fact the first of the month when suddenly Mouchette in the flower-bed ... when suddenly Francine ...

But that Marie at her post at the corner of the terrace was apparently not in the least upset when Mademoiselle Francine didn't pop into the kitchen to see her as usual and that therefore she wasn't at all bothered about the possibility of Colette going to see Madame Idoménée, the cook did apparently manage to join the niece in the aunt's room, in short that the greatest calm was apparent that evening in people's hearts as well as in Nature, exquisite well-being, the sun is setting, it has been a hot day, the prospect of dinner in the shade of the trees revives everyone, affection, pleasant chatter, it must have been nine o'clock, in fact Marie gets up and rings the bell, the ladies and gentlemen sit down to table, the conversation quite naturally starts off with the subject of the Auguste Serinet affair, the poor man was found dead in the wood, old Lorpailleur says she was recently talking to the widow a woman who has always been highly-strung, impressionable and odd, and now she's taken it into her head that her brother-in-law might well be not altogether unconnected with this misfortune, he was always jealous even though nothing about the corpse could have given rise to the slightest suspicion, it was a natural death, she maintains that some strong emotion could well have been the cause of death, her husband had a bad heart, to which she replied, I'm referring to the school teacher, that a man of his age, barely thirty, no percentage of disablement for social insurance or whatever purposes, couldn't have reacted in that way either to fear or to any sort of threat just consider, that sort of accident is unforeseeable, what did Mademoiselle Ariane think, they had got to the cheese souf-flé, she replied that she wasn't a doctor, that if the doctor had decided that it was a natural death there was no reason to question his decision, one could only pity the woman, sorrow sometimes takes on unexpected aspects but she is young, it will all pass, she will marry again, I have been told that young Magnin, do have some more Abbé, no ceremony here, she herself put some more soufflé in the plate of the old glutton who wagged his index finger at her coyly, you'll never change, what are you doing about the sin of gluttony, the good Lord et cetera.

Or that they knew next to nothing about young Pinson except that he was very reserved with the ladies, that his behavior had never given rise to any gossip and that the good people really wondered why he had not taken Holy Orders, he could only be attracted by higher things, there weren't a hundred and one different sorts of men, he must be unhappy to have got on the wrong track like that, they did say that his anticlerical background must have put a spoke in the wheel at the age when a vocation is normally determined, and what would become of him in his old age all by himself such an affectionate person without a good wife to mend his socks and wash his underwear and cook for him, he was much to be pitied, that sort of thing.

But Mortin in his bedroom was wondering how the trag-edy in question which was a good ten years old could have cropped up again out of the blue, the suspicions of a deranged woman who saw a connection between a news item and the misfortune of that poor widow who would be neither the first nor the last . . .

Or wondered whether the tragedy didn't have something to do with what he knew of certain far from laudable practices but which were after all excusable, you see what I mean, and which could have created this wild panic in our midst which . . .

Such a lovely night . . .

A July night over our little gardens, the moon illuminating a bare wall or a couple dreaming on a bench or a form creeping about under a tree or even . . . but everything looks so strange in this half-light, one must pull oneself together, one must be reasonable, Mortin at his window would be thinking of something like his life, failure along the line, death gaining ground, friendships forfeited, the image he had had of himself and which had gone up in smoke, in short all the clichés you can think of . . .

He had known young Pinson well, yes, but so many years before, death had passed that way too, why all this torment on such a beautiful night, as if his whole life had shrunk to the proportions of a single day, hardly possible to sleep any more, every thought, every movement represents the sum total of those that came before, a hell to relive hour after hour, freshness faded since . . . since . . . impossible to calculate.

Or that Mortin, remembering young Pinson who had disappeared so long before, the gay parties at Broy, a few years of living it up and thumbing your nose at the populace, that they had been young, yes, that was it, a flash in the pan, but how much dust and ashes later, since . . . since . . .

Impossible to calculate.

Write it down.

But Mortin drafting this news item.

Write it down.

Hopping, skipping, and jumping.

The shadow in the forest coming closer and closer, now only eight yards, the child was picking raspberries, or else his little fishing rod made out of a reed and a bit of thread that his mother ... now only five yards, now only three and whoosh the fish bites, the shadow makes off, the child has disappeared, all this in the space of a few seconds, life only hangs by a thread there's no other word for it.

They were drinking their port, then, and old Lorpailleur was recalling the delightful afternoon at the guest house, those charming children had given a concert Mademoiselle Loeillère's pupils that is which began with a poetic evocation or what do they call it, a pilgrimage that's right, poetical pilgrimage, followed by a sentimental pilgrimage or vice versa, with recitations, dances and musical interludes by that eminent pianist their professor, all the same it was encouraging to observe that culture still holds a place of honor in our midst, poetry and all that, which indicated on the part of the populace, for the mothers and some of the fathers were in the audience apart from the guests who have so few amusements, a breadth of mind, an interest in the things of the spirit which was far from auguring ill of the future, when one thinks of the present-day level of the people those for instance who listen to the radio or watch television not to speak of the total mediocrity and almost indecency excuse the expression of the programs and also of young people's alienation from the humanities, yes certainly our little community has merit but she didn't say, I'm referring to the schoolmistress because she didn't yet know it, that it was probably during the concert that the child had taken advantage of the absence of his parents who were at the guest house with his sister to go over to Malatraîne where he must have met ... for he did not in fact go home to his parents that evening but objectively it had to be admitted that the boy, after all he was fourteen, was no longer a child and that he had probably already ... which came to the same thing as to say that he had that particular vice in his blood and that he would have come to it sooner or later so the harm wasn't as great as people would have them believe.

In short ding ding it's nine o'clock the sun's setting but the light is still admirable, the ladies and gentlemen sit down to table when all of a sudden Mouchette who was under old Lorpailleur's chair leaps into the hydrangeas, the school teacher shrieks and Mademoiselle de Bonne-Mesure bubbling over with laughter ... or was it Francine as the mistress's expression was so irresistible ... starts explaining ... or that she had leapt from the hydrangeas into the rhododendrons and terrified old Lorpailleur and that Francine et cetera, the aunt's remark about Nature ...

The soufflé.

The gibelotte or something of the sort.

But Mademoiselle Ariane was so impatient when nothing and no one had arrived at half-past eight that she called Marie who was not yet at her post at the corner of the terrace, she was putting the finishing touches to you know what, and asked her whether Francine had given her to understand that she would be late she who was always so punctual, to which Marie apparently replied that she had no idea meaning that no one had told her anything but that Mademoiselle should be patient, her watch is half an hour fast, it's only eight o'clock, by the way would Mademoiselle like me to make some toast for the cold consommé, it's so good, to which Mademoiselle replied yes and serve it in the Wedgwood bowl, my goodness I am impatient because she was, I had something important to say to Francine before the guests arrive, by the way do you know or don't you know whether the schoolmistress has had wind of the Poussinet

212

affair, it is Poussinet isn't it, personally I should be amazed if your accomplice, that was how she referred to old mother Idoménéé with whom Marie used to gossip in her spare time or was it Lorette but that's of no importance, very much amazed if she has held her tongue but Marie with her innocent air she's so cunning answered no meaning that she had no idea, Mademoiselle must excuse me but I haven't spoken to her since yesterday morning, with all this extra cleaning I've been doing my fatigue has come back, my legs as you might say feel sick, I can hardly stand upright, for since the butler had left or something of the sort she had been trying in every possible way to persuade her mistress to employ the gardener's wife or was it Lorette for a month, now Mademoiselle Ariane refused as she foresaw the endless complications that that would cause in view of the indiscretion of the woman whichever one it might be, all right said she all right, you go back to your stoves to put it mildly and she went back to her embroidery not without continually raising her head in the direction of the drive, she was so impatient . . .

And when Mortin after the delightful concert asked Madame Apollonios to tell him why she had made such a fuss about her seat or was it the other one that's of no importance, she replied that it was always the same thing at every delightful concert, couldn't they once and for all allocate her own place to each lady, for herself she would choose the third from the left in the front row because of the little reflecting mirror that Monsieur Edouard had put up which got in her eyes and one thing leading to another started talking once again about the marriage or whatever, our little Nenette she's so affectionate, to which Mortin either replied evasively or didn't reply at all.

All right she said go back to your muttons and was going back to her own when suddenly Francine appeared in the drive

on Idoménéé's arm, she had just been overcome by a fit of
giddiness or something of the sort, Mademoiselle Ariane leapt
out of her chair and went to help her niece who said it's
nothing, may I go up to your room for a bit just to pull myself
together before you know who arrives, which was why Mademoiselle her aunt completely forgot what she had wanted to say
to her and the rest of the evening was spoilt to put it mildly by
this unfortunate omission ... then the arrival of old Lorpailleur and the curé and the port under the plane tree which in
the setting sun had taken on a pinkish hue up above and a
bluish one down below, you see what I mean.

Now during this time Francine was reading from beginning
to end the letter she had found on her aunt's dressing-table
which was none other than a detailed account of the delightful
concert written by Mortin who knowing that old Lorpailleur
was to be at the manor that evening and having more than one
reason to believe that she was aware of the relations that once
existed between Professor Duchemin and Mademoiselle Loeillère ... between Magnin and Lorette which were recalled by
one of the ladies who very innocently pointed out that Nenette
bore a striking resemblance to the builder, it hadn't fallen on
deaf ears, people had smiled or blushed whichever was appropriate, the poor wife Madame Magnin that is apparently
left straight after the concert, and this all the more seeing that
the week before a rumor had been going the rounds about
Magnin's excursions over Malatraîne way round about nightfall, the poor chap had been laying snares on his brother-in-
law's land, you see the kind of ill-natured gossip at a time when
over-heated imaginations ... that the builder then was interested in young people of all sexes and from there to seeing a
connection ... or that the bogus Legion of Honor and former
admirer of our poetess was a nasty piece of work who was
blackmailing her, the poor old girl was obliged to turn over to
him the whole of her takings from the concert under penalty of

being unmasked I mean about the authenticity of her signature for the old paralytic was in fact the authoress of the poems in question and therefore the only one responsible for the libretto but that Mademoiselle Loeillère's claims could after all be considered to have some foundation because she was the one responsible for the production and for the presentation of the whole ensemble, a work which took up all her time during the whole year, and that over and above that the disabled woman had given her permission according to Loulette or at least was quite devoid of any pride of authorship and had not the slightest need of the takings to live on as she had entered into an agreement with the people who had bought her little house which brought her in an annuity or something of the sort, in short what people thought was a contribution to the very modest resources of our poetess what you might call the butter on her parsnips was in fact what's it called now a pledge or goodness knows what, let's say tribute-money paid to that vile beer-swiller so as to shut his face I mean stop him talking, so that people might well have wondered why Mademoiselle Loeillère went to so much trouble, she might just as well have lain low and not given any concerts but they would have been wrong because an old artist, unless she's already in her second childhood or even if she is, still has a compulsion to appear in public, it's the mystery of creativity, of psycho psychi equilibrium, in short this is something to do with the primary sources of . . . in short that's how it is and it's extremely touching to put it mildly.

A letter which was none other than a faithful account by Latirail of the council meeting in which they discussed the demolition of number twelve, a thing which was of prime importance to Mademoiselle de Bonne-Mesure who had to find out by fair means or foul whether old Lorpailleur had by goodness knows what machinations in some way or other incited Monsieur Monnard to raise the question with the gentlemen as

215

she had always refused, I'm referring to Mademoiselle Ariane, to allow that building to be pulled down as it had belonged to her grandfather or as near as makes no difference but she alas had no say in the matter any more as she had sold it to the parish that was it, so it was simply a question of principle for she was a great stickler for principles and she wanted to know whether yes or no old Lorpailleur was responsible for what she called an act of treachery, for she didn't mince her words any more than she did her ... in short she was furious, which explains or could explain her faintly unforthcoming attitude when old Lorpailleur arrived not getting up out of her chair contrary to what Loulette had reported, in any case she had every right not to in view of her age and status, and calling Marie in the presence of the schoolmistress to ask her whether Madame Idoménéé had told her about you know what, in actual fact to give herself time to adopt a suitable attitude towards her visitor, it was tricky, her imagination may well have put her on the wrong track or goodness knows what tittle-tattle about the integrity of the mistress on whose behalf Loulette produced some very simple though cogent arguments so it seems, the cause of her having become so unpopular being her crusty and unsociable nature, a manner which in her opinion was less suspect than the opposite that's to say a bonhomie which however natural it may appear nevertheless conceals every kind of compromise, calculation, atrocity et cetera, and she cited as an example old mother Tripeau who had made her fortune out of the local people who go on patronizing her shop even though they are well aware, it's very odd, very instructive, that the business of giving sweets to the schoolchildren or whatever conceals a profit motive that neither Madame Moignon nor Mademoiselle ... in other words that it was only the fact of her unsociability that laid her open to suspicion, gossip and hate, whereas in fact it was if not the only at least a considerable guarantee of integrity, which between ourselves didn't necessarily mean that old Lorpailleur . . .

Which was none other than a faithful account by the Lorpailleur sister, her name is Edmée isn't it, of the relations between Monnard and the schoolmistress and which caused Mademoiselle Francine to work herself up into the sort of state you can imagine, what, that bitch with her holier-than-thou airs and her mourning crêpe, she slept with excuse the expression our parish clerk and that half-wit . . . it was enough to send you off your head, such a distinguished man, her eyes were bulging out of hers, I'm referring to her head, Francine's, and yet the report couldn't have been circumstantial, it had started soon after the death of old Lorpailleur's mother, Monnard coveted a piece of ground that the girls had inherited and hadn't been able to think of any better way to get in their good books than to take them on one after the other starting with Edmée the less repulsive one who had turned him down and then tackling the schoolmistress who was only too delighted, which was the reason why the former out of jealousy revealed this sordid liaison to Mademoiselle Ariane who as she well knew was not entirely disinterested in the piece of ground in question given its proximity to the Grance ponds and for certain other reasons which would take too long to explain, in short it revealed that the operation after many vicissitudes, wrangles and so on was on the point of coming to a conclusion advantageous to Monnard, which explains why Francine took her time in her aunt's bedroom, she was trying to think of some way of inducing the schoolmistress into some sort of confession and wondering why Mademoiselle Ariane hadn't told her, the thing was that she had arrived so late that the lady of the manor hadn't had time and . . . or if Marie had intercepted the letter and only just now put it on the dressing-table . . . in short the niece had to find an excuse then and there to speak to her aunt alone and found it . . .

217

Or if this revelation about the relations that existed between Monnard and Francine had come about through Mademoiselle Ariane meeting the Lorpailleur sister the very same day as the incident of the altar-cruet, they had bumped elbows while they were taking the holy water you know where, they were coming out of church, that's apparently how they made each other's acquaintance ... more likely an anonymous letter whose source Francine could well imagine given her rivalry with Edmée who had been jilted, just imagine the perfidy, was the schoolmistress in league with her sister, but on the other hand how was it possible to assume that the aunt had been fully informed about her misconduct and was even so capable of concealing that fact to her niece by kissing her affectionately on her arrival, this ran contrary to everything Francine knew about Mademoiselle Ariane, her rectitude, her sense of honor, so on and so forth, in short she found the excuse she had been looking for, went down to the kitchen again and asked Marie ...

Because as she hadn't recognized the writing on the envelope as that of any of her mistress's usual correspondents and given what she had been told that morning by Madame Idoménée she apparently thought that it was an anonymous letter, which implied that she had opened it ... or if Marie was in league with Sintier the postmaster who used to commit certain indiscretions with the aid of a kettle I mean who used to steam envelopes open and had therefore known before the letter was delivered what was in this piece of filth ... in short in her zeal to distinguish the true from the false she was becoming tiresome and Francine upbraided her for this before going to join the guests, her imagination was playing tricks with her, she ought to know that Mademoiselle Ariane was above the village tittle-tattle and that it would never make her act any differently, she would take it upon herself to tell her aunt, she asked Marie to ring the bell and then went back to the terrace.

218

But old Lorpailleur who was not unaware of Francine's liaison with Monnard was promising herself that this interview would be a great treat, furthermore she thought she knew that Lolotte that very morning had informed Madame Idoménée of the rumors that had been going about since the previous week which the lodge-keeper's wife had certainly repeated to Marie who couldn't have prevented herself passing them straight on to Mademoiselle Francine that very minute, she had in fact just noticed, I'm referring to the schoolmistress, the niece coming out of the rhododendron walk and going towards the servants' quarters in other words the kitchen, just so long as that is of course old mother Idoménée hadn't told her all about it the moment she came in through the gate, but that was really not very likely as the relations between masters and servants were not such as to encourage expansiveness, Marie however was the exception that proved the rule, she had known Francine since she was so high she had been her nanny or something of the sort, which meant that the teacher when she saw Francine coming up beaming all over her face apparently started to sing a different tune, Lolotte couldn't have said anything to the lodge-keeper's wife and Marie still didn't know anything about the rumors that were going about.

You won't say no to a finger of port, Francine was addressing old Lorpailleur having herself been to fetch the decanter and glasses which were not yet on the table contrary to what you know who asserted, but that's of no importance, just a finger replied the schoolmistress, by the way did you know that Madame Moignon was so rash this morning as to start moving her husband's truck, she only has an ordinary license, not one for a heavy goods vehicle, and she ran straight into wasn't that stupid the little wall that the doctor has just had built under Mademoiselle Mottard's windows, was it clumsiness or perfidy, for Francine in her car the previous week had nearly run into a child coming out of school and there was a rumor abroad that she frequented somewhat too assiduously the Tanner's bar, a worthy emulator in this respect of her aunt who didn't turn her nose up at the juice of the grape nor at having dealings with the populace not to mention any others than those that were abroad at the time, I'm referring to the rumors, for instance shortly after Francine was born, she was reputed to have been the daughter neither of her father nor of her mother but of her aunt and Magnin and then to have been adopted by her parents who were sterile or something of the sort in spite of the waters of Lourdes, so on and so forth, who in so doing killed two birds with one stone, an heir and saving a reputation about which the accused, I'm referring to Mademoiselle Ariane, couldn't have cared less at the time i.e. shortly after Francine was born ...

Or that Mortin at his window ...

Or that death had anticipated all the gossip and suddenly they had all become silent beneath the plane tree, nothing and nobody any more ...

They wondered, apparently, why this sudden silence, was it normal, and this stiffening and this ... yes, that was it all right, it had crept in unobserved, it had got hold of Mademoiselle Ariane and then Francine and then the two commoners with their noses in their glasses and now it was spreading out beneath the plane tree, decay would not be far behind, as regards this beautiful July evening ... in short no one quite understood how it came about that these four people or to mention only one of them Mademoiselle Ariane should have collapsed, I can still see her slumping down in her armchair with staring eyes, her arm hanging by her side, Francine can only weep and the curé mumbles a modest prayer ...

This sudden silence, this estrangement, how to describe it, absence ... but they had to pull themselves together, make

220

the effort which would definitely not cost them any more than to keep silent for ever and ever, saying, I'm referring to Lolotte or who was it now, that people were making much more of this business than was reasonable, it was surely a very ordinary occurrence, why make such a fuss, why be so shocked, people only had to think on the one hand about what was happening elsewhere ... everyone certainly had some relation, some acquaintance ... and on the other hand about themselves, she went so far as that, something along the lines of treachery oh not that it was so very serious but that with time it had got more entrenched, had become impossible to swallow and made us as sick as a dog the moment ...

So that she had almost got to the point when she could make the dead take up their beds and walk, make them sit down at a table beneath the plane tree and stiff as they were converse in the candlelight, hardly opening their mouths, barely touching the food, they took on a kind of majesty, they suddenly increased in stature, out of all proportion, they came up to the lowest branches and their fixed smiles beneath the unguents reflected goodness knows what evidence ... or deficiency ... a void, but an agonizing void this time, like a solemn echo of their condition when they were alive.

And that people might have wondered what Mortin was up to at that moment in his room, he knew about the relations between ... knew about the affair and having solemnly announced to his guests that he had started to reconstruct the tragedy, maybe he was writing something about it how could anyone know, a minor detail without any connection but which had made an impression on him as they say, a doubt or a deficiency, could it be out of affection, he was so secretive, he practically never confided in anyone, messing about with his papers in his room, then, disconnected elements of what might have been ... how could anyone know and so involved in it all that an impartial reader would have got nowhere, scraps of conversation mixed up with flashes of inspiration, idiotic renunciations which made lost joys appear completely out of proportion, a really hopeless mess that nobody could possibly swallow ...

And so involved in it all that it seems that death surprised him with his nose in his papers, a position something like that of a drinking man lapping up the final drop from the bottom of his glass, however that was precisely what it was, death you understand, ah if he'd only known he would have come to terms with it but there you are ... in short all the clichés you can think of on the subject and on so many others, it remained to be seen ...

To come back to the housemaid who was dismissed from Bonne-Mesure it was apparently not because of her relations with the butler but because of an indiscretion she had been guilty of in her mistress's bedroom, she had read a letter on the dressing-table about the more than dubious dealings between the lady of the manor and a certain Vernet concerning the sale of a piece of ground near the Grance ponds, how could Mademoiselle de Bonne-Mesure have allowed herself to get caught up in it, in any case she had made up for her error not as a consequence of the indiscretion but of the information that the lawyer had been obliged to give her even though he had probably had a hand in that same piece of dishonesty without the reason that you can imagine ... to cut a long story short the woman what was her name oh yes Colette had found herself being sacked and had revenged herself by taking a piece of silverware which she had immediately turned into cash by the good offices of a second-hand dealer who was a relation of the bogus Legion of Honor, a transaction which nobody at the guest house or in our little circle knew anything about but which came to the knowledge of you know whom ...

Now it was not impossible that Mortin had overheard a conversation between some of his guests in which they were discussing this housemaid who turned out to be a protégée of Madame Apollonios, an orphan for whom she had found a job at the manor, a species against which we should be on our guard, she herself hadn't been informed about her unscrupulous action, ought they to tell her or not, an indecision which could well have seemed contradictory in view of the permanent resentment the ladies felt towards her but which in fact was based on their hope that if they asked her she would speak to Mortin about a little domestic problem that had arisen at the guest house at the time and which the old eccentric was the only person who could deal with, given her close friendship with the proprietor.

And that the interview that morning between Mademoiselle Ariane and Magnin apparently had nothing to do with his relationship to the orphan but was simply about some work which was to be done in the former smoking-room which was an extension of the dining-room as the lady of the manor had decided to have a door made in the back wall or shall we say to enlarge the window, an operation which presented certain difficulties in view of the proximity of the nineteenth-century construction which encroached on this facade and in view on the other hand of the moat which had not been filled in at this spot, a question that that idiot Moignon apparently confused with what Magnin had told him of the difficulties they encountered when they were building the little wall under Mademoiselle Mottard's windows, you see the proportion the slightest little thing assumes in these ladies' gossip, it's enough to make you despair of our traditions of logic, clarity, reason, so on and so forth.

For the orphanage had at first found it very difficult to accept the outcast for certain reasons which are difficult to state as the case contained so many ... and then to release

223

her for the opposite reasons which would take too long to explain, in short this institution, which was a private one at the time I'm speaking of, was called Sainte-Fiduce, had a great reputation in the district and was regularly visited by priests, archpriests and top-level confessors sent by the bishopric to say the least, it had a certain what you might call authority because of its principal, a lady what was her name again who was of gentle birth if you please, mannners, breeding, an eminence, in a word a distinction which was so intimidating that in the council meetings however strange it may seem they took notice of what she called her warnings or her reservations and old man Monnard himself, I'm referring to the father that's to say the grandfather . . .

So that the Vernes man after the housemaid's dismissal had disappeared from our midst and when they were searching his place they found some compromising letters addressed to you know whom which the examining magistrate hadn't really known what to do with but in extremis he came up with a solution that was considered elegant which consisted of visiting the accused under cover of good-neighborly relations, in short it was being hushed up neither more nor less.

And this must have been the reason for that anonymous letter that upset us all so, the first time that such a thing had happened to us, tongues were wagging, imaginations ditto, to such an extent that this insignificant business, just a little female flurry, had taken on such proportions, you could see signs of it everywhere, you could sense that people had come to some sort of an agreement, the whole of our local history for years had been called into question, no one came out of it unscathed, I need no further example than the suspicions directed against that poor what was her name the eccentric woman at the guest house, people said she was in league with Vernet and the examining magistrate himself, or even, though you'd never have imagined it in your wildest dreams, Mademoiselle Thing who went to communion every morning being suspected of having had an affair with Topard which is supposed to have resulted in the orphan at Sainte-Fiduce neither more nor less, which explained the interest of you know whom ... really it was all too much and thank God the war came and we had other fish to fry, a blessing in one sense, fraternity. solidarity, patriotism, they cement our hearts, don't they, farewell trivialities, farewell tittle-tattle, you turn over a new leaf and start off again on the right foot, Providence arranges everything for the best seeing that in fact as we both agree the principle parties concerned are no longer with us, the Vernes fellow first and the baker and the gendarme and young Pinson, not to mention the victims of the Spanish flu or whatever, talk about a clean sweep, a mopping-up operation ...

All of this came surging back into poor Mortin's consciousness so far as one may presume that is of course but what else could have kept him so absorbed at his window at his age I ask you, the past neither more nor less, the reflection, the redolence of the past, she wasn't so far off the truth that good woman that good woman I have her name on the tip of my tongue, after all this time she doesn't bear him the slightest ill-will, she is resigned by nature and yet how she suffered from his indifference, such a haughty man at that time, he's certainly had to draw in his horns since, that guest house you must admit he might have finished up better than that but I have never heard him complain ... what was her name again tcha after all this time you have to admit ... in short all that jumble of ill-natured gossip you couldn't tell what to make of it always given of course that you really wanted to make something of it but so many years later where was the interest I ask you, everything had changed in our midst, the Claudettes, Bobettes, Lorettes and all the rest of them were married, they had children, they had settled down, they had become respectable, so on and so forth and the fathers had settled down too, it was the children's turn now, what a hornets' nest, the poor little angels would go through it in their turn and end up one fine evening at their windows at the age and time in question ... hopping, skipping and jumping ... hobbling, wobbling from the wash-basin to the larder, careful you don't fall, careful not to catch cold, careful ... you see what I mean.

Hushing it up, neither more nor less.

This prison I'm in.

Right in the middle of something else, to have been standing on your doorstep and like the rest of them been a witness to that ... that ... and now so isolated, it seems as if July had hardly ... as if ... that's not the important part ... fighting against that stiffening in the candlelight, I can still see her, her soul or whatever it is that they call by that name ...

Death beneath the plane tree.

That sudden silence, that estrangement, how to describe it ... but they had to pull themselves together, make the effort which would definitely not cost them any more ...

Well yes then that morning at the cemetery had been mortal, we had all caught our deaths of cold and when I say cemetery it all started in the church, the coffin wasn't there yet but the draught was oh yes, we were all standing by the font, I can still see Monnard with his scarf ... or Mottard who had attended the dead woman, last gasps, and Mademoiselle his daughter hobbling wobbling, her poor nose frozen, her hands tucked into a melusine muff or was it rabbit that had belonged to her mother with a little cord that went round her neck, and all the local councillors plus

Léventail and our roadman, people were trying to make suitably dignified conversation, they recalled the dead woman's career, teaching for twenty years doesn't time fly, and one thing leading to another everyone was chipping in with his own dear departed and the whole gang of them were getting into the act, all pushing and shoving you should just have seen it, the deceased mothers and fathers, the in-laws, so on and so forth, an invasion like a revival meeting which was just as if they were excuse the expression re-celebrating their own funerals or as if today's one was just a rehash, a lousy old rigmarole of a litany which people had started bawling twenty years previously at the very least and which there was no way of stopping, you'd find us chuntering away at the intercession for the dead until kingdom come.

There's certainly no shortage of funerals said the roadman.

Ah no not of funerals there isn't.

I can still see the one in question, we all caught our death of cold, poor Moignon not the tinsmith the other one, he was for it pretty soon after, it was as if he were rehearsing the ceremony *in petto* with his nephew that great ape you know the one I mean, the verger was getting out his register and beckoning to us, come on, sign, don't be shy, under the eye of Saint Anthony, a bit like the lost property office, but that family never had much luck, the coffin still didn't come, at one moment little Jean-Claude sneezed, he hadn't got a handkerchief, a lovely long splodge of snot on the lapel of his coat, Mademoiselle Cruze drew his attention to it, the child flicked it off, and the excrement took wing and went and stuck on Magnin's umbrella which made us laugh, when suddenly Blimbraz opened the doors, he'd been tipped off by Verveine who had just appeared, this was it, our faces reassumed the appropriate expression but the only thing that came in was the draught, someone said it's still too soon, they've got caught up in a traffic jam at the crossroads, they shut the door again and the harmonium which had started wheezing stopped in its tracks, we still had a good half hour to go, Magnin said that at the service for his mother-in-law they'd been two hours late and I thought of all the delays in funerals, so much time salvaged for our pious reflections, only we couldn't really take advantage of it, the pleasure you get out of wallowing in them you might just as well find in avoiding them and in fact we were all talking about everything else under the sun except perhaps that old bigot Mademoiselle Lorduz you remember her, when the doors were finally opened and this time by the undertaker's number one and in came . . .

But the whole thing could almost have had to do with something quite different, a sort of thingummy what's it called now where the actual event goes far beyond what you see of it, as if we ourselves were being washed up *in posse* by the tide while we were bawling away *in petto* the lousy old litany that they would soon be flinging in our faces to give us a bit of a push in the right or wrong direction and the sacred words Requiem and other Liberas . . . in short a sort of comedy fabricated *ad hoc,* think on these things, clots, for thou art dust, all the clichés you can think of.

We had taken up our positions at the back of the church at eleven o' clock, I can still see poor Mortin flanked by his guests, three or four of the ladies, ought they to move up into the nave, there was a mortal draught, wait for the family what the hell were they up to good God but there's not much point in expecting any *savoir-vivre* excuse the pun on a day like this, people started mumbling a few modest prayers or various little details they happened to remember, it all came flooding back, no need to cudgel our brains, as if the only thing amongst all these modest ceremonies that could take us back to square one was the intercession for the dead ... to cut a long story short *in articulo* ever since the beginning of time amidst wreaths and crowns, the *Libera me* and other litanies intoned *in petto* for years and years found us gratuitously snuggling down in the coffin instead of that particular day's delivery, you see what I mean.

And apropos of the family who still didn't arrive as they were caught in a lousy traffic jam Mademoiselle Lorduz was telling us that at her grandmother's funeral or was it the gendarme but it came to the same thing the party had lasted three hours including the service that is, a Mass *in extremis* for the repose of her soul ... I can still hear them bawling out her *Libera me*, she was fascinated by all the funereal trappings, the litany so measured and rhythmical you ought to have heard it, not forgetting the sight of catafalques, aspergillums, pallbearers and what not, a fat lot of good that did us, as if the tears we had been holding back *in petto* since, since ... or if this comedy ...

To cut a long story short we had agreed to meet at the Swan at about nine and make our way to the church together, a comforting recipe, a little white wine to cheer us up and then on to the ceremony, I can still see Monnard or was it Blimbraz after so many years, everyone was very gay even though we were all susceptible to chills, colds in the head, anginas and what not, along the rue Neuve, it comes out or as near as makes no difference at the rue Saint-Antoine and at the church which, like the fief of lost property—but that family had never had any luck ... that poor woman that poor woman what was her name again had been carried off just six months before the tragedy in question, a thing we were quite unaware of at the time and not

without good reason but which we remembered at the aforementioned day and hour because Mademoiselle Crottard had
also now I remember nominated the poor thing what was
her name as her heir, no doubt about it it was one thing or
the other, either it's a question of failing memory or . . .

Gathered together there at the back of the church, the
parish councillors, our little group, some friends and a few
Liberamaniacs, we could hardly feel our toes any more it
was so freezing cold and that draught good God when
suddenly the doors open in earnest, the coffin comes in
followed by the family, a vision which strangely resembles the
other one . . . the other one . . . I mean the previous one, it
was some years before, imprinted in our consciousness,
smeared like cow-dung over our primroses and other har-
bingers, so that under our very lively eyes excuse the pun
there was nothing inopportune about it, I'm referring to
death, and that we could have tugged at its sleeve to remember ourselves kindly to it, as if that shadowy figure
because of the fear it inspired in us . . .

The coffin had come through the doors followed by the
family in mourning, the mother with all her crêpe deployed,
a real puppet-show bat, black gloves, black stockings on her
goat's legs, box-calf handbag from Tripeaus', always the
same old story, on the arm of the father in a bum-freezer,
wing collar, patent-leather shoes, his poor face bloated with
sorrow, pernod and all the rest of it, plus the son, the sister,
the cousins, the whole crowd, an old ape-woman who was
she, an old bistro-keeper from the Auvergne, an ancient
theatrical virago all tarted up with mascara and vaseline
followed by the nice clean schoolchildren and the pupil-
teacher you remember her the one who got tumbled by
young Magnin the year of the Mission how long ago was that
how long ago . . .

230

So we all stood to attention or something like it, the father gave us the sort of glance that the occasion seemed to require, was it meant to convey sorrow, gratitude or dignity, difficult to say, he probably didn't know himself, when you have all known each other for so many years the attitudes we each assume ought to be familiar to all the others but no not at all, we were just quite simply and stupidly one after the other adopting a funereal attitude at the appropriate day and hour, in short we moved up just as much as was necessary to join the body of the soul of the thingummy what's it called now, the grief of the ones being shared by the others, a sort of collective header into the valley of tears or the den of nightmares, panics and other little pleasures which will spice *ad vitam* the course of our existences.

A perfectly ordinary funeral, like mine, like yours, what could come out of it, modest prayers, *formulae in petto*, as if the august ceremony or the fear it inspired in us … in short nothingness, no more anything, no more anybody, night had fallen, the spell was lifted, the thingummies what are they called now.

Or that Mortin at his window on the day of the funeral saw the procession going by and spotted little Jean-Claude in the traffic jam.

Or that poor Loiseleur woman so long ago, the schoolmistress you remember her, had never had anything to do with that business, he must have been mixing it up, I'm referring to Léventail, with the other affair, Marin was it, or Marchin, you know the one I mean, that intrigued us all so, the articles that fellow wrote who was it at the time do you remember, the murder of that madwoman what was her name again by the Descreux fellow that was it, it certainly dragged on and on.

Or that according to other people how can anyone know . . .

Those four figures rigid under the plane tree, the draught Mademoiselle what was her name again so feared was already blowing out the candles and carrying up to the very top of the century-old tree the Liberas and all the rest of the mumbo-jumbo.

After the intercession for the dead we would have shaken the mitts of the family who were wedged in between Saint Anthony and the front, the father, the mother, the sister, so on and so forth.

Or been to have a good booze-up.

Leaning with his elbows on the window at his age poor thing what else could interest him.

A funeral neither more nor less.

Libera me Domine and the rest of it as if the cow-dung that was being chucked in our faces.

Libera me Domine as if the lousy old traffic jam.

De merda aeterna excuse the pun.

A modest little dirty trick to help us recover from our emotion, don't get me wrong it's one thing or the other.

The ladies' gossip, it helps to pass the time.

Or that the shadow as night was falling.

Or that that poor child what was his name again.

Those dear little faces they give you the shivers.

In short a fiasco or something very like it.

Then for so many years, an uneasy feeling how to describe it, maybe a sort of thirst but it's all so long ago.

Still see him that July morning on his doorstep.

As if the tragedy rehashed, digested and all the rest of it.

No more question of getting over it, no more question of finishing with it.

A fiasco *ad vitam*, mucked-up spells, and that's perfectly all right.

232

Such as were being hatched elsewhere.

Things what do they call them now, half-seen, spied on, do what you like, they rise far beyond the tree-tops.

That lot of old crap, lousy old mirages and other junk in our creaking nuts.

Mucked-up spells.

No more question of finishing with it.

A thirst but to quench it do what I like I can't.

A thirst yes, as I see it.

AUTHOR'S NOTE

It seems to me that the interest of my work up to the present has been the quest for a *tone of voice*. This is a formal problem which may perhaps explain my connection with what has been called the 'nouveau roman'. But it would be a mistake to consider me a partisan of any 'school of observation'. If we are thinking in terms of objectivity, the ear has equally tyrannical exigencies. And the tone varies from each of my books to the next. There will never be an end to my research in this field. I shall always be looking for something new, and it will always be my fate to have to choose, each time, one tone among the milliards that my ear has recorded.

It is not what can be said or *meant* that interests me, but the *way in which it is said*. And once I have chosen this *way*—which is a major and painful part of the work, and which must therefore come first—it imposes both composition and subject-matter on me. And once again, I am indifferent to this subject-matter. The whole of the work consists in pouring it into a certain mold, and I have learnt from experience that it is the mold which, line by line, makes the pudding. I am always being surprised, on re-reading my work, at having written about various things which I should have thought did not come within my province. I only accept responsibility for the errors of tone, and there must, alas, be some.

The question of the co-existence or co-birth of form and content has recently been the subject of some interesting studies. Once my book is finished, I am convinced that this co-existence is the only poetic reality.

Why speak of poetry apropos of a novel? Because this is the term which I consider appropriate to the work of the artisan that I am. It is my disgust for the novel as it is

234

classically accepted that constrains me to use this more general term for creation which may imply poetry, or the opposite. There is no pretension in this.

If I say *recorded by the ear*, it is because spoken language, or rather its non-codified syntax, which encompasses the slightest affective inflexion, fascinates me. This evolving syntax, which has always been attempting to adapt our language to the exigencies of our feelings, is the only syntax I feel is worthy of interest. I am not trying to codify it—this is the last thing I should want to do—but to register it. And this not in the least because I am attempting to be an encyclopaedist, but simply because I am an egotist.

It does in fact seem to me that every sort of artistic sensitivity—my own therefore included—deserves to be expressed as accurately as possible. And the only words and syntax I dispose of are those which do just this. I say this to reassure my readers. If they find in my books any poetic material, or psychological reality, in short, anything other than verbiage, they will certainly not be doing me an injustice.

There may well be a new point of view, a modern kind of sensitivity, an unusual sort of composition, in my books, but I can't help it. The fact that I become aware of it the further I go in my difficult profession doesn't make the slightest difference to my assertion that the only thing I am really interested in is the *voice* of whoever is speaking. Our ear is just as powerful a recording instrument as our eye. And I think I may safely say that our habitual tone of voice, the one we use to ourselves and to those who are closest to us, is a sort of compound of the different tones, apart from those which are hereditary or which come from books, which we have recorded since childhood. If it is interesting in, say, a letter, for the writer to examine, after the event, this natural tone of voice, how much more interesting is it to analyze its component parts and make them, one by one, into a book. Which is to say that I have never tried to reproduce objectively, like a tape recorder, the sound of someone else's voice, I have quite enough to do in reproducing my own. This consists more than anything of an artistic exigency which is simply the expression of one individual, and not that of anyone else. And it is a commonplace to state that it is only in so far as the artist remains fiercely himself that he is able to describe the society of the times he lives in.

I say the voice of *whoever is speaking,* because for me the preliminary work consists in choosing from the component parts of my own voice the one that interests me at the moment, and of isolating it, and then objectivizing it until a character emerges from it, the narrator, with whom I identify myself. This is why there is always an *I* in all my books, but it is always a different one.

And to call it *preliminary work* is not accurate, because it is an unconscious work which goes on during the unproductive periods after a book has been published. These periods, which may be long or short, are hard to bear. The tone to be chosen must first mature, and then it is not so much that it is chosen but that it imposes itself. If I still speak of choice, it is because the different tones that I have been working with up to then still remain in my ear, and I am tempted each time to re-utilize them. I don't do this between one book and the next, because each time I feel, probably wrongly, that I have exhausted them. In any case, once I have registered them, they bore me. But the temptation remains, because I find inactivity, the fact of not writing, of not producing anything, painful. And so, in these blank periods, I am dependent on this process of maturing.

It is also inaccurate to say that the tone is found at once. It has been the exception when this has happened to me. It has started off as something more like a tonality, which becomes more specific as it is worked on, in the course of the book, that is, and which finally becomes a tone, maybe only on the last page. In any case it is only on the last page that I become aware of the rightness, or approximate rightness, of the tone, even though I may here or there have felt as I went along that I had found the right note, which encouraged me to continue.

One thing is certain, though, and this is that I never know at the outset what I am going to say. For a long time I thought this a weakness, but there is no way of avoiding it as it is my only strength, the strength that enables me to continue. Some time ago, with every line there was the pleasure of a discovery. Nowadays it is often a chore, but it remains a discovery. I may add that I am more and more obsessed in my work by a regard for composition, which I didn't have to begin with. But I maintain that this composition is, with every new departure, unforeseeable. It was only gradually that I became aware of this fact, and I have from time to time given things a push in this or that direction—to produce what is not necessarily the best of my books. For my confidence in the mechanism of the subconscious remains essentially unshakeable.

People have spoken of the plots of my books. Rather than plot, I would prefer situation, and this is imposed on me by the chosen tone. If a plot seems to be in the process of being woven, it can only be as a result of the thread of the discourse, which can only unwind in a void. They support each other mutually. This discourse, then, consists of various stories. If I say that these stories don't interest me, it is because I know that they could have been different. This doesn't prevent me from accepting and even liking them, as I would have liked the others, the others that I still have to tell, so long as I don't weary of the search for an initial tone.

When the moment comes to start writing, I am fully

conscious of what I am doing as I release the mechanism or, if you like, as I open the tap to the subconscious—let us say, to the feelings. This work could not be more spontaneous. It is almost a sort of fully conscious automatic writing, that's to say with the direct infiltration of the *possibilities*, of what could be developed, and I force myself to develop a minute part of this in spite of my distaste for every sort of development, and for the novel in particular. Why this asceticism? In order to discover, finally, my own kind of truth, which is idiotically moral, but so profoundly embedded in contradictions that it is the only thing I am capable of doing.

If I haven't found, or if after a few probationary years I haven't even been looking for, a poetic form within the strict meaning of the word, it is because it seemed to me that it was only the form of the novel, or let us say of the narration, with all its possibilities of spontaneous development and its difficulties of analysis, that was capable of forcing me to explain myself and thence enabling me to communicate with the outside world. For example, when I decided to write *The Inquisitory*, I hadn't anything to say, I simply felt a need to explain myself at great length. I started work, and I wrote the phrase: *Yes or no answer*, which was only addressed to myself and which meant: *Out with it!* And it was the reply to this abrupt question that released the tone and everything that followed. But I still believe that it was this tone that necessarily had to emerge from a thousand others when I started. I had to see it transcribed before I could accept it.

It remains to be seen who speaks in the tone of *The Libera me Domine*. This time I don't know. Contradictory remarks are reported by someone ... who hasn't revealed his identity to me.

Robert Pinget

OTHER BOOKS IN THE FRENCH SERIES

THE PARK Philippe Sollers translation A. M. Sheridan-Smith $4.25 $2.25 paper

SENTIMENTAL TALKS Two Novels Daniel Castelain translation Patrick Bowles $4.95

LAW AND ORDER Claude Ollier translation Ursule Molinaro $4.95

PASSACAGLIA Robert Pinget translation Barbara Wright $6.95 (summer 1978)